CUTTHROAT

Editor in Chief...Pamela Uschuk
Fiction Editor...William Luvaas
Poetry Editor...William Pitt Root
Managing Editor...Andrew Allport
Assistant Fiction Editors...................................Julie Jacobson
Matt Mendez
Assistant Poetry Editors.................................Howie Faerstein
Teri Hairston
Mark Lee
Assistant To The Editor...Susan Foster
Design Editor..Alexandra Cogswell
Interns...Whitney Judd
Joseph Madden

Contributing Editors
Sandra Alcosser, Charles Baxter, Frank Bergon, Red Bird, Janet
Burroway, Robert Olen Butler, Ram Devineni, Rick DeMarinis,
Joy Harjo, Richard Jackson, Marilyn Kallet, Richard Katrovas,
Zelda Lockhart, Demetria Martinez, John McNally, Jane Mead,
Dennis Sampson, Rebecca Seiferle, Luis Alberto Urrea, Lyrae
van Clief-Stefanon and Patricia Jabbeh Wesley.

Send submissions, subscription payments and inquiries to:
CUTTHROAT, A JOURNAL OF THE ARTS
P.O. Box 2124
Durango, Colorado 81302
ph: 970-903-7914 I email: cutthroatmag@gmail.com

Make checks payable to Raven's Word Writers Center or
Cutthroat, A Journal of the Arts. Subscriptions are $25 per two
issues or $15 for a single issue. We are self-funded so all
Donations gratefully accepted.

CUTTHROAT THANKS

Website Design..Laura Prendergast
Pamela Uschuk
Cover Layout...Alexandra Cogswell
Pamela Uschuk
Magazine Layout...Alexandra Cogswell
Pamela Uschuk
Logo Design..Lynn McFadden Watt
Front Cover Art..Jerry Gates
Early Fall Off Forestry
Oil Pastel on paper, 22" X 28"
Back Cover Art...Jerry Gates
Time Portal
Oil Pastel on paper

AND THANK YOU TO:

Alexandra Cogswell for her expertise in designing our cover and our magazine. Susan Foster and Joseph Madden for proofreading. Andrew Allport, Howie Faerstein, Teri Hairston, Richard Jackson, Julie Jacobson, Marilyn Kallet, Tim Rien, William Pitt Root, Pamela Uschuk and Patricia Jabbeh Wesley, for reading for our contests.

Special thank you to Warren Alexander, Doug Anderson, Patricia Ascuncion, Jeffrey Bahr, Paul Beckman, Earl Braggs, Simmons Buntin, Lucy Clark, Cathy Conde, Alfred Corn, Alison Deming, Chard DeNiord, Cindy Domasky, Keith Flynn, Olivia Garza, Dick and Gay Grossman, Hedy Habra, Cynthia Hogue, T.R. Hummer, Richard Jackson, Patricia Spears Jones, Patricia Killelea, Willie James King, DJ Lee, Marilyn Kallet, Tony Lubberman, Leslie McGrath, Charlotte Lowe, Marilyn Nelson, Alan Perry, Elise Paschen, Lucyna Prostko, Joani Reese, Amanda Reavey, Lawrence J. Reynolds, Lindsey Royce, Jane Sobie, Melissa Studdard, Eleanor Swanson, Bill and Cindy Tremblay, Melissa Tuckey, Dan Vera, Patricia Jabbeh Wesley, Mary Jane White, Eleanor Wilner, and Stephen Zorich who donated to our GoFundMe project to help fund Cutthroat, A Journal of the Arts.

We also thank our subscribers around the world.

CONGRATULATIONS TO THE WINNERS
OF OUR 2018 WRITING CONTESTS!

FINAL JUDGES:

Patricia Spears Jones, Joy Harjo Poetry Prize

Susan Mona Powers, Rick DeMarinis Short Story Prize

David Quammen, Barry Lopez Nonfiction Prize

FIRST PRIZES, $1300 plus publication

"Human Words" by Meredith Stricker of Carmel, CA
Joy Harjo Poetry Prize chosen by Patricia Spears Jones

"Women With Large Dogs" by John Tait of Flower Mound, TX
Rick DeMarinis Short Story Prize chosen by Susan Mona Power.

"After Lennon" by Julia Mary Gibson Los Angeles, CA
Barry Lopez Nonfiction Prize chosen by David Quammen

SECOND PRIZES, $250 plus publication

"Human Results" by Jenn Givhan of Albuquerque, NM
Joy Harjo Poetry Prize

"A Small Bright Room" by Sharon Solwitz of Chicago, IL
Rick DeMarinis Short Story Prize

"Visibility" by Sarah Priestman of Richmond, VA
Barry Lopez Nonfiction Prize

HONORABLE MENTIONS, publication

"Nocturne Domestica" by Samuel Piccone of Henderson, NV
Joy Harjo Poetry Prize

"Vison Confidence Score" by Kimberly Blaeser of Burlington, WI
Rick DeMarinis Short Story Prize

"The Ten of Wands" by Sarah Elizabeth Schantz of Boulder, CO
Rick DeMarinis Short Story Prize

"Sharing Rus" by Michele Feeney of Phoenix, AZ
Barry Lopez Nonfiction Prize

Finalists 2018 Joy Harjo Poetry Prize

"Home Remedy for Miscarriages" Josephine Yu
"Goldilocks" Rebecca Olander
"You Ask What I Am Doing, So Far From Home" Ingrid Wendt
"Portrait of Endangered Sturgeon Release Party" Andrea England
"Sober In Margaritaville," Lynn McGee
"Stranger's Rice," Richard Oyama
"To Keep Away Crow's Feet" Tyler Dettioff
"Human Remains," Robbie Gamble
"Wish," Kelly Spence
"Hallucinations (sensory)," Kay Lin
"The Dream Catchers" Maximillan Heinegg
"Day of the Giblet" Jeanne-Marie Osterman
"In Case of Emergency" Partridge Boswell
"Chimayo" Janice Gould
"Rotted Blues" Tony Barnstone
"Call & Response" Scott Withiam

Finalists 2018 Rick DeMarinis Short Story Prize

"The List" Stanley Stocker
"Viva Bush" Reilly Nolan
"Can't You See The Walls?" Mark Connelly
"The Sound of Water" Joseph Boone
"Val And Hollis" Mary Salisbury
"Figure In Green and Blue" Miranda Hersey
"A Day of the Dead Story: The Sugar Skull" Seres Jaime Magana
"Clean" Kay Lin
"Air Drop" Sandra Hunter
"Road Trip" Gary Powell
"The Empty Vessel" Hajar Abdul-Rahim
"Profile" Doug Crandell
"People Like Them" Anne Leigh Parrish
"The Gauntlet" Barry Kitterman
"Empathy" James McDermott

Finalists 2018 Barry Lopez Non-Fiction Prize

"Beauty In The Embers" Wendy Gaudin
"The Feasting Tree" Elise Atchison
"End Of The Road" Sean W Murphy
"Muscle Memory" Ryan Ireland
"Old Tijkko" Lara Palmqvist
"An Arab Man and an English Woman Walk Into a Bar"
                                              Adriana Paramo
"No One Knows Where the Caribou Go" Alexis Lathem
"Trail Time" Lucy Bryan
"Family Album" Angelique Stevens
"Forked Tongues" Mary O. Parker
"The Behemoth of Loss: Man, Mammoth, and Melancholy"
                                              Heather Altfield
"Shower Moment" Carol Jeffers
"At My Window, With A Broken Wing" Stephen Policoff

We dedicate Cutthroat 24 to Maj Ragain, poet, race track officianado, fisherman and Buddhist who inspired us and supported us all along and to poet Art Smith, fellow dog-lover and colleague at University of Tennessee, Knoxville.

ROGUE WAVE IN THE ROSE BUSHES

Maj Ragain

I told Lu after the rose bush
Had snapped back and thorned
her cheek, after she had lost
her silver earring in the flower bed,
after we lay quietly walking in the flower bed
on the bedroom ceiling.

Let's leave it all behind now,
clear out the bank accounts,
throw the breaker switches, tell the neighbors
come get what you want *Jesus Loves Me*
all over Mom's I'm-in-the-nursing-home-now
1995 Cherry Delta Royale Oldsmobile,
run it through the car wash with the windows down,
half a dozen times, you and me riding up front.
Let's get waxed and make a run toward
the moonrise, a notch off full.

Because when it comes, that rogue wave,
we won't have time to babble more than a mouthful
of words, kicking around in the blue light,
streaming silver shards at each other.
Then we'll be swept away
into the cold. Then the dark.
This moment, the air is cinnamon,
sandlewood, sweat honeyed,
here on this high ground with you.

From CLOUDS PILE UP IN THE NORTH, Press 53

WALTER'S ETERNITY

Arthur Smith

It's always early summer
Inside me—or late spring, birthdays,

The slightest breath of dew still
Mist on the rose leaves, bouquet

Of apricots and dates more
Redolent in the morning

Open to the world.
Me too. The towering

Palm trees pigeon-holed with pigeons
Crapping on anyone trying

To get to their ramshackle nests.
The old man two houses down

With my father's name, I would see him
As I climbed the tall palms—

Always walking the streets, with purpose,
The blocks back and forth, the grid

A city's laid out on, his pants cinched up
Mid-chest though I never made

Fun of him, his hunched walk, his back
Broken in an earthquake, a fact

I learned in school he lived
Through in 1906 when he was six.

Hard to imagine. I know a woman
Who fled Bosnia when the hostilities

Intensified. She was a child.
Age means nothing. Age means

You're counting. Is there an end
To sadness? However long

We wander the streets, here away
From the bay area, away from a homeland,

Looking for our mothers,
Sisters, fathers, lovers, the ruins

Of our lives burning in the fires, in the rubble,
In the work of living, in my mind.

Published in Cutthroat 12, 2012

Table Of Contents

217 **NONFICTION**

RIDER ON THE STORM
Black and White Photo
Ann Leshy Wood

POETRY

HUMAN WORDS

Meredith Striker

"...the gate of heaven is everywhere"   Thomas Merton

is heaven a chain link fence for a luxury car lot
        or the crook in a sleeping woman's arm
burned out light
nest in grass
a pause
in digging up the jack-hammered water main
        heaven as mended cloth
or armistice, cerulean blue canoe
                a man lying dead drunk by a storefront
rusted winch, safe-house
a wren
        this small, saintly blot
                        this sad empty pen
what would you leave out,   what scrap-heaped
        holy, outmoded wreckage, what useless, unloved
                pile of bones
                        and skin
                        doesn't belong

                what about leaf blower, dirt eater
                dust devil, brush whacker —
                why shouldn't I expect paradise in the roar
of a septic tank pump
as weeds glisten at midday with no trace of guilt, shame or agitation
                fields sheltered by dryness
                        which shrives them bare

habitat restoration
    to heal human words

        to sway like fish in waterlight of aqueduct shallows
            float green and unmetered in psalmed sound the hum
      of electric wires strung across Wasco irrigation ditch
almond orchards outside San Ardo oil rigs fracked and churning over
delicate and hidden fault lines how strange to open like winged petals
drifting in air past crop-dusters
into Great Silence
the way I did not shape
the reticulate form of the thumbprint
that identifies me nor my DNA
nor last night's rain
that washed my dreaming
      I am moving without moving since the vastness
of the sea moves for me
    is the actuality of the world
        as I watch a white sea bird take the devoted
        shape of disappearance
            we are made of the same substance
            our gestures coincide
                where we lived, once, on earth

HUMAN ███████
███ RESULTS

Jenn Givhan

Today is *not* the day I scratch
the wounds.

Let's play hang[wo]man now

I'm hallelujah hellflowering—on my red couch
I moved to Tejas & back
    2-thousand miles through jasmine

& cenote night-
blooming, I'm sitting in cupcake crumbs surrounded
by chocolate my chihuahua will scrap for later
I will fight a little black dog I rescued from the shelter

& I'm watching Lady Gaga in pain in booty shorts
getting shots in the fleshy pad of her hip to manage
the trauma, take off the wigs & admit *I too am alone*—

but these cupcakes are delicious today
on this day the nurse practitioner's office has called &
the test results are in & by God I am not this moment

in my sweatpants & messy bun & caramel frosting
on my fingertips I am not this moment
dying.

    The first time I had booty sex
I was 33, my Jesus year, & a year later I'm praising
because a moment ago before the call I was truly
[dead]. The [real?] first time was *accidental*

or *rape*. I was 15 the year
I never had my quinceañera & fell in love
with a boy/man I'd search for & run from/to

my entire girldom/womanlost [managing the trauma]
& Gaga says the year she sold 13 million albums
she lost Matt & the year she sold 30 million
she lost Luc & now the Super Bowl &—

At first I think Gaga you're a queen you're a goddess
if I could reach that many girls/women & empower them
the way you do, what Luc or Matt could ever

touch me again? What D█████?
                                    & then the symptoms
I ignored while he [loved] me. Nightsweats. Bleeding-

gums. Blood flowers in the toilet water, amaryllis
killing me, softly. Sores. On my fleshy pads. I'm a hypo-
chondriac he said, each night in the hotel bed

asked if we were good, asked if he could
stay inside me & I thought this was [finally] [self] respect &
buzzed *yes.*

The nurse practitioner is a woman named
Marlene I specifically requested on the hotline [please
God send me a woman to heal this pain]. She searches

the Death/Love/Sun tarot spread across my breasts
the calaveras whose skeleton hands hold my broke-
ass romance [all your lover's revenge]. I am so sad.
Did I mention that?

                        Marlene's no-
nonsense, a true scold in her voice & I'm 15 at the clinicas

again wishing I could've told my mom about the HPV J██████
gave me [instead of the baby my body let go]

the curettage burned—hellflowering I'm telling you
& no one knew except the lukewarm baths I took for days
praying for the lotus flower I lost the little cactus girl
somewhere &

        D████ said it was nothing like then
—before he'd left me, when he'd promised
he was screwing only [me] & I believed

I'd grown up, as if growing up meant
more than managing [the trauma]—
                    Marlene says
Honey you've got to take better care of yourself. You got kids?
I nod, tears in my eyes. *All men lie,* she tells me.
I thank her for the sex advice, silently, humming
as she requests the tests, charts
my heartbreak. *Your kids need you.*

            At AWP a woman who'd read all my books
came to me crying—the way I cry at the lilies dying
on my bedside table, my tarot altar to the Universe
that today is *not* the day I learn to tie

the noose [please God help me] [unbandage the trauma].

None of this matters in the nurse practitioner's office.
I am Honey, be careful. I am Mother who has not taken
care of herself & by extension, her babies.

   I am Carrying
this burden I've carried more than half my life down the stairs
to the blood lab. Pull the tab, number 102, take a seat, pull
up a vein. Open. Open. [God heal this wound].

NOCTURNE DOMESTICA

Samuel Piccone

There are ghosts inside you that haven't eaten in centuries;
I bought a nightlight for your side of the bed
hoping to chase the shadows from your body,
unblacken the toothy bruises on my neck.
I wanted the plastic luster of a half-moon
to turn bite marks into the glossed feathers
one finds thrashed and littered after a kill,
a sign there's nothing left to consume.
But in the dead quiet of afterglow,
night is a slow blue pang, and it drains me,
how you kiss like love is something to feed.
Every wound I manage to close peels open like a husk.
What if marriage is like this, just two people in a room
afraid to starve alone? Like nightjars with fractured beaks,
all we have is the hunger on our tongues, petrified mothdust
under our talons, a bed that deepens with each lick.

TREE AND TOWN (PINE)

Patricia Spears Jones

Aleppo pine casts a shadow of sweetness
Across wooden benches, the Mediterranean
Crossed daily by all manner of ship, the aquatic
Children dive and bob and flash their health
Their wealth, their well-being. Ancient trees
Old city. But an older city wracks and reels
Assault by assault. Who is left behind as walls
And houses, hospitals and campuses fall
The genius of modern warfare is the artfully
Targeted weapons that burst the lives of ordinary
People. There the pine trees may hold at a corner
Where once a good neighborhood stood, familiar
Shops with stuff to buy, barter, and family names.
Oh yes, the ordinary citizen's complaints, the groans
of the restless, then nervous population.
We see in pictures what we accept too easily
The mortal price for rebellion; the suavity of tyranny
The tyrant's suits lined in silk; his moustache trimmed
Daily. His routine contempt for the people whose
Love he demands. His routine contempt for
The land he shadows.

SUNDAY MORNING, CASSIS FRANCE
August 19, 2018

Patricia Spears Jones

Mourning doves coo
Three small ships in the water
Waves contrail clouds over cliffs
There is no
Still life
Dynamics of sun
Slow rising pink with noise

Time in tides routine
Water aggresses
Water retreats
Bells shimmer brass tone
Soon laughter
Soon laughter
Clouds mass
Clouds retreat
Boats bring in
Fish sloppy with salt.

SINGING EVERYTHING

Joy Harjo

Once there were songs for everything,
Songs for planting, for growing, for harvesting,
For eating, getting drunk, falling asleep,
For sunrise, birth, mind-break, and war.
For death (those are the heaviest songs and they
Have to be pried from the earth with shovels of grief).
Now, all we hear are falling in love songs and
Falling apart after falling in love songs.
The earth is leaning sideways
And a song is emerging from the floods
And fires. Urgent tendrils lift toward the sun.
You must be friends with silence to hear.
The songs of the guardians of silence are the most powerful--
They are the most rare.

FIRST MORNING

Joy Harjo

This is the first morning we are without you on earth.
The sun greeted us after a week of rain
In your eastern green and mountain homelands.
Plants are fed, the river restored, and you have been woven
Into a path of embracing stars of all colors
Now free of the suffering that shapes us here.
We all learn to let go, like learning how to walk
When we first arrive here.
All those you thought you lost now circle you
And you are free of pain and heartbreak.
Don't look back, keep going.
We will carry your memory here, until we join you
In just a little while, in one blink of star time.

For Shan Goshorn December 3, 2018

SWEET FIRE

Heidi Vanderbilt

...sweet fire licks me clean
I'm just a dream child full of desire...
— cris williamson "Dream Child"

when I was a Florida child
the beach rolled under my toes
coquinas starfish horseshoe crabs
washing up angel fish jellyfish conchs
the Gulf of Mexico smelled of women
tasted of women
ask me how I knew that
when I was small

ask who called me *Obaby*
who pressed my face between her legs
who shoved her fingers into me
before her tongue
who circled back behind the sandbar
carrying my small canvas Keds
my shovel and pail my bathing suit
in her hands

Punta Gorda, Boca Grande, Gasprilla, Sanibel
this land was wild then, houseless, cypress kneed,
roiling with geckos and cottonmouths
out at sea dolphins pelicans a catamaran
I map my childhood in long cuts into flesh
here the Caloosahatchee River and the Peace
and there an unnamed delta of welts and burns
as with all cartography there are gaps
a few months missing hidden in deadfall
but this map my map is missing a half decade
that disappeared into the gulf

she dug inside me

now I fall hard for a spike haired dyke
her eyes like seaglass Ferron-voiced
beach sand in the corners of her mouth
the backs of her hands are turtle shells
her palms peel my cheeks from my teeth
this dyke who calls me *baby* who kisses me
turns the volume all the way up
licking those almost healed wildlife tracks
along my arms my legs my breasts
presses her tongue hard
against the enjambment   I can't feel

AH-MEN

Courtney Felle

Ah-men! Ah, men.
It always comes out sounding like praise.
Funny that "oh, those goddamn girls are at it again"
never carries the same ring to it.
It sounds like a deflation rather than a worshipping.

When I was in the third grade, there was a boy who had a crush on me.
I was a cute eight year old: straight-cut bangs, pink frilly dresses, that tee shirt
with the monkey from Justice that everybody owned.
It was back when they called it Limited Too and I,
I was limited, too. I didn't like to pay attention in class
because I already knew all my multiplication facts,
and I wasn't allowed to read or teach myself anything new.
I had to wait for everybody else.

The boy who liked me sat across the table from me. We had assigned seats.
My teacher said she wouldn't take complaints and wouldn't move us,
no matter what, end of story. But this kid: he's the elementary school version
of a "nice guy." Like, he'd lend you the last purple crayon out of his 124
                                             crayon box
with the fancy sharpener attached when you just had that crappy 12 set,
and he'd consider it a huge advantage to you like you were the one
                                             with all the power now,
and he wouldn't say anything if you accidentally pressed too hard and
                                             broke it,
but he would expect you to hold his hand on the playground later and
                                             let him kiss you
on the cheek.

He'd always stare at me during lessons and it felt like I was the indigo dye
we looked at under the microscopes during science one day. He kept peering
into the lens to get the focus right and see all the individual cells.
It made my skin crawl.

Like most of the little girls in my suburban elementary school, I'd been
taught to cover up:
wear baggy clothing, high necklines, like we had boobs that would peek out?
But it meant I had extra fabric bunched around my stomach.
I would hide books I'd brought to school underneath my shirt and raise my hand
to go to the bathroom. My favorite was *Matilda*. I must've read it at least
four times
hunched over in my little red-walled cell. There were three stalls and I
always took
the middle one. If anyone else walked in, I would curl my feet towards me
and crouch
above the bottom sight line.

Since I was eight, I wasn't very subtle about what I was doing. In my mind
I was a sneaky super-spy, but really, it doesn't look natural for a kid
to hug a rectangular object into their stomach and disappear for twenty minutes.
So my teacher stopped me—not pulled me aside, mind you, but yelled at me
in front of the entire class for wanting to learn more than she was teaching.
Apparently, I was a "delinquent." Except, really, I was just really, really bored.

A couple days after this happened, we took a math quiz. It was a
multiplication table
we had to fill in completely: 6 times 7, 2 times 9. It only went up to ten,
but I knew my facts up to twelve. I wrote them in the margins so the table
would look fuller, like in it there was everything I could possibly know.
I got a hundred on the quiz. The kid across from me had a bunch of red marks
on his paper. We didn't get number grades because it would've "categorized us,"
but I'd say if it had a number on it, it probably would've been mid-eighties.
Not bad,
but not stellar. The type of grade you get when you spend a lot of time
making googly eyes
at the girl who sits across from you instead of actually practicing the math
you're supposed to be learning. I hid my quiz so he wouldn't see my score
because it felt like bragging even if he saw by accident.

My teacher congratulated him on trying so hard for his grade. She
commended his work ethic
and gave him a gold star sticker. I got no gold star sticker. I also got
food poisoning
on the day we were supposed to celebrate the end of our multiplication
unit with tacos

and missed the whole affair. My mother said she would've gone out to
                                        buy us tacos
and we could've had our own personal party, but my teacher had called
                                        her to say
I'd been sneaking off to read and I was in trouble. Not for wanting to read,
                                        but for not
following the rules. Even though my sassy eight-year-old self maintained
                                        that technically
there was no rule against what I'd done, and even if there had been it
                                        would've been
a really dumb rule, my mother said she didn't care. I had to follow the
                                        rules anyway.
Part of being a grown-up was following a lot of dumb rules for no reason
other than that they're rules.

Ah-men!
I'd press the retweet button on that.
Funny little axiom that almost proves its sender self-aware,
but then they keep doing their conformity routine
with the little bouton flourish at the end and it's like,
oh, maybe not.

Ah-men!
Same boy in seventh grade made fun of me
when I got glasses, and when his friend reminded him
he used to like me he scoffed and said,
"We were stupid kids back then and maybe
I was a little stupider than the rest."

My nerd status was in itself reason to dislike me.
Reason to stick feet just a little farther into the hallway to trip me.
Reason to blame any classroom mishaps on me because it's not like the teacher
would believe it anyway. I was Miss Goody-Two-Shoes and they knew it
and everybody knew it and it wasn't 'cause I actually had strict morals or rules
for myself, it was the irony that because I questioned everything and was
                                        so smart
about doing it, everybody assumed I accepted the guidelines I hated.
For the most part, I put up with it because smart kids who don't put up with it
are called "problem children" and get demoted into lower classes
because of "behavioral issues" that are really just refusing
to deal with arbitrary adult bullshit, and as much as I abhorred

arbitrary adult bullshit, I wanted to stay in my advanced classes
to keep knowing more stuff.

Ah-men!
Can we amend our amens so that they include women somewhere?
Crazy thought? For all the other little girls like me who feel like they
don't have a space
to breathe on the playground? Like they have too much ambition to
have friends
because they want to be taken seriously?

Ah-men— Ah-men—
The problem is not a lack of amenities,
but the fact they're all in place for people who aren't like me.
Because I never had a 124 pack of Crayola crayons with the fancy
                                        sharpener attached,
but my brother did when he was in third grade
because "they helped him be excited about learning,"
and what I needed when I was eight were
Hello Kitty sunglasses and Minnie Mouse nail polish.

Ah-men! Can we make it ah-men-and-women?
Just for once can I hear ah-women? Or is that wanting to replace you
                                        in the hierarchy?
Are you admitting you're already on top are you admitting you're clawing
                                        to stay there
are you admitting my argument has substance—

I'd say I have a point, but I don't have the tools to make my crayon sharp
                                        enough to have a point.

GILMORE ROAD

Joan Larkin

When you fell in wet snow
downhill from where your car
balanced all night, one wheel
hanging over nothing, wind
hissing secrets in the pines,
your mind still making words—
So *this* is how it happens—
no one heard your sigh
or saw your ghost rise
from the soaked husk of you.
Wind hissed as they gathered you in,
shouldered you carefully onto their truck,
never having heard your music,
ignorant as I of your new address.

THE BODY INSIDE MY BODY

Joan Larkin

Can't see itself, its tongue
dangling from a bracket. The body
inside my body sways, a door
swollen in a wet month. The body
inside me is all thumbs. Has a dog's
stomach, a dog's habit
of scraps. It droops, sleeps,
is growing a sharp little tooth.
Prefers the pronoun *she*. Is sick
of the reek of ether. Wants
the breath it lost trying to escape,
that afternoon in Hell's Kitchen
pitching itself headlong
down three flights to the street.
Has had it up to here with the scalding.
Doesn't blame them but wants
the whole carcass unburied. Wants

what any body wants, to wake
under stars and taste wind
while vultures hiss in the low branches.

UNDERNEATH

Chris Bullard

in the disassembled city
named streets still proceeded
from the collapsed main gate

the guide said use them
as guideposts to imagine this place
when it ruled the world

but all we saw were yellow flower
helmets on stalks slanting
out of the roadbeds

cut blocks canted to the side
some loose and trembling
others halved or split

seeds had slid under the stones
like bribes slipped
into a senator's robe

we asked the name of the flowers
they weren't the same
as those we have at home

just as in America we don't
have the same kind
of monumental civic ruins

though we might expect
a few dandelions rising next year
from Pennsylvania Avenue

UNDERNEATH

Chris Bullard

I will not be accepted into the heavenly orchestra,
Father, but if it's any consolation, neither will the night-

time fiddlers at Signal Mountain's Mountain Opry.
To make seventh seat in heaven, you have to practice.

You used to say my playing sounded like children
crying. I have not played in a while, you will be happy

to know, but I sometimes walk to the opry and listen
to the bluegrass, daydreaming of white table cloths,

potato salad, throwing the football in the yard.
That special southern upbringing I never had.

I do not sit down – I stand in the back and watch.
In the life after this, I will rest in a folding chair

and let my memories of music fade into palimpsest.
Like most deceased musicians, I will find comfort

in silence. In this life, I am young and you are old,
and my skin is yellow while yours is growing pale.

I have seen how people look at you and wonder
if you are the father of a Chinese violinist boy.

Father, what would you say if I told you that I want
to pick it up again, that wooden hourglass,

the stringed skull of Suzuki method? Just so
I could carve out our biographies, put our lives

into a song that answers all of their questions,
save the living the trouble of having to ask.

A song for clicking tongues behind white teeth.
If only their silence could be as calming as music.

ALONE AMONG OUR ANCESTORS

David St. John

We named the bombs *Fat Man* and *Little Boy*
and we dropped them on Japan two days
before my mother was born in China.
My grandmother's name translates roughly
to *piano in the snow*, and my grandfather's,
to nothing worth knowing.
                                     I never met them.
Together, they named my mother *Kai-Sen:*
"the sound of victory," and they fled
the mainland for a better life. For seventeen years,
this was her name, until a Canadian missionary,
her English teacher in Taipei, found its two syllables
too difficult to pronounce. She changed her name,
and then my mother became someone else.
My father was a fat man, and I was a little boy
when I told my mother that I didn't want to learn
Chinese, that I was American - basically white.
Not like my friend, Edsel Hsu, whose parents
chose his English name out of a book.
                                     I regret
not learning the language, that it took me until
my father's death to ask questions about her life
while we swiveled on old chairs that left black marks
on the kitchen floor linoleum. Recently, she says
her English name, *Grace,* feels insufficient
when someone asks what her name is
and her thoughts struggle to become words.

I ask her what I would be named if I were born
in China, and she does not understand the question.

CONCEALER

David St. John

Your face was like a diamond - carved
       by the beams of the officer's flashlight.
           I watched his fingers snake through your hair

onto the soft skin between your ear
       and jawline. I watched as his thumb
           pressed between your lips, into your kiss.

I thought I was going to die, frozen
       in the backseat, alone and unable
           to feel my body out of fear.

We did not die, but instead
       experienced a different hurt,
           a cold blade from ribs to throat.

The next morning, I sign the papers.
       The skin around your eyes is soft
           and filled with blood, like a ripe plum.

Together we are released into the world,
       and, in the car, you gently dab your eye
           with a sponge first, and then, a brush.

HARVEST

Naomi Shihab Nye

(For Palestine)

The American doctors come to see
what we are living through when we pick olives.
They are our witnesses, working for peace.
My uncles stand with buckets in both hands.

The doctors say they are shocked to see.
We don't know what it would feel like,
not having guns pointed at us.   Guns
have been pointed at us all our lives.

America, don't act surprised, you bought them!
Just tell us how to be a farmer, with guns.
Or celebrate a birthday, with guns.
No guns invited!

The doctors say they will go home and tell
what they experienced. Their kindness is
a balm. We think people know already, and care.
But where is that news?

Some say Israel would be happiest
if we just disappeared. Like in a magic show?
Our magic is that we are
still here and were always here.

LATE NIGHT PSALM

Richard Jackson

The moon snaps its rope across the stubble field.
Clouds lay in shreds across the hillside.

The black hole that is the barrel end of the assault rifle.
The screams that are trapped there like dying stars.

The dreams that drift away with the early seeds.
The milkweed seeds later hovering like doves.

The gun wavers, tracing the direction of a weathervane.
There is no compass to tell us where we are headed.

The dimmest stars knife their light into the pond.
The songs of crickets barely rise above the grass.

Radio waves pass through us unheard and unseen
The killer's dreams speak a language of silence and fog.

All the promises float by like last year's dried out leaves.
The shadows of these deaths return to stain the soul.

How many burnt out planets inhabit our galaxy?
How many doors are shut tight in our own souls?

In the muzzle of the gun too many futures are trapped.
In the muzzle of the gun every meaning begins to explode.

Why the sunset is now an open wound on every sky
Why the heart never heals with a prayer or kind words.

Why when a child falls their shadow stands back up, for
hidden in the dark center of the cypress a mockingbird sings.

Tonight these few unspeakable words flashed into being
as if in these headlights, then returned to their extinct language.

There are regions of the heart inaccessible by any map.

NABOTH'S TRUTH

Richard Jackson

There are always shards of light that are never
swept away. There are so many pages missing
from our histories. Even now the words for Truth
lie muted by the roadside. Newspaper filled with
stories you should read float over you like hawks.
But like me, you don't want to believe them.
They say I cursed God so they could stone me
and then steal my garden. My own people!
It was a king who thought you could do anything.
But you know that, and you have one like that
of your own. It was his wife who plotted with two
liars to accuse me. Everyone believed what they wanted
to believe. Even your own truths seem to dart
in and out of sight like fireflies. The lies hover
like yellow jackets around the garbage. What
you will be left with is something like the shells
left after the pigeons in the park. Our prophet
sounded like an owl in the night, but the king
would not listen until the truth finally ended him.
It was dogs that licked the blood of his wife.
But that is not my truth. I live in a waking landscape.
My soul hovers over you still, like a dragonfly.
It wasn't just a garden it was a history, the story
of my family. We do not have long. In a while
you will hear the sound of locusts stirring beneath
your feet, but you may not know it. There is no truth
that will not upset you. It doesn't care what you think.
Like the rogue planets spun off from dying stars,
invisible now, until they will, like the Truth, collide
with everything you thought you once believed.

A WORLD WITHOUT ANGELS IS NOT A WORLD

Richard Jackson

What is that world that appears behind the threads of our
firelight's flame unravelling in the infernal air, maybe
a vision of a few late buzzards harvesting abandoned shadows,
a world whose shadows ferry themselves across
the evening waters, shadows that blend with the bats
that skim the surface,

                and what is that world that midnight
street cleaners wash away with the discarded prayers
of the day, where the steel crane lurking over the church
points to the river where the sandhill crane gazes
towards an empty future, a world of forgotten dreams
pooling in clogged gutters,--

                aren't these the visions that reveal
to us the lonely hours of the soul, worlds where the open
mouths left on distant battlefields cry out to us? Above them
a few milkweed seeds pretend to float like angels.
The moonlight stretches its rope across the field.
Months later, a fleck of blood still stains a white rose.
Above it all, no angels, only the shredded clouds that
seem to have no place to go, a sunset that wants to
appear as an open wound.

                My love, where are we?
what are we to do when all the reflections seem empty,
when the tent of stars seems to shroud the world,
when the only embraces seem to be given by shadows to
the shadows of shadows? For a moment, the pale, brooding
moon has no answer. Maybe hope is here, in the white ember
that suddenly comes alive.

Maybe, as the mystics pray,
we must drink the silence of the Angels believing
there is a world inside this one that flashes into being
the way those passing headlights light up the trees for
a moment which is more real than what the clocks have
ever measured, like a love that is invisible except
when it is not. So maybe Blake was right and we must
see eternity in that fleck of blood on the rose. *Brother
Sun, Sister Moon,* Francis preached to the anxious birds,
for they, too, knew, like him, a world inhabited by Angels,

like the radio waves that pass through us unheard and
unseen, just as your radiant glance, even now, has lit up
those regions of the heart inaccessible by any map.

THE COLUMBINE

Richard Jackson

The silence within each word, the simple syntax of wind
whispered against the chimes, the owl's answers echoed
in the dark spaces dappling the immense, impossible sky
between stars, drifting as they have since the beginning,
everything becoming only what it will become, though
I could not have seen that in 1996 under the tree I still
can't name, nor most of the flowers you plant except
the red columbine, little lanterns lighting what we believe in,
the earth that returns what we give it, those transplanted
gardens of your dreams, the star that watches over
your face each night through the window, itself drifting
through time to disappear just as the morning doves
cloak the day's news, a world that hovers like the invisible
black holes that perforate the center of our galaxy,
what the untranslatable words of your sleep also cloak,
so that I should touch you as softly as that starlight did,
for it is true that every star wants to be the daylight,
every flower, every word wants to blossom the love
it harbors, showing a way like the light of your columbine
whose seeds will migrate next Spring into galaxies of color
we never expected, constellations that will whisper our love.

THE TRAIN WRECK OF LOVE

Anita Endrezze

My heart is burning alive
for you.
The Van Gogh stars are spinning for you.
The trees are greening the sky
for you, moths circling the flame for you.
The moon howls your name,
crickets are silent for you.
 I hold a tin can to my ear
and hear the deep male thunder dancing for you.
In the river, tiny hearts battle upstream
for you. Clouds become deltas
for you. Trains divide the air into whistle and poem
for you, hurdling across the yellow wheat plains,
lost in tunnels that praise the darkness of you.

Birds and storming violins find their songs for you.
Oceans flood the red hills for you,
longing to touch that which is opposite.
Passion and ice. My heart burns,
my heart burns. I offer you the terrible gift of love
the fractional annihilation of self.
 I offer my torn and bleeding heart
on love's altar. I offer the atlas of my body.
For you, I offer the name of my lost angel.

HOW TO TASTE CHOCOLATE

Anita Endrezze

1
I prefer dark chocolate
for its slightly bitter taste.
My edible life.

2
I am Ixcacoa, Little Chocolate Woman,
your sister-goddess. With such tenderness
I offer my body, the spicy brown elbows
and caramel thighs, the red wrapped heart.
The wanton self-sacrifice of love.

3
Touch your tongue
to the night, the velvety sweetness
the tiny star brickles
and white chocolate moon.

4
Chili flavored, mint, sea salt.
Lavender, cherry, orange.
Pick one and go sit on a hill.
There are the windy birds swirling
across the broken sky.
And you're sipping tea
from a thermos cup,
dissolving

lavender fields.

SMALL SPACE

Anita Endrezze

I'm my own small space
and there's meaning
in that   Yet
what's inside of me is oceanic
40 teaspoons of salt
sweating love
(tiny fish- shaped tears)

23 feet of convoluted coils
digesting (oatmeal and pizza)

99% carbon (diamond eyes)
oxygen and hydrogen
(O the weight of an earthbound soul
who longs to breathe clouds)
nitrogen and calcium
phosphorus
My bones weigh 4 lbs
broken and age-porous
(sister to the dying coral)

It's crowded in here, a jelly bean jar
full of 37.4 trillion cells,
and universes of microbes surfing those cells.
(I am a cosmos of infinite beings)

My rib cage is an altar to my heart
(light the candles of love)
My pelvic bones an earthy cradle
(children slept there)

Each of my eyes has a blind spot
where the retina attaches
but my eyes see past the hole

(the way we see tree branches
and not the sky between)

I can see 10 million colors
the crow's iridescent wing
turquoise veins in a rock I hold
(red willow twigs in blue rain)
the pink flush of a lover's skin

Albert Einstein's eyes are in NYC
in a safety deposit box
(mine are in a medicine woman 's dream)

My hair is strong enough to support two elephants
(if ever I needed to twist a rope
and ask them to stand on it like acrobats)

Some knew my secret roses
when I was worshiped (a brown goddess)
I was young, my body a river of desire
Now, I'm a clay vessel and earth
calls to sovereign earth
This small body will mother
the dawn songs of a forest of birds

I'm everywhere
50% of the dust in my home
is yesterday 's me

(the way a lightbulb
doesn't confine light)
the space of me
is beyond me

I'm the space between the muscle
and the synapse, the word
that is a poem

NIGHT PSALM

Anita Endrezze

"The world around sends up its holy chant"
From a poem by my relative,
Slovenian National Poet Oton Zupancic (1878-1949)

In the soft summer twilight, pale blue
horses float through moonlight.
This far north, night falls late
and incomplete.
Robins sing slower at midnight
while ivy grows an inch,
tendrils tangling stars.

If you're far from home, lost,
and the tide of war is rising,
and your dreams
have stuttered slow,
and the world's fist
is a body blow
against your tenderness,
be the resolute ivy.

Be the light that lingers
in the darkness.
Be that holy chant
in the robin's song,
the waves rippling,
in the fragrant dawn.

RELIEF

.chisaraokwu.

> *Ogidi*
> *Akola, Agu*
> *Onitsha:*
> *these frontlines*
> *blurred lines, refugees in line*
> *for the hungry end.*
> *— 1969, Aba, Nigeria*

imagine
children carrying
stretched blue-veined
balloons for
bellies, like sacks of water.
imagine pin-bursts.

hollow eyes
wake at dawn to yolk
hanging from
the sky.   boys,
girls open their mouths & dream
of shapeless hunger.

eggshells crack.
out pours sun & light
Caritas
gives us
an egg yolk for our portion:
no chickens, no goat.

many are
the ways to divide
an egg yolk
but never
with your teeth. 'twould be a waste:
balloons burst ∧ crude graves.

i begin to see me how you see me and forget i knew me once

after "No Mirrors" by Sweet Honey and the Rock
.chisaraokwu.

in mother's house:
windows windex'd clean &
sparkle mirrors shine bright.
here i am pink with fairy wings.
out there speck of dust calcium &
spit clinging to windshields. swipe
right. clean the freckles from my left
cheek. swap brown eyes green
then swipe white. new
eyes. see them mirrors
everywhere. i see me in their
eyes   see me: i am a type
of white / an imitation
of black / an indictment
of red / an accusation of
yellow – a useless rainbow
invading sky blue
eyes & i
forget i knew
me once.

JUNCOS AND BUNTINGS

-For Binoojé

Ty Dettioff

Look at the rainbow
in the fog
above the barn
where the pigeons
throw themselves
into the hayloft.
     You can see it
at this angle from before
the time you told me
how hard it was the day
my car broke down.
I slept in town that night
     miles away
from you and your womb,
both only warmed by the bog
and our two snoozing dogs.
Don't hold your breath
but this is what it sounds like
     before I cry.
Mourning doves coo hard
like fresh sheared lambswool
and this sharp horizon lacerates
queen anne's lace in the ditch
but the mountain ash in the field
have berries that
     just hang in there
happy to feed every single
nuthatch and chickadee,
even the juncos and buntings
that visit for long winters.

You can see it
miles away
before I cry.
      Just hang in there.

CLEANING TROUT

Ty Dettioff

A young man with a switchblade pen
can't decide if he will fight or write
about loss. A young woman
with clay molded false nails
a blue-gray she says is sparkled
stole classroom glitter and pressed
her fresh-did nails toward the bottle bottom.
Her reach was to repair mens' stares
from side-eye trout
back to gentle bears.

She watched benevolent gardeners plant seeds
whisper *grow grow please grow*
season into combines and thrashers
to harvest spoils. She won't be
the grain truck
or the good luck
but the *get fucked*
her ma screamed at the match
that lit her pa's clothes.
She wept lighter fluid.

Youngman's father rips lids off
tallboys of Beast with his teeth
and drinks like a fish.
After clanging can after can
his butterfly knife mouth rusts shut
a cocoon of tiger swallowtails and fruit bats
claw his rippled mouth's roof.
He never sleeps dry
or without sweating, suppressing.
He remembers young women with false nails
who stole knives to clean trout.

TO KEEP AWAY CROW'S FEET

Ty Dettioff

I watched a dozen red wing black birds
fight over a single maggot in the church parking lot
as funeral barkers repeated the priest.
The birds smeared that crawler into a grease
to bake on the blacktop. Maggot resin
waxed their beaks. Soon I will gather fiddle head ferns
and place their fuzz on my tongue.
I thought about paving my driveway,
left it dirt instead.
I won't reseed the lawn either.
I can smell the bog's breath.
Thickets are not fallow.

Last winter I crept to the crawlspace
slept away four moons. When I awoke
I could only stomach tubers and a few berries.
But I wanted meat in my mouth.

Mayflies hatch and we tie bait
to match. Fingertips gaunt and sharp
from feathers and thread, a tight quilt
knit to moisten trout tongues.
Fly rod flits cast spells over swamp streams.
I do not understand trout rising in the thaw
but I damn sure know the comfort
in the underbelly of a bog.
Worms and maggots ask questions
all winter long between roots and decay.
I plug my ears with mourning dove songs.
I tilt with the earth away from the sun.

Together we burrow blindly
like voles chase winter grubs.

If we traveled like birds we'd grow fat and pretty.
My hands would soften.
I'd moisturize my crows feet and fallow heart.
At every funeral I'd say the same thing.
I'd knead spruce sap against my gums
and ask the needles to have mercy on my tongue.

THE MOUNTAINS

Anele Rubin

The snowy mountains
and the shadows they offer,
the comfort
of mountains in a darkening sky
for all the cold
for all the bitter cold,
still you can remember
easily now as the shadows
are deepening, you can remember
how in spring, the sun lingered,
the last rays on the mountainside
as if caught there in the peaks…
and then later we were glad for the glare's fading,
for the cool night air to bring relief
from scorching sun and biting flies
that drive a horse mad, a horse who now
is clenched for the bitter
icy cold that makes the water in the bucket
hard and mean, that puts icicles on your face,
that makes you walk slow and think slow
and only the chewing and chewing keeps you warm,
the hay and grain, and the woman
the old white-haired person
kissing and fussing and shoving apple and carrot pieces
up to your mouth as the sun goes down and she trudges back
through the snow, down a hill, and into the farmhouse
looking back at you with such concern
you long for summer
and her walking lively again.

DOG-EARED

Patricia Colleen Murphy

With sharp scissors you snipped
their silky ears. Sent the tips falling

like leaves leaving our beautiful dogs.
Ears I have kissed, caressed more

than I have, lately, the doe-ey hair
on your arms that many years ago

made me fall in love with you.
I picked up the parts. Thought about

stitches, several that could make
the ears soft again, smooth, pat-

worthy; I obsessed over nerves, veins.
Would blood flow back? Would rust coats

grow again? But the ears were already dry,
flaky as rawhides. We had been fighting and

you cut their ears to punish me. My perfect,
literal companions. Who know no sarcasm.

Who show their care in wiggles. You cut
their ears off. Their silky ears. And even

though it happened in a dream, I woke
knowing I could never forgive you.

A LULLABY

Marina Tsvetayeva

Over deep-blue over the steppe
From stars of the Great Dipper
To your forehead, but . . .

                                --- Sleep,
Deep-blue stifled by pillows.

Breathe, in but not out,
Gaze, don't just glance.
Volynia's-one-eyed-moon,
Caspian-lullaby.

Over flattery over a walking-stick
Like beads of dew that fall
Fingers begin their work . . .
Footsteps --- stifled by pillows

Lie down --- but don't move,
Tremble --- but don't cry out.
Volynia's-tangled-limbs,
Caspian-caught-in-lies.

From the sea from the Caspian's --- deep-blue cape,
An arrow whistled, but . . .

                              (sleep,
Death stifled by pillows) . . .

Chase --- but don't touch,
Sink in --- but don't sink under.
Volynia's-tinkling-chime,
Caspian—kiss.

13 February 1923   translated by Mary Jane White

A LETTER

Marina Tsvetayeva

One doesn't wait for a letter like this,
Like one waits for --- the letter.
A soft scrap,
Around it a ribbon
Of glue. Inside --- a small word.
And happiness. And that's --- all.

One doesn't wait for happiness like this,
Like one waits for --- the end:
A soldier's salute
And into his chest --- the lead
Of three 44's. Into his eyes, red.
And that's that. And that's --- all.

No happiness --- I'm too old!
My flower is --- wind-blown!
Waiting for the courtyard square
And its black muzzles.

(For the square of a letter:
For ink and magic!)
For mortal rest
No one is too old!

Nor for the square of a letter.

11 August 1923

translated by Mary Jane White

BORING OLD SEX AFTER 35 YEARS

Ann Fisher-Wirth

This year my students are into it—
sex every which way, licking, sucking,
masturbating, fucking, ac/dc,

lineups, straight, bi, group, anon—
they write about it in poem after poem,
about the fluids of their bodies,

shit, piss, blood, snot, barf,
smeared, leaked, and the hardon,
the cock, the clit, the spurt, the cum—

they are "undoing the self
and challenging gender identity,"
and I love them for their sweet

brilliance and youth, their carrot-dyed hair
and tats and huge hoop earrings
and reinvention of the wheel. Me? well,

been there, done (some of) that, but never
quite so frank about it. What I want,
these days, these years, is the same old guy

in bed each night, my honey, my bear,
and the privacy of our bodies,
what works, what doesn't, what sometimes,

how we manage and don't mind, what's weird
about us and just ours, how I speak
in tongues and he knows every syllable.

'TIS A CONSUMMATION

Ann Fisher-Wirth

When my kids were tiny, all they wanted was to hang on me.
Probably my mom felt bereft when she came to visit, when after
the first thrill of her presence they would turn to me instead—as
now I feel bereft when, after the first thrill, my grandchildren
turn to their mothers. There is nothing like the idolatry of the tiny
child, that bodily adoration, no way you can be close enough.
The hand slipped into yours as you cross the street, the body
climbing over yours, sprawling and cuddling as you read a story,
the bone-breaking hugs. It's everything, everything.

One day long ago, while my kids and I were visiting, my mom
and stepfather drove us to the zoo. Tired, they waited outside
while we went to see the animals. When we emerged all sticky
with cotton candy and popcorn, they were lying on their sides in
the grass, in the dappled sun, softly talking to each other, and
I thought, *they are so trusting, as they rest against the earth.*
Already the tumor that killed him had begun to grow on his face.
Soon the earth will open and they will slip into their graves.

My love, my love, we too. Free from the chemicals of embalm-
ing, I will be a natural woman, you will be a natural man. Death
will wrap us in its cloak, filthy with sticks and feathers. But then
at last when our flesh is gone to worms, if we are lucky our
bones will mingle, and we will become mud, grasses, mycorrhi-
zae and springtails, bluets in spring, the toothed dogwood tree.
Our children will know where in the woods we are buried, and
maybe our children's children will plant daffodils on our graves.

AN ELEGY FOR ART SMITH

Patricia Jabbeh Wesley

Some days were created out of the womb of a woman
only for grieving, for the flow of tears, for sitting
with your hands on your lap,
just shaking your head because you've just lost
a dear loved one.
Today is that sort of day, so gloomy, all the darkness
of earth, coming out of the wounds
of unspent years in protest against death.
If this were in the evening, the stars
would not come out. This is when the moon
stands still when children decide to tease
the moon and make it follow them.
But the moon does not follow because
something as horrible as death has happened.
This is when even a metaphor stands in awe
between a doorway and its own door.

I am in grief, Art, that you are dead.
That you died three days ago, died the way
a poem dies in its own heart, died, the way blankets
fold themselves after their owner
takes leave of them, finally, the way birds fly
South, the way the hills collapse after days
of torrential rainfall.
That dying only a poet does because
after all their words have broken through
the doors of many hearts, they take leave
as if they didn't say a word
to push off the call of death.

Art Smith, I did not know you before you came
like fresh wind at dawn, drawn only by poetry
or like leaves fly in search of new ground,

after fall's strong winds toss them into your yard.
The news says you are no more, Art, that you are gone,
the way we lose everything, the way
we lose ourselves, the way words are lost
from lips, the way our world folds under us.
But you are not dead, buddy.
You are only gone from us and from the body
of things as we see them with our bare eyes.
You are here, in this room, where I sit,
laboring over your poem. You are alive,
dear Art, as the wind lives on.

ON SEPTEMBER 11

Patricia Jabbeh Wesley

A Memorial to the Unknown

On September 11, I always think of the homeless
and all those unknown, the forgotten, street people,
those who sit in alleyways, on the stairways,

those who belong to nobody, the forgotten we see
along street corners, their shabby coats unfolding
stories we're too busy to read, their eyes, sunken

and alone, the aloneness of our manufactured world,
enfolding them as they wait as if waiting for us
or for tomorrow or for a god under the shadows

of buildings so built of steel, we thought they were
invincible, those with no name, whose names will
never grace a stone or wall or the lips of a grieving

mother or child or wife, those who were forgotten
in the count, the beggars, too ashamed to be beggars
until that morning when the first plane flew into

the first tower, and looking up, the second also fell,
the homeless with his old coat torn at the sleeve, his
food in a small cart he tooted around a city so alive,

the city forgot him, and I wonder how Heaven
remembers such heroes, and even as they ascended
into the Heavens, I wonder if somehow, the rich

and the poor, the homeless, the unknown coffee boy
at the corner bar, the unknown child who fled home
away from family until family forgot he was still

alive, and I wonder if (these) rising dead held hands, poor,
rich, the beloved and the unloved, and all those who
shaped the world before the world shattered us all,

and how I wonder how it felt holding hands like us
in our common tragedy, the gone, and those whose
bodies were so crushed, but in death, they rose

and rose above their killing, the beloved father
and the motherless run-away child, the street walker,
the black, the white, and the yellow skin?

Since no matter who we are, dying is dying,
the common denominator since blood is blood
and grief is as deep as grief and all our tears flow

all the same, and the heart pounds like a heart
in grief and in pain, no matter who we say we are.
I wonder as we remember, if they remember us.

LAST KISS:
VALENTINE'S DAY 2008

Susan Foster

After they cut the tumor   from your neck
I held you close   and you laughed   to see that I had
brought the Kiss.   Every year for thirty-six years
I have given you this Kiss   giant whirled merry-go-round
of chocolate   wrapped in shining foil
glistening   gaudy   garish   pink
as a young girl dressed for Valentine's Day.

When the children were asleep we'd sit at the kitchen table
and carefully undress the succulent chocolate
its pink foil falling   like spring petals   in the wind
the merry-go-round slowing   and only us
twirling   dancing   until at last   in the round curve
of our kiss   all the world was gone
while Moonlight Sonata   played somewhere
in the deep   winter   night.

Nine months it took   until
the strength drained thickly out from your body
as leaf-clogged rain   seeps slowly   into the ground
just nine months   until you
would be as helpless as a kitten
in my arms   until the bright   dancing   laughter
of your life   would slip away
and I would find the Kiss   unopened   still
     its pink foil   shining

THE FOREST FOR THE TREES

Melissa Studdard

It's all my fault
for making love to the avalanche.

House dusted gray now
with rocks and debris, spruce trunks
jutting from the bodies of windows,
ragged as broken bones poking through skin.

I only meant to lie in the driveway
until God's distance thawed.

Then the sky would be full of hot
air balloons and Mary Poppins types,
float-singing beneath ebony umbrellas.

But like a dune transfixed by the ocean
I opened my legs to the crashing.

Such a sad story! And the whole
time, what I couldn't see: God
already there, drowning inside me.

INCANTATION FOR PAIGE AND KAVEH

Melissa Studdard

Speaking of vows, someone mailed the bride
an envelope filled with finch's wings. As if love
could ever be so simple. The groom said, *Bring me*
this new dialect. I want to fill it with couplets. The bride said,
First, show me the ladder in your throat. When they handed
each other the promise, it looked like hoops of gold.
But really it was a sunrise that will go on and on. After all,
every poem is widest where it's been stretched by lovers
walking in twos. But this must be how all marriages begin:
someone carrying an envelope filled with enchantment,
someone opening it without breaking the wings.

INSIDE THE BEIGE BRICK HOUSE, THE BEIGE ROOMS

Melissa Studdard

and beige-shirted people sit beautiful as unbuttered
biscuits, their awful loveliness upon me. They want me

drier than wheat and so still no marbles can roll

from my head. I want summer flashing the yard
red with begonias. I want Ladder-backed Woodpeckers

knocking at the gables, and Crepe Myrtle blossoms

blown down like hot pink cotton in a storm.
I'm embarrassing like that. A walking faux pas no one

wants to be seen with at the mall. I know love like

the arms of a cactus. I know the scent of earth revealing
her secrets after a much-needed rain. I buried

everything they told me to bury. Then, I dug it up again.

RETURN TO THE LAKE HOUSE IN EVERGREEN

Angela LaVoie
> *After the concussion*

I. Boat Ride

One year after speaking our vows, we rented a canoe.
I wanted to. No whitewater bucking me from a raft, but still,
the canoe a shimmering fish I couldn't catch.
I laughed when you and the deckhand helped me to my seat.
Horizon swirled. I asked you to paddle us out midlake,
each ripple of water a dagger forged from sunlight.

The log-and-stone lake house, where we spoke vows, tilted.
I tried to focus, asked if you remembered our wedding.
I did not. Asked you to tell me again the story
how we snagged the sold-out venue. Two cancellations
and the lake house was ours. And you
with a diamond for me still in your pocket.

Sky fell into lake. I held onto the canoe, both sides,
asked to paddle, almost tipped us, but we stayed safe.
A few more strokes before passing the paddle back to you,
if only I could take back that whitewater trip.
I needed to know a boat could still hold us, my arms still paddle.

II. At the Inn

We had homework—physical therapy.
Twenty-five paces, out and back.
Supinate, pronate, let my foot grab the earth.
Each bump and dip, a mountain to the ant.
You, standing at the far end, there to catch me.

One year before, you'd stood at the end of that long
aisle of petals, waiting. Surely, you must have known that day
I'd reach you. And now, these few months later,
my feet falling into melting sky.

OR COULD I FINALLY BE ALLOWED TO LEAVE MY ANALYST?

After Remedios Varo's Woman Leaving the Psychoanalyst

Hedy Habra

I am leaving his office with my hair standing on end. No iphone at hand, or else that would have made a great selfie. I walk out with a steady stride, tired of these useless sessions. After all, am I not reconciled with my dark side? No more makeup to hide the once widening circles around my eyes: I'll let the gray show on my temples, allow my electric hair to rise and curl at will, catching sunlight and moonbeams in its spires. I don't need him anymore but he doesn't seem to know it. There's still work to be done, he says, wants me back over and over again. I have no more stories to tell, no more foggy areas to recover, forge and weld. Has he become addicted to my voice, or does he see his own shadow reflected in my dreams? See, this is the story of my life: analyzing instead of being analyzed, entertaining instead of being entertained.

THIS WAS BEFORE EVERY GIRL GOT HER JACKAL IN THE SUNLIGHT

Shelly Taylor

Above the clouds is light
and below is still dark in the cities and outside them in the forest.
When the hands were to be kept busy   the hands were to carry the jackal light.
Christmas trees had been carted off   it was a new year for them.
You start off with snow and make something.
This was before he laid her naked on the kitchen floor
and they had each other's bodies   dark and snow out back the yard.
Jackals howl open into the moon and children love the drone of voices
howls through the trees   even in cities.
You can play by the train tracks all your life
or go west for real   which is really to go under
to be of no more   I meant death but that's way too taboo.
Luck is a lot like that and jackals cannot be made pets.
Neither frogs but that has to be learnt the hard way.
Luck is knowing you are going to make it
whether hard up or not howling by the train tracks
real good dog by your side won't bite your fingers off.
Every man I ever wanted had a pocket of rusty nails for me
hard luck thing you are far from Georgia. Children with pretty smiles
know how that works. Above the cloud line is sun and that's what matters
hard freeze too   boys on the kitchen floor.

GODDAMN EVERY DIRT ROAD

Shelly Taylor

Flooded to Daffodil Bridge   we are 33 and 34 respectively
our childhood drunkenness years later each Christmas a dirt road
named Daffodil. Cast gold those 2am fireflies   how dark
despite the headlights   these sleeping things come up from the earth
river going somewhere we couldn't see for to bend
they flicker   make you a girl again in a hayfield on a hay bale
in a meteor shower   the next day Norma Jean died
you wrote God may my word light a fire to it alone
for every soldier bows from the hip   metals you pass to your children
navy ships and girls with legs showing in France   the Riviera heat all day
on their legs no matter what—we were brave girls running
behind the dark part of the barn for dare   legs furious
every turned corner   ten dollars the crocs won't get you
one houseboat summer you put your body in the river
and though it is cold   you put your body in the river
practical thing once won a bikini contest in Mexico God
Daffodil and Norma Jean with the skinniest waist we do not forget.

TRAVELING MERCIES

Shelly Taylor

I am my great grandmother's   keep me hungry.
I came back two knees a dirt road   ochre the desert body
braced for the stone always rolls back down. Women
bore children   placed their bodies at the end
of tobacco rows   taught the older ones watch for snakes
rock the basket if the baby got to crying   you don't know
how hard we worked   hid our money under planks
the earth of the oak. Compliant was a woman   keep her
hungry and pregnant. I got a little arson in me
said set fire   fight   all the way back to Georgia
put my head on her lap. Inappropriate I got   I mother-fuckered
every waking entity   got on home when the cotton popped out bolls
despite the rain   now the prettiest girl I've ever seen is barefoot
the 7/11 for cigarettes   two 10s in the back black tinted windows
hair all curled up for occasion. Of the beautiful array of new teens
walking barefoot the dirt lane parallel to the busy road where we were
buying tomatoes at a stand   mama said they'll be pregnant in a year
if not more and the man whose stand it was hollered
I loooooove lil chilluns. You cannot make this shit up nor dip
a plate any better place than this. She was a good woman never
said nothing cross about nobody   the proud will be troubled
in the final days. The wills imposed on them turned them a way
I like the one who goes awry   twists when she isn't supposed to.

BRUSH FIRE

Chard DeNiord

I was drawn into it by the flames that stilled my eyes in a stare
that fixed on the shadow inside the blaze which opened as a mouth
from the other side and sang, "Everything you've ever done
and are doing now will turn to smoke." The fire that burned
the pile of sumac, alder, and oak spread in me as well, as if my heart
were the cedar tinder beneath the pile, so when I walked
I scorched the earth and when I sang the sky accompanied me
with silence. I felt my blood turn to oil as I threw more limbs
onto the fire until nothing was left in the hunger of flames
except a few sticks still crackling at the center with an acrid smell
and a cloud of smoke that rose like a soul; no, a gown no, grief.

SAPPHO AND ANONYMOUS IN PROVINCETOWN, CIRCA 1995

Chard DeNiord

We sat on some steps of a stairway that rose to sky above Commercial St.
in Provincetown.
                    Sappho smiled like Lilith, then lit a cigarette.
                                                            I said
"What is time when we're together *killing* ourselves?"
                                        We were waiting
for *The Lobster Pot* to open across the street, so we had twenty minutes
or so to talk about this and that—Tony's psoriasis, Sappho's dogs, Jerry's poem
in this week's *Atlantis*—just where we'd left off the day before
in our gossip about Marcabru, Levine, and Tsvetayeva.
                                        The stars pierced
through the dusk like so many eyes of the dead.
                                        We grew quiet for a minute
as Sappho dragged on her cigarette and I lit one up.
                                        The distillation
 of ocean's breeze enveloped us like a veil the gods had woven from molecules
in the atmosphere—the same divinities who'd sat just where we were sitting now
before they evanesced the day before to fog and clouds and birds, leaving their
emptiness on the stairs, which was also their presence: Venus, Mercury,
and Mars.
        Our cigarettes glowed like distant lamps, as if we were already
in the Underworld enjoying our fate with Baudelaire, Catullus, and Chatterton.

What did we know about our fuel?
                            Only that it was filling us with poems
as we talked and breathed, breathed and smoked in that eternal little while
which only I remember now, now that Sappho's gone—*that time* I call it
merely to please the gods who ask for only the right details.

We loafed together
in that forever of waiting to enter *The Lobster Pot* where we continued to talk
some more as we cracked our shells and sucked the meat from inside the claws
that fell to our plates.

THE WAY INTO

Whitney Judd

I see a virgin on her knees
angel in the street light

Moses to build a fire a city burn
mock memory like broken necks

of those old who crane too far to
look back and second guess

stills a kindness in the city haloed
with the burdened light in

the crack of the street for the whiten
tearing sheet windows hang

bare to show blood its purity
- a child grown too old soon

who pleads the shriek of a lover
this white robed brittle woman

who now finds the pavement's watch
vigil to her slow laying down

with any lover who will hold her
for a moment to hide

the darkness on again and off
she is - homeless, thrown out:

this ascent of ancient neglect
we whisper of passing,

a hard fall, Mary and a christ
forgotten things still.

I have seen a virgin, the fall
and angels consumed --

a prophet on her knees burnt to
a golden calf, fires

of heat and smoke and of no light
in silence looked at the

end things hollowed in this immersion.

TOWER

Richard Dinges

Beyond city's edge,
where sidewalks end,
trees volunteer.
Weeds grow freely
along tarred roads,
uninterrupted by too
many rules. Our
address is a village
where we do not
live, miles past hills
that block its great
tower, an old white
granary of unknown
use, all words long
ago distilled into
one last language.

KITCHEN TALK

Mihaela Moscaliuc

"That's something," my mom exclaims, "you, me, bica,
her mother too," as her index pinches the blackhead
that's claimed for generations the same precise spot.
Don't! I threaten under my breath, *don't even look,*
especially when someone's around.
Hands in dishsoap suds, I turn to make sure
my husband's out of sight.
How is he supposed to relish
the solfege of my spine with his tongue
if he catches my mom's appraising eyes
or the drift of her genealogical narrative.
Jesus, what's with you Romanians, he once lost it
when, only days after being grossed out
by couples engaging in the flagrant deed
as they took turns straddling each other's backs
on the packed Black Sea beach,
we almost soared off a cliff
as my cousin leaned toward her driving lover's neck
to nick one out.
Mom can't understand what the big deal is.
"America's neck-deep in dreadful habits."
Like? I dare her. "Like always paying others
to care for your intimate business.
Seventy dollars so you can call it 'back facial,'
as if you can't tell your face from your ass."
"Or your elders. Even the ones you love
you dump in 'homes,' then make yourselves feel better
by quoting the high cost. 24/7 among people
with whom you share nothing, some the kind
you loathe enough to have counted as enemies."
My love steps in and hugs me from behind.
For once I'm grateful he doesn't know
my tongue, as mom's segued to bathrooms.

"And you overdeodorize, God forbid
you get a whiff of our own shit. No wonder
you can't look your dead in the eye."
They're shut, aren't they? I joke so not to ask
how she got from flushing toilets to the dead.
What's with this heated conversation? my husband asks.
"Oh no big deal," she serves in English,
"We battle about national tradition.
And pimple wars. She won."

GIRL ON THE RUN

Herbert Plummer

There you are again, running in front of me,
your back-kick like a mare's magic movement,
your dark hair so close I could tie it in braids.
Stay forever five feet ahead of me, so I can reach out
for you, reach for the halt of an embrace,
the sweet stillness that never comes.
So that the sweat stays wild on your skin,
your shadow sweeping closer and closer, then beyond,
past the ache of longing, past my own voiceless, extended hand.

ROTTED BLUES

Tony Barnstone

A strange time has come to America.
We keep children in cages.

Sometimes across the parking lot I hear a woman screaming
after her husband comes home.

I think they are making love.
But I listen carefully because it sounds like pain.

She screams very softly at night,
a knuckle grinding my temple.

I spend a lot of time angry at the television.
Eating angry, drinking angry

"Son of a whore!" shouts the guard, sitting on the writhing boy
while another pries his mouth open and shoves pills past the tongue.

Then he stops shrieking.

Today the ocean groans and shifts its weight against the shore
like a patient in a bad dream.

They have the girls fight like gladiators, tearing cheeks, jerking hair.
The winner gets Skittles and potato chips.

They tremble and wobble and have trouble walking.

They tell us a dash of lead in the water makes you strong.
That isotopes will protect you from cancer.

Don't worry about the seizures, the taste of metal on your tongue.

I heard the gunshot last night, but didn't get out of bed.
To do what? Investigate in my pajamas?

The sun is a red coin or a stoplight or a feral eyeball.
And it's looking at me.

This, I guess, is that.
Isn't that what the mystics say?

Therefore, what my country does is also what I do.

Therefore, the news is a dentist's vibrating needle scraping under the gums.
But the roots are rotted through.

RAISING MY SON IN THE TIME OF PENCE

Jennifer Martelli

The beach grass bends
left: I see the blades' underbellies, beige below
green. Back when my son was born, an artist carved
half-moons into nine tall gray stones
circling a bronze sundial up here, beyond the dunes
and the roses on the crushed rocks. Four boys
I don't know kick a hacky-sack back
and forth on their bare tender high arches:
they play within the long
shadows of the stone circle--their chests
tattooed blue
by the moving light. No one can cross
through their game, break
the arcs. No one.

WHITEWASHING THE WHITE

George Wallace

> *'Estos días azules y este sol de infancia'*
> *-- Antonio Machado*

Look, Antonio, I'm back in New York City, every day I wear the blues, every day I drink in this bar and play the loveable intro-spective fool, you taught me to do that, and I listen to the beau-tiful people and pass your name around like a hat, even as the fascists of the 21st century are closing in -- Antonio Machado, Machado Machado, every day I carry your name in my pocket, in my wallet, a secret poem, pensive in my sad old dying days and thinking about you at the French border, 64 years old and pensive too, Franco on the march, your last days on this earth Lorca dead and Manuel your brother trapped in the National-ist zone -- and yet these are blue days in New York City too, not childhood blue, gray, very gray, winter gray and a different shade of blue from yours, the peril in the world today is not the peril you faced back then but it is real, and the Generalissimo never died, Franco's not dead, and every day I feel it, fascism on the rise and I cannot reconcile myself to the news -- govern-ment of pigs, they have us on the run, the oligarchs and the si-lencers, they have their trolls and their torturers, they have their stooges on the way with gruesome tools

And in the barstools and buzz of artificial light, in the dead black bottles of Cuervo Gold and afternoon chatter, I hear the ruthless ones, spinning like a field of dying daisies their sad counter-rev-olutionary songs

And do you remember the hat I wore in Barcelona in 1970, Antonio, the rain was running into my eyes and you laughed and

said do not worry, my friend, Franco could never kill the dark
mystery of the common people -- you were serene, circumspect,
rich with outrage -- and yes the Spanish men were surly, and
yes the Catalonians were biding their time -- and yes it was in
Barcelona that I first read your words, *'there is no road, the road
is made by wandering,'* and followed you like a cross, carried
your words like a pilgrim or a soldier might -- to the Balearics,
to Marseille, onward by ferry to Athens and Crete, to Arvanite
villages in southern Italy – to the crooked and the cut-throat, to
enclaves and broad glamorous avenues

O Mediterranean sunlight, whitewash the white, celebrate the
blue eternal!

February 22 1939, the day you died, your legacy in your pocket
(and your elderly mother beside you, ready as you to pass over
from this world into the iron fist of the grave), we all make our
preparations and I could go on about this forever but I'm here in
New York and you are gone, beautiful Antonio Machado, *'alma
de fuego,'* spirit of flame -- and yes there's a lot of cold around
here -- therefore Antonio, whenever my little Jesus heart, like
yours, goes out, I take the mystic blue taxi to you

MY FOURTH OF JULY POEM

George Wallace

I know sometimes the life of Gregor Samsa
seems superior to this & in fact we're in deep
soup at the moment it's tempting to just say
up your nose America -- not to mention fuck
you -- but i have also watched you sleeping
in your bed of hopeful roses & I'm ready to
open up my heart & yours & give this thing
another try, i.e. figure out how do we extricate
our sorry asses this time because no America
you are not earth's first or only miracle but
you are a pie chart of spectacular dreams a
launch pad of untold generations, no quit in you,
malcontent ecstatic jack of hearts resurrected
ready to give it all back in the flesh -- o bodega
open 24/7 o ribbon of highway o whiskey in
the jar jesus you are a rattlesnake of mean
ambition sometimes with secret fangs but i
love you anyhow like Ricky loved Lucy like
Kerouac loved jazz I love your poolhalls &
palm trees your applefarms your Clark Kent
manners your mild heroics your boogie nights
& rodeo lips I love your neon Romeos & fishnet
roulette I love your truckstops goddammit --
you million dollar bandstand whore of a nation!
i love how you court disaster race neck and neck
with doom but always come out on top besides
there is only one New York City & California's got
the shit babe, dreams are born here & if they die
they are reborn again & yes the East Coast's old
& the West Coast's sliding into the sea & i know
it's all temporary & of course the Trail of Tears
Jim Crow union busters pussy grabbers stream
polluters the creeping fascist at the White House

window -- intern camps & kids in cages -- but god
dammit & god forgive me for saying this but hell
it's Fourth of July I wake up one day a year &
celebrate America with all its imperfections --
yeah you, you stupid goddamn beautiful country,
your big hands your long stride your fireworks
& sudden magnanimity -- yeah & Woody Guthrie
John Reed Walt Whitman Crazy Horse Cesar
Chavez Langston Hughes Robert Johnson
Rosa Parks Maxine Waters Alice Paul & Gloria
Anzaldua too -- every man who takes a knee
or marches or strikes, every woman who lands
in jail or chains her body to the gates at 1600
Pennsylvania Avenue -- & tomorrow when the sun
gets woke, I'll roll up my sleeves spit in my hands
& jump back into the fight -- with you & with you,
saints & comrades all! & just like Woody Guthrie
we'll beat the fucking fascists together again –

together
like we did
last time

PONY RIDES IN BROKE TEACUPS

George Wallace

the circus is back in town and with it the borders that separate us, the flags we wave in each other's faces, in the name of tribe the gutsplitting categories, mistrust, disbelief, impulse crimes we've yet to commit, the circus has come back to haunt us, and in the name of self-protection and our children's children we ignore the higher truths of our humanity, yes, the old mistakes are back in town,

free admission in the name of fear

affliction upon affliction upon ourselves, amen, born of the desire to be safe, to be cared for, to be well off and to belong, we who are loveless, we who offer false token, we who cannot hold back the hate and cannot inject it fast enough into our veins, nobody writes about this anymore, nobody offers us fair warning, fair or unfair there is a spider at the bottom of the glass and we have drunk it down

these bellies full of chains,
which rattle us to our bones --
these pony rides in broke teacups --

the choking dust of corrals we round our hearts up in, in the dark, forgetting entirely where we left them

A RAINY AFTERNOON IN NEW YORK CITY

George Wallace

i remove my coat
i take off my hat
i shake out my
umbrella, take
a seat at the bar
and place my dog-
eared copy of
   'heart of aztlan,'
  rudolfo anaya,
on the countertop
dear bartender
capitalism is a
sin and i am
transient in the
western world --
i have no nation
save you -- the
solace of hard
places and open
spaces holds no
meaning to me
there is no man
woman or child
from albuquerque
to new york city
who can make
consolation pour
from a tap like you

the human geography of all the americas cannot map my current joy

AMERICAN FREEDOM SONG

George Wallace

francis scott key waves his red white and blue suede shoes and
sings o beautiful for spacious skies, o what a morning burning
with stars and money and plenty of gunpowder

a single jaundiced eye surveys the seven seas, there is no other
ocean for us, we own them all, let freedom ring, surrender
dorothy this is your captain speaking

paul bunyan takes an axe and crushes everything he sees; elvis
grabs a lo-jack and cruises time square in heroin dawn - you
can't take that away from me no no

and trayvon had skittles and the cop had a gun

and we're keeping the poor folk down in freedomland & you
want me to salute that? look me straight in the eye, tell me
straight to my face you don't know how much you and your kind
have stole

even if I love you dan'l webster and the way you put your pants
on one leg at a time and outtalk the devil

even if I love you henry david thoreau and the way you won't
pay for war on mexico and canoe the Merrimack

even you margaret fuller boring as a cruise ship
even you ralph waldo emerson holier than thou
and johnny appleseed (tinpot capitalist) and oliver wendell
holmes (autocrat of the breakfast table)

and walt whitman and walt whitman, chest hairs waving in the magnanimous sun, free as an elevated railway that's jumped its track, walt whitman whistling with sweat and incubating groovy ideas for a nation with no ideas of its own

this is the sweet smell of allegory in the morning, and flowers are napalm and automotive parts are rainbows, and america is a rusty shopping cart hauling veterans to the walmart parade

and miracles fall from rooftops like wall street suicides, and rich men give birth to tennis courts, and women giving birth to each other
and children will always be children and innocent in the bitter-sweet chapel of jarring citizenship

and an immigrant organ grinder making a lonely buck on a lone-ly streetcorner

organ grinding, organ grinding, organ grinding -- there, i said it three times -- a sweet, impractical, tubular, enigmatic american freedom song

SHORT FICTION

FIRST PLACE, RICK DEMARINIS SHORT STORY PRIZE

WOMEN WITH LARGE DOGS

John Tait

When Scott runs into Claudia during his walk, at the corner where the railway bridge cuts Pioneer Street, it's a fortunate happening. Scott first met Claudia at a music festival the month before, a friend of a friend, hit it off talking in the beer tent. Their conversation now, between bridge and bus stop, goes equally well. Claudia is as pretty as Scott remembers, wrapped in a wool sweater against the chill, her red hair tied in a kerchief that she tugs on shyly as they talk.

The problem is Claudia's dog, which is huge, some sort of mastiff, rigged on a chain leash that looks crueler where it winds around Claudia's wrist than where it harnesses the animal's shoulders. While they chat about music and mutual friends, the dog, which must outweigh Claudia by eighty pounds, pulls her toward the graffitied underpass until she sways. It lunges the opposite direction next until she's leaning fully away from Scott, cantilevered, on one leg more than two. Claudia rolls her eyes, makes conversation through clenched teeth.

"Calm down, dummy," she says to the dog. "Jesus."

Scott tries to get the dog's attention. Dogs most often like him. But this one's not interested, nostrils working, dark eyes searching somewhere in the mist. He's a thick, flat, heavy animal, impersonally aggressive. Like a panzer tank.

It's hard to talk on this street corner with the dog pulling Claudia nearly off her feet, and so they make vague promises to stay in touch then part, the dog hauling Claudia in one direction while Scott travels the other. And he's annoyed at himself for not asking for Claudia's number again, annoyed at the drizzle that's started while he's still blocks from home, and annoyed most of all at that bothersome, interfering animal.

Why does such a small woman have to have such a big dog,

Scott wonders, just like he's wondered in the past about other women and other dogs. For protection, sure. For companionship, okay. He gets that a big dog provides more of both those things. He understands, and yet, as he thinks of Claudia being dragged down Pioneer Street, it confuses him too.

When he arrives home from his walk and sees the coy text from his friend, Karen, saying Claudia just asked for his number, when Claudia texts a quick hello the next morning, Scott manages his excitement. He's already getting ahead of himself, maybe because he's been single a while, maybe because it's fun to imagine what life might be like with this small woman with her big dog: epic hikes, three-way tug-of-war in the yard, movies on a sofa with the animal across their knees.

Though he's already experienced all of these things, Scott remembers, just a few years ago, surprised at why he would have forgotten.

Scott calls to ask if Claudia wants to get coffee after work that evening, and she agrees. He's about to head out when she phones.

"I feel terrible about this. I've got to cancel. Carl got into the garbage. It's going to take forever to clean up. And I probably need to take him to the vet. I'm so sorry."

Scott tells her they can do it another time, though what he's really thinking about is that name, Carl, which makes him think of some unsmiling creep with a sports jacket and expensive haircut, some broad-shouldered dude that cuts in to dance with your date.

"Yeah, he's got great timing, this guy," Claudia says then laughs as if Scott would know this about Carl. *"Don't you, dummy? Don't you?"*

Scott laughs too, if only because he understands that one reason some women have big dogs is because a small woman and a large dog can have a world that's theirs alone, filled with their own adventures and whimsies and lore. Scott knows this because – well, he just knows.

*

Muriel told Scott early on, when they first started dating, that her dog had saved her life. Scott and Muriel had been friends back in grad school, had flirted a little then though they were seeing other people, had fallen out of touch for ten years before reconnecting when Scott came to Cleveland for business. During that reunion visit, Scott stayed over in the cottage Muriel rented by the university, and they got drunk and confessed their feelings as the stars were coming out, kept talking until sunrise, an avalanche of conversation about all they'd missed in each others' lives -- relationships, jobs, friends, even the dog snoozing beside them.

"Yeah, B saved my life," Muriel told Scott as she sat and held his hand in the weedy yard behind the cottage, her voice hushed, her free hand scratching between the animal's ears. Scott never asked what exactly Muriel meant by that. He knew she'd had at least one health scare in the years they hadn't talked, had spotted a bottle of antidepressants on a shelf in her cottage's small bathroom. Though she might have meant it literally for all he knew, that the dog had pulled her from a burning car or icy river. He never quite found out.

The dog, Beatrice or B, was a big, friendly mongrel of uncertain age, a foundling with scars on the side of its snout -- happy and affectionate, clumsy and comical, with large, mournful eyes. Muriel sang songs she'd composed for B, had conversations with B about neuroscience and Motown and supplied B's earnest responses. Scott enjoyed it the way you do listening to any two old friends, even though he didn't understand half the inside jokes.

There was one problem with Muriel's dog. B barked whenever Scott touched her owner, when he kissed her, when he sat too close. It was not angry, not a warning or remonstration, just a flat, inflectionless sound, a comment. Scott lived hours away, and when he arrived for a weekend at Muriel's, it was the same ritual always. He and Muriel would hug in the driveway, and B would bark. They would kiss in the front room, and B would bark more. By the time they were sitting at the glass top table in the back, the dog would be barking steadily, indefatigably, until they pulled their chairs a respectable distance apart.

It wasn't a huge problem, this chaperoning. And the dog mercifully never barked while they were in bed, though it would worm its way between them in the late hours, so Scott often found himself balanced by morning on the mattress's edge with sticky paws pressed into the small of his back. But he remembers that barking, the dozens of interrupted conversations and unexpressed sentiments, just barking, more barking, the steady, incessant racket of it.

"Is she jealous?" he asked Muriel once, even though he could see nothing resembling that in the animal's dark eyes.

"Dogs don't get jealous the way people do. They're protective of their station, of their sphere. It's more abstract. Less personal."

"What's causing it then?"

"Beats me." Muriel shrugged. "Maybe she's just a barkin' fool. *Right, B? Who's a barkin' fool?*"

"I just wonder sometimes if she's picking up on something."

"Picking up on what?" Muriel had turned to face him, and he felt some danger in proceeding, in theorizing too recklessly.

"I don't know. Forget it."

"Are *you* jealous?" Muriel asked after a time and laughed.

"Of course not." The question annoyed him. If he was jealous, it was only that the dog had been there when he hadn't, that decade of Muriel's life he would never know, all those happy and difficult years.

Muriel was a post-doc at the university hospital and worked long hours in a lab there. Often during Scott's weekend visits, he ended up spending more time with B than with her. The two of them developed a camaraderie as housemates, as creatures with shared interests. They took long walks through the lush neighborhoods around Muriel's cottage. They watched baseball on TV and ate meals together. A few times, when there were thunderstorms, Scott sat and held the dog in his arms while B cried and cried, no matter how he comforted her. It would go on for ages, the plaintive whining, until the thunder stopped and the animal would collapse, exhausted, across his knees.

On nights when Muriel worked late in the lab, which happened often, he and B would sit, waiting. When Muriel called to say she would be delayed yet another hour, they would both of them sigh. And when that hour passed with still no sign, they would look from the window to one another, a mute recognition passing between them.

"She neglects us," B would silently say to Scott with her mournful eyes.

Scott would silently agree.

"She said I saved her life," the dog would sigh, resting her head on an armrest.

Scott would nod, would commiserate.

When Muriel finally arrived home from the lab, even later than she'd warned, B and Scott would both, in their own ways, sulk. The dog, after the initial greetings, would retreat and stand, flat-eared and sullen, in the kitchen. And Scott would pout too, though he hated the peevishness in his voice, the reproachful tone that led to arguments.

"I don't feel like you're supporting me," Muriel would say. "My career, I mean. When you talk like this, I feel like you don't view it as important."

"I came here to see you. I drove a long way. We only have a few days together."

The dog would watch through the kitchen doorway, a mute spectator, until Scott and Muriel grew tired of arguing and hugged, and then B would bark and keep dutifully barking until they separated.

Later, lying in bed, dog and girl pressed into his sides, Scott would continue the argument in his mind, declare that it was not selfish to expect a little more of Muriel's time. That it was not presumptuous to expect her to match his efforts. That he wasn't just mad about himself, that he wondered if she'd thought about what life was like for the poor animal, alone from early morning to dark. What did B do here in the long periods when Scott wasn't around to walk and feed and keep her company? He thought about thunderstorms, and it only made him angrier.

But the next morning he would hear the two of them waking together, girl and dog, the drumming of the dog's paws on the wood stairs and the girl's quick footsteps, the singing and laughing in the kitchen then outside where he would find them huddled like plotters by the glass-topped table. He would watch them there, Muriel and B under draping willows, an icon like a Madonna and child or a Pieta. And he would wonder then why he ever could have been upset.

*

Claudia gets back in touch with Scott a few days after their canceled first date, calling from the veterinary hospital, explaining she's still there with Carl. Her voice cracks with fatigue.

"He's still pretty sick. They don't know what he ate. They had to keep him on an IV all Tuesday night. It got pretty scary. He's a little better today."

Scott commiserates, asks if there's anything he can do and is surprised when Claudia says there is.

"I feel weird asking this. But I've run through my favor bank with Karen and my other friends." She sighs. "Could you move my car?"

Scott hesitates. "Your car?"

"Karen dropped me here this morning so I wouldn't have to pay for parking. I totally forgot that my neighbor's moving and needs space for his U-haul."

"Yeah, I can do that."

"Thanks. It's the silver Toyota out front. There's a key in one of those little magnetic boxes inside the wheel well."

Scott copies the address into his phone, drives over. The car is an old Camry, pretty dinged up, the rear bumper barely hanging on. He pulls it around the corner and parks under a tree, texts her that he's done it. Claudia calls immediately.

"Oh my god. I owe you one. I'm not sure how much longer we'll be here. But when we're home, we'll definitely do something. You and me."

"Sure," Scott says. "Sounds great."

Before he leaves he glances at Claudia's little red brick house, at the small backyard that contains a few well-gnawed toys, a wood table with a rainwater-filled coffee cup, a battered wooden chair with a knotted leash wound many times around its legs. Scott takes this habitat in for a few moments longer than he should, until he worries a neighbor might mistake him for a burglar casing the joint, gets back in his car and departs.

*

Scott and Muriel talked often about buying a house together, maybe at some halfway point between their workplaces, a place where they could spend weekends and maybe move to permanently in time. They outfitted this house in their imaginations: the recessed reading room, the twenty-gallon fish tank, the elevated dog house for B to survey the back woods.

"Maybe we could get a second dog too," Scott suggested once.

Muriel turned to him, laughed. "What?"

"I've been thinking about getting a dog. For myself back

home. And when we're together, the two of them could keep each other company, be buds."

"What if they don't like each other?" Muriel's voice, to Scott's surprise, had risen, sharpened.

"Dogs work things out between them. You told me that."

Muriel's eyes were wet now, he saw, arms folded across her middle. "Sorry, I'm trying to process this. I guess I don't understand. Why you feel B's not enough."

"I wasn't saying that. I was just thinking out loud. You're right. I have B. We have B."

They talked about other things – picturesque road trips, a destination wedding -- though all of these plans occupied the same fanciful geography as the house they never bought and never even looked for.

In their last conversations before the break up, Muriel told him that she felt there were parts of Scott that she didn't know, and that she felt "unknown" by him too. Though he was a little surprised, he didn't disagree. The final parting was bad, Scott standing halfway out the doorway of her cottage, a loose bundle of his belongings escaping his grip. Muriel tried to hug him a last time, and B barked, and he pulled from her grasp out to his car, drove off without looking back.

Scott has thought a lot since about what went wrong, what ruined things. Maybe just long distance. Maybe the ten-year interruption in their friendship. Sometimes, in quiet moments, he finds himself blaming the dog, though that's the silliest explanation of all, and thinking about it makes him feel traitorous. But he keeps coming back to that, the reason he and Muriel never connected, never progressed. From first to last touch, with every kiss, every conversation, every intimacy -- that barking, that ceaseless, stupid barking – a sound he might have heard, if he'd been able to hear anything, as he pulled away in his car that final time.
*

Claudia is home from the vet when she next calls Scott, her voice lighter, less burdened, though she yawns a few times. He asks about Carl.

"Oh, he's fine. *Aren't you, dummy?*" Claudia sighs. "Listen. I definitely want to do something, but I'm pretty wiped. And I have a ton of work to catch up on. Next week maybe?"

Scott hesitates. "Sure."

"I was thinking I could make you dinner. Do you like pho?"

"Maybe I'll just call you some time." Scott is surprised at how the words come out, curt, a little chilly.

"Okay." She's confused, he can hear. "I mean, if you don't want to . . ."

"It just seems like you have a lot going on. But yeah, I'll call."

Claudia hesitates a moment before she says goodbye.

Scott hangs up, doesn't totally expect they'll speak again, might not be disappointed if they don't. Maybe the initial excitement has waned. Maybe the timing is off, the narrow window for such things closing. Other opportunities will come, he's been telling himself. And it may be better to wait for someone else, for something different. A girl without a dog. He's wondered why he's returned to this same situation, same configuration. As long as he does, he'll be the third wheel always, the interloper uncertain of his station, needing to pull and protest just to be noticed. Yes, it will be better to wait for something else.

Around this time Muriel leaves a message on Scott's phone, the first in months. Her voice is halting as she greets him, as she draws a few uneven breaths then asks him to call. He listens to the message several times, doesn't phone until a week later.

They chat briefly, small talk and jokes, though he feels the weight beneath her words.

"There's something else," Muriel says.

He has already guessed what she is about to tell him, the only reason she would have called out of the blue with that particular quaver in her voice.

"It happened fast," she sighs. "A tumor in her liver."

"Sorry," Scott says, finds himself wishing there was some easy way off the phone because, though it makes him feel selfish and petty, he isn't sure he wants to talk to Muriel about her dead dog, to share her fond memories.

"I just thought you'd want to know. I remember you two were pretty tight."

"She was a good dog."

"Yeah." Muriel's voice hitches before she laughs. "It felt sometimes like you had more fun here with her than with me, right?"

Annoyance bristles in Scott for a moment. "No, I wouldn't say that."

"Sorry. Just a joke." Muriel sighs. "Okay, I shouldn't have said that. I know it was a sore point."

"It's not a sore point."

"Hey." Muriel inhales. "Just so you know, I've been thinking a lot about what happened back then, my part in it. I can see now that I was selfish, that I did make you do most of the work. Which was unfair. And I regret it."

Scott can think of the vindication he would have felt hearing these words just a few years ago, isn't sure what they make him feel now. "It doesn't matter."

"Sorry. I've been doing a lot of soul-searching lately. I'm still not used to her being gone. It was so quiet at first." Muriel laughs. "Though check this out."

The text arrives, a photo on his phone of Muriel at her glass top table. The puppy in her arms looks like a cross between a German Shepherd and a dire wolf, its bony paws already massive. Scott says nothing.

"What do you think?" Muriel giggles. "Hello?"

"No, it's cute," Scott says. "It's . . ."

"What?"

"I'm just surprised."

"Why?"

"I don't know. It's just –" Scott considers halting, maybe should. "It's just you always said B was your life-dog. Your one-and-only."

Muriel is silent a moment. "But B's gone now."

"Yeah. But you didn't even wait a month."

"Fuck you." Her voice has tightened, maybe near tears. "Why the fuck are you saying these things?"

"Sorry," Scott says. "Sorry. The puppy looks great."

But the call ends soon after, tense and curt.

*

When Scott runs into Claudia in line at the post office, it's uncomfortable at first, three months since they last spoke. Scott considers pretending not to see her, though soon there's no avoiding it.

"Sorry, I meant to call, but I've been busy," he says, and she says it's fine, that she's been busy too, though the flicker of hurt in her eyes says something else.

They talk briefly, part awkwardly, Claudia saying again that they should do something. Scott nods at this, smiles, heads off.

When Claudia texts the next week, asking if he wants to come downtown to shoot pool, Scott is surprised, moreso when he finds himself agreeing.

She has Carl with her, of course, huge and healthy, straining on his chain. The dog greets Scott sullenly, its large nose blowing, hot as a hair dryer, into his palms.

"Well, here we are," Claudia says when they reach the pool hall, starts tying Carl's leash to a post by the entrance.

"Could we just walk or something," he says. "I don't really like pool."

Claudia squints at him, nods. "Okay. Sure."

They do walk, talk for longer than Scott imagined. On the drive over, Scott thought of keeping this brief, letting things drift however they did, maybe toward friendship. And so he wishes the conversation now wasn't so absorbing, that Claudia didn't look so distractingly pretty, to the point that he's as startled as her when they see the time on the old clock over the jewelry store.

"Shit. I totally forgot the meter." She reaches for her purse, glances at the dog then at Scott. "Hey, could you . . . ?"

When Claudia offers him the chain leash, Scott doesn't take it at first. Though he doesn't resist either as she loops it around his right wrist, pats his shoulder then the dog's massive one. Then she's jogging away before Scott can protest, and he can only watch her go, Carl watching too, suddenly alert. Scott holds the leash tighter, wonders how much the beast outweighs him. The dog stares and sniffs, tilts his head back to view Scott before he sits, settles, lolls. Scott feels suddenly foolish, standing braced like he's on the deck of a ship in a typhoon.

He places a few tentative fingers between the animal's shoulder blades, scratches until he hears a rumble of pleasure. For a moment, it's almost pleasant, the two of them waiting under the trees. It makes him think of another moment, another dog, him and B pausing in their treks through the treed lanes near Muriel's cottage, resting amidst birdsongs. That dog gone now to doggie heaven, Scott remembers, still a little amazed.

Scott never knows what it is that sets Carl off, some squirrel or cat, some distant noise, but suddenly the dog is up again. Scott grips Carl's leash, calls his name, is able to halt him briefly, though the animal leans into the taut leash like a ploughhorse, ears up, hackles quivering. Scott looks around for Claudia, wonders if he has time to call before things go very bad, is reaching for his phone in his pocket when the dog moves again.

This time Carl lunges full force, and though Scott is prepared he really isn't, feels both shoulders wrench painfully. He tries to dig in, but the soles of his sneakers skid over the turf, over asphalt. Even when he plants a foot on a curb, it only buys him a moment before he's yanked forward. Soon the two of them are trotting, then jogging. Now, a calm, analytical part of Scott's mind suggests, it will be even harder to arrest the beast's forward motion, to wrest back control. He tries once, when the dog slows, but he's overmatched, can barely believe the strength of the thing.

There is another possibility, of course, unwinding the leash from his wrist, letting go. It might be the most sensible action. But the animal is heading directly toward Pioneer Street with its four lanes of traffic. And so he hangs on, wonders if Claudia has returned yet to find them gone.

Halfway down Arbor, Scott trips on his own feet, topples, nearly dragging, leaving the right knee of his jeans and some skin on the pavement, his left palm scraping too as he pushes himself up. When he stands, it's at a strange angle, still off balance, and he feels the relentless pull of the leash in his twisting joints like he's being tortured on a rack. Then the pop in his right shoulder that he can hear above his footsteps, the pain rising further than he could have imagined. And after that he can do nothing but limp along and try to keep up.

The dog pulls them into one of the quieter residential streets just before busy Pioneer, straining harder, wheezing, the chain disappeared into the flesh of its straining neck. Scott feels the agony in his dangling right arm, the lesser pain in his scraped knee. The blood from his abraded left palm makes it hard to grip the chain. They pass a young guy in a security guard uniform who asks if Scott's okay but doesn't move to help, a group of giggling teens who spectate from a porch.

It is laughable, Scott knows, being hauled down the street like a toy by a huge dog. The rest is silly too, whatever he's hoped for from this. He should have refused the offered leash. He should never have come out with Claudia at all, should have obeyed the inner voice that screamed for him not to.

Somewhere in a shaded subdivision Scott finally does give up, gathers enough slack to unloop the leash from his right wrist, lets the dog go. Unrestrained, Carl races ahead. Scott limps after, breathing raggedly, stopping to lean on a mailbox, leaving a single bloody palm print on its pale brick. He watches Carl in the distance, leash trailing like a comet's tail. Then the dog is gone, and Scott is alone in unfamiliar streets where kids walk bikes, where a television plays too loudly someplace.

Now the phone in his pocket is ringing, Scott feels rather than hears, though his left hand is too bloody to answer it, his right hand dangling unusable, shoulder hurting savagely when he does just about anything. He keeps walking, turning the same corner the dog did, surprised that this street looks familiar, the gaudy Madonna fountain in one yard, the peeling gazebo in another. He nearly laughs out loud as he turns a corner and sees the small, red-brick house with the enclosed backyard. He should have known.

But Carl isn't there, in the front or the back. Scott searches all around, even comes in through the gate in case the animal managed to jump the fence. Because he can find nothing else to do, Scott fills Carl's empty water dish from the outdoor faucet, rinses the blood from his left hand. When his phone rings again, he's finally able to answer.

"Hi," he croaks. "I'm at your place. You better come quick."

The fourth car that rounds the corner is Claudia, parking out front, hustling out. Hand clapped over her mouth, she takes in Scott with his dangling arm and torn knee, stares around the empty yard then, the panic mounting in her eyes.

"He can't have gone far," Scott manages.

Claudia hurries to her car. Scott follows, sits in the passenger seat, clutches his right arm against his body so it hurts less. He's bled on her seat covers, he sees.

For the next hour they circle from Arbor to Merrimack to Dove to Arbor again.

"I'm really sorry," Scott says to her more than once, and though she mutters that it isn't his fault, that it's hers, her expression is tight.

Around dusk Claudia pulls to a stop outside her house.

"It's getting too dark to see," Scott says. "Maybe we should wait until morning."

Claudia nods, is trembling now. Scott puts his left arm around her shoulders, nearly yelps when she leans fully into him.

"What's wrong?" she says, pulling back.

"I think my right shoulder might be dislocated."

Claudia blinks rapidly. "Oh. Do you need --"

"Probably."

She puts the car in gear and pulls out, reaches to squeeze his hand. Her warm palm feels good against everything else, feels dizzily pleasant.

In the ER waiting room, Claudia sits with Scott on the bench after he signs in, holds his hand, weeps every few minutes until he collects her with his good arm, tells her again it will be easier to search in daylight. She nods, smiles bravely, is on her phone then, calling, listening, calling again.

"His name's Carl. My name and address are on his tags. No microchip. He's big. He's very big."

They search for the next week with no luck, driving downtown, checking shelters, posting signs. Claudia has begun coming home with Scott each night to eat, to sleep. One evening Claudia looks through her laptop for new photos to post, pauses at one of herself and Carl, the dog sprawled across her lap during some merry camping trip. She draws in her breath -- a sob, a spasm -- traces a finger down the screen but manages to smile. And Scott smiles too because it's honestly a great picture, because there's something complete about the image, a girl and her big dog, something self-contained, needing no other adornments.

Then they're out the next morning and the one after, further patrols until the streets blur. Though Scott occasionally thinks he sees something, a glimpse in an alley, some shape moving low and fast, it's always just a windblown plastic bag, a roving tomcat. The glint of what might be a trailing leash is always just sunlight on a car mirror or a puddle. The baleful face that appears on the shelter website is only familiar the first moment, then it's just another big dog.

As Claudia cries in his arms at night, as he holds and comforts her, as they make love late, both exhausted, Scott wonders sometimes if she blames him, at other times if she can intuit the truth of what he's begun to feel, that he is happy with just this, that though he will continue to help her as long as she needs, he will be happiest if they never find Carl.

But he will keep helping her look, up Arbor and across Sycamore and down busy Pioneer, so close to the place of their chance meeting months back, the impatient dog nearly pulling her off her feet. Of course, he will help her keep searching.

A SMALL BRIGHT ROOM

Sharon Solwitz

Thea has multiple projects at work, including the mess over in London, but if you crave something—even if you don't think you've earned it—you can still ask. She has thus achieved a labor-free week during Allan's spring break. They can go to Paris or Puerto Vallarta, any fucking where! Melissa, aglow with late-in-life pregnancy, will stay with the boys. "She promises not to give birth till we get back," Thea says giddily, fiercely.

"What about Nathan?" says Allan across the breakfast table. A cup of tea lies before him and a new book on cancer cures.

She knew he'd say that. What about us? she would like to reply but doesn't want to sound whiny. Is there an attractive way to say, And what about us?

It's Sunday, Groundhog Day, overcast. Shadowless, supposed portent of good things. As if in support of Thea's bid for action, a bird alights on the unmaintained flowerbox beyond the kitchen window. It plucks among the dead stems. "We have to live," she says, clamping down on a tremor that threatens her voice. Sounding like an actress in a soap. Remembering back when she'd wanted to act. *Cowards die many times before their deaths.*

"Yes but not . . ."

He stands then seems to forget his next move. She knows what he didn't say: Not without Nate. "What can happen in a week, Allan? He has energy. And his test scores, you saw the letter? Honey, the boy is going to Harvard!"

"Yes. But I don't like the look of—"

"Don't look. You start to see things."

He sits back down, looks into his cup as if for a response to her. Not that she, sour with claustrophobia, expected one or even wanted. She wants to burst out of the cramped, frightened sheath that imprisons them. Nate has been ten months in remission—please can they quit worrying?—but Allan remains vigilant. He drains his teacup, coughs, catches his breath. "Why give them college entrance tests in

116

eighth grade? Is smart everything?"

"Allan, please don't disagree with everything I say."

He looks suddenly right at her. "I don't mean to."

He is genuinely consternated. Like a warm gust through the window comes love for her husband, widening the walls of her heart. When he might be at fault he will ponder. Give the matter full consideration, wanting to do right. She leans across the table, takes his hand and presses it to her cheek, then her mouth. Oh Allan. Thus they toss back and forth the hot potato of their mutual fear.

And here is Dylan, in unreflecting good health. He slides in his socks across the kitchen tile to the refrigerator, opens the door and starts in on last night's dinner. Bits of rice and chicken fall like snow. "How many times have we told you to eat sitting down?" she says in her witch-voice. Mocking her irritation although there is some.

"How about a bowl of cereal?" says Allan. "Or a toaster waffle?" Dylan seems not to hear. Thea proffers an empty plate; he waves it off. Not hungry. Sighing theatrically she hugs him, Dylan, the age Nate was when diagnosed. At twelve Dylan is beautiful, sturdy verging on hefty. "Quit that," he says, though he doesn't yank away.

"Just an excess of love, sonny," says Allan. "Be grateful."

Thea laughs. Continuing to love her nutsy husband. Loving her love. "Think of the children in India," she says to their son. "Starving for affection."

"They're not starving," says Dylan, a reader of news on the Internet. "They're the world's tenth largest economy."

The parents laugh, together now. Their senses of humor do not align with their younger son's, who suspects mockery but can neither return it nor let it go. Craving mastery of wit, he can best his friends most of the time but not his parents yet. Thea feels for him. According to the tests (she believes in tests, has always done well on tests) he's as smart as Nate but with lower grades, a lower boiling point. A personal sense of not-quite-competence that one day she plans to explain as her genetic gift to him. In the meantime: "Why don't you guys go bowling today?" she says to Allan. "If you don't have any other plans?" To Dylan: "Go see if Nate wants to go." She likes them out enjoying, and she busy apart so she doesn't have to inspect it. In the sweet silence of the empty house at the end of winter she'll clean the kitchen. She'll send accommodating emails to the forces that threaten the corporation's London project. She'll start dinner; they are having company. She likes to move fast, do one thing after another with no space in between for useless thinking.

Soon they're gathered in the living room, a merry group, the boys, the dad, Dylan's friend Ethan from down the block. Abbas, Nate's best friend from grade school, they will pick up en route. On a small pulse of joy, she wraps her arms around her husband, tilting her face up for a kiss. He kisses only the top of her head. Her disappointment is out of bounds, like so much else.

Alone, she moves faster than before. The sink and kitchen counter are clean, her note with the attached new contract already in the in-box of the Business Association of Hampstead NW3 (where more millionaires reside than anywhere else in the UK). Other courteously cogent notes have been sent to the Heath & Hampstead Society and the Ladies Pond Association, though their objections seem pro forma. She was trained in Design but in London what she does mostly is schmooze. Locate the tiny interface of self-interest that will allow a project to move forward the next minuscule step. How did that happen? Despite Nate's illness she still holds firmly to the belief that good things are in store for her, and all of them. She washes the lettuce leaves, spins them dry, stows them in a sealed plastic bag in the fridge. In her mind is a far off, shining, gardenlike place where *good things reside,* and she races toward it, in hopes of resting there.

But not today, even with the chicken bathing in its home-made marinade. The feeling of constriction has returned, the sense of being walled up like the prisoner in Poe's "The Pit and the Pendulum." When the table is set and there is nothing else to do besides call Melissa to hear how many pounds she has exultantly gained and how hard the baby is kicking, she skypes Edward Harrison, with whom she sleeps when work brings her to London. Not every night of her stay—this is key—just two or three of the five or so available each month. Were it every night—as if they couldn't get enough of each other—she might have to rethink this. The only person she's told is her sister, and they don't say "affair" though of course that's what it is. Edward, they call *the Young Brit* though he's nearly her age. "So," Gaby will say, "how's the Young Brit?" and Thea will flush and laugh and tell her.

There was a time with Edward when Thea felt on some risky edge. The night after their first night together, alone in her hotel bed she was saying to herself *never again*, and the phone rang on the nightstand. "I want you," he murmured, gulping air in his house in Brighton, and she felt his desire coursing through the long wire into the soft shell of her ear. What a gift, his wanting. For an ecstatic thirty minutes she waited and dreamed while he drove the miles back to her. The next morning at room-service breakfast he said the word *love,* though in the third person and as a rhetorical question (Could a decent, church-raised chappy fall in love with a married woman?) and her chest had swelled with crazy, frightened yearning. Love conjoined with passion? However irresponsible (if not sleazy), it also took courage, self-abandon. People died for it, and not just Emma Bovary: intelligent, strong, charismatic women, and men too. Her mouth had softened, moistened, wanting to open for him, wanting and resisting till she thought she would lift out of her chair. Words of a Hebrew prayer came to mind: *Open thou my lips and my mouth will declare thy praise.* Was this heretical?

But time cools even extra-marital passion. In the course of Nate's illness Edward became her refuge as much or more than her lover, someone with whom she could rest her brain. Was this more or less reprehensible? Either way, one day the London project will end, and with it their connection. Thus guilt and fear merge and sink to the bottom of the pond of her conscious life. She leaves Edward a voice message.

"I have a free week coming up. Would you like to meet somewhere new to us?" A building contractor, he might be able to hand over responsibility. "You choose. Anywhere but Chicago or London." She gives him the dates, tightening her voice against some lurking whine. Minutes later he calls back with Paris in mind, for him only two hours away by fast train.

At dinner Thea is unusually warm and bright with their friends, less so with Allan, from whom she is mentally defending herself. Friends gone, she goes straight upstairs, gets in bed without brushing her teeth, opens the book she is reading, a historical novel from the time of Henry VIII when a passionate, brilliant woman needed a king for access to power and it didn't last long. But it's the twenty-first century. Why can't she take this short trip, with Allan running the kingdom of Nathan's imaginary recurrence? She too fears for Nate, but Allan's fear is so vast and deep it almost nullifies hers—nullifies her, even. Once upon a time he professed himself *grateful* for her attraction to him, grateful—bravely putting himself at her mercy or maybe just aroused to the point of self-abandon. Where is that man now?

When Allan enters the room, she is trembling under the covers. Images of husband, son, and lover have been circling like bats. Cold in her nightgown, she wants him beside her, arms around her.

"I'd like to move up the scan date," he says. "What do you think?"

She can't think about scan dates. After two clear ones Nate has been graduated to scans every six months. The doctor they call bad and the one they call good are on the same page here. The next scan is in June. Her fingers make little rips in the pages of her book. "Why wait," Allan says, "if there's a concern?"

She shakes her head while he's speaking. "Listen. I bought tickets to Mexico City for your spring break," she says though it isn't true. It could become true. She hasn't bought her ticket to Paris. She could cancel with Edward. It wouldn't be hard, even. "I booked us a house in Oaxaca!"

He looks dismayed; she rushes onward.

"There's *no* concern, I mean there's *always* concern but he was clean in December, not a speck. We're going, get used to it!" She pictures Oaxaca, where they went once before the kids were born. Bougainvillea, *las ruinas*, trying to speak Spanish. Allan had a better ear. She thinks of Edward in London. London and Chicago, distinct. The men, distinct. Thus she safeguards her marriage. In almost every way she prefers Allan to Edward. She puts her book down, takes off her nightgown. Make me forget Paris. *Por favor, esposo mio.* Spanish rolls over her tongue. Please, dearest love.

He kisses her—mouth, neck, the top of her breast. But they are husks of kisses, non-urgent, please-don't-be-angry. She's an old rag of a woman. A horny forty-something fanning the ashes of her sexuality into a flame that can't heat anything. She folds her arms over her bare chest, makes a last, sad stab: "The results. Of the scan. Whatever they'll be, do you think our fun will change them? Please,

please, try to be rational about this."

He puts a hand to his face. He doesn't look at her nor she at him. "Did you buy trip insurance?" he says, oh so neutrally. But she knows what he's feeling, *all alone in the worry department*. She also knows he knows what she'd say if he complained about his isolation: *There's no room for anyone but you in the worry department.*

"I lied," she says. "I haven't bought anything yet. But this is *très* time-sensitive. Say yes, darling, it's your last chance. Peace and prosperity rest upon your decision." Dizzy with her mutually exclusive planning, she waits for him to be amused. How easily she used to amuse him.

Allan's spring break and her week off arrive; she flies to Paris. As expected, Allan encouraged it. "You've been working so hard," he said. "You deserve a break. Have fun. I love you."

On the plane her head hurts. She is not superstitious, so where does it come from, the notion that this badness will call down divine punishment? This is Allan's mode, sublimely irrational Allan, believing that Nate will remain alive and well if and only if he, Allan, makes sacrifices. Allan used to overeat and now he under-eats, hoping the fact he looks and feels better won't count against him. Abstaining from sex takes more will power but for the most part lately he has been holding up his end of what she imagines to be the bargain. Poor Allan. Dear Allan.

She almost dislikes Edward.

Still, sex is ardent the first day and night in their hotel in the fourteenth *arrondissement*. She loves the word "arrondissement." *Quatorzième arrondissement!* Then sex between is merely pleasant, then routine, as are the restaurants and museums. The vast Hall of Mirrors scares her, images of her and Edward everywhere she turns.

The last two days she eschews all physical contact with Edward, she can't even hold his hand. He's hurt, and she, pained by his pain, elicits his views on subjects that interest him though she already knows these views. She ventures a complaint about Allan, a facet of her life that she has kept private till now. "He just doesn't know how to stop worrying!" She tells Edward a story about Allan that his mother had told her, full of affectionate mockery. In third grade his classroom teacher mismarked a test of his, a speed test in long division. Two columns, in one of which all his correct answers were x-ed in red. Allan brought the test home weeping. "I think it screwed up his reward and punishment system," says Thea.

He says, "I might like your husband."

She tells another Allan story. When Nate's belly started to swell, the first doctor missed it. A pediatrician with glowing Yelp reviews, residency Northwestern, one of Chicago's Top Fifty Doctors according to *Chicago Magazine*. He palpated and felt only little-boy paunch, leftover baby fat before the growth spurt. "Allan blames himself," Thea says. "I can't talk him out of it."

"I'm not sure," Edward says, "that I want to hear more about this."

He looks sad in his British way, or perhaps annoyed; she can't tell. She stops talking. He may have other girlfriends; part of her hopes so. Should she break up with him for his own sake? Would that be kindness? Sooner or later the London project will end. Things end. It's a view she holds but can't quite comprehend. She's aware of that.

Glad to leave Paris, she's weepy with joy to see Allan pull to the curb at O'Hare. She loves their kiss hello, loves buckling herself into the passenger seat with him at the wheel.

But he doesn't pull away from the curb, though the airport cops are waving them on, and cars thick behind them. His ears are pink. Before anything else, before she can wonder or worry about what he's discovered, before he puts the car in Drive, he has to confess: Nate has a scan tomorrow, Elkin okayed it. "To get me off her back," he adds. "I know, what a welcome. And you're jet-lagged. Forgive me, Thea?"

"No, it's fine!" she says, wishing she too could ask for forgiveness. "I know you had to, and it's okay, it's probably a good thing if it'll make you feel better. It might make me feel better too." Frantic little bursts between breaths. She holds his hand while he drives. She loves his hand and the way he drives, the unreflecting competence. She loves their house, the world of their family. Hugs all around. The following day at Children's she is cheerful and energetic throughout the procedure, the clicking and humming, while Nate cracks jokes and Allan sweats inside his lead apron.

As in December, results don't come the day of the scan. Two days later someone calls to schedule an appointment. At the hospital, parents only. This is the system, bad news or good. Beware the small, bright room, Allan had read in some cancer blog. Though in the last small bright room, he tells her and she remembers (seated beside him in this one), the news was good.

He is chatty today. She wants to respond in kind but she's holding her breath. Peeking out from her casing of so-far-so-good, closing out what can't be changed or fixed. She will not be sad or frightened if there is a choice.

And yet, on the plastic couch across from the doctors, even before either doctor has spoken, it seems unaccountably worse than December. Mentally clogged, she takes in only sensations. Threads of white in Dr. Elkin's short black curls. A hardened brown splotch on the coffee table. In order not to pick at it she presses her hands together. Gail Elkin does all the talking while the good doctor (Paul) looks blank. What's his last name? There was a time when she knew it. Elkin is speaking, but Thea can't get a mental image. *Five small tumors, one the size of a walnut. A spot near his heart.* What kind of spot?

She can't look at Allan but seems to hear his heart beating. His hand is wet, and his shirt under the arms. His speaking voice, though, is low and calm. "So what's the plan? What do we do?"

Dr. Elkin is stern in her curly helmet. She will not inflate expectations. With Nate's aggressive first line treatment, there's a limit to what his body can stand at this juncture. Radiation is out. The point is to do no harm.

"We are going to do *something*," says Allan. His hands squeeze into fists, but Elkin, small and compact, doesn't blink. The case will come before the tumor board. Nate will need more tests. They are to make an appointment at the desk.

Driving home from the hospital, while Allan describes his own plans for Nate's treatment, Thea keeps her face to the window, knowing instinctively that he won't like her tears. She is weakly surrendering, while he, pulsing alive with adrenalin, will never surrender. He's ready for this, glad for the appointment tomorrow so he can discuss with the doctors some of things he's learned from his books and Google Scholar. Most exciting is angiostatin, a drug that stops tumors from developing their private circulatory systems. It not only sounds miraculous, it *worked*—on a girl with the same kind of cancer as Nate's, he actually talked to the girl's father, her cancer became a kind of chronic condition. For a year, but still. He can't remember why she died but he recalls the names of the drugs she took to prolong her life: Thalidomide, which deformed babies in the 1970s because you need veins and arteries to grow arms and legs, makes perfect sense against tumors. Thalidomide along with a maintenance dose of Etoposide, also called VP-16. A small dose. Nate probably won't even lose his hair. He can live with Nate in a chronic condition. He rather likes the word chronic, its root in time. A chronic condition persists. Endures. Without cease. Endless.

Some of his words settle in her mind. VP-16 sounds like an IUD she had that gave women pelvic infections that sometimes made them sterile. She wipes her eyes, but the tears keep coming. Noiseless. Weird. Allan's voice hums in her ears. At the end of Lake Shore Drive Allan turns onto Sheridan, and she says what has just popped into her mind. Since Nate was diagnosed he's been good to the point of saintly. Even more after his Jewish summer camp. He thinks he and God have a pact. "What will he do," she whispers, "when he learns he's going to die?"

Allan swerves and nearly hits the car in the lane beside him. He pulls to the curb, brakes with a lurch. "He is not going to die."

She makes herself look at him. She tries to understand his thinking. Both of his parents are alive and healthy in their eighties. The month before Nathan got sick Allan finished a triathlon among the top ten fifty-year-olds. His blood pressure is lower than hers. "People can *live* with cancer," he says. She nods, dizzy at the thought of what he is seeing, a tie, a stand-off, Nate 1, Cancer 1. Hospital stays like last year, but Nate with hair. "These are facts, Thea. Cutting edge. I've been talking to people. Researchers."

She wipes an eye with the heel of her hand. You're a PhD, she might have said, not an MD.

The hospital's second line treatment, chemo lite (so-called), doesn't seem light. Every wisp of Nate's hair is gone by the second week. His ankles swell, the whites of his eyes turn yellow, it's hard to pee, he's catheterized, there's blood in the urine bag. And for the first time he seems depressed. Allan is indefatigable with the funny movies and joke books, while terror has all but blanked Thea's mind and she exhausts herself trying to conceal it. There is no refuge nor does she want one. Edward has skyped several times but she can't talk, only writes, it's bad, I'm sorry. She's dizzy with sorriness. In the past, despite her failings as explainer/empathizer, the Bad Doctor had at least seemed on top of the situation, but now after minor objections she pulls the hospital regimen and replaces it with Allan's, not as if she believes but as if it doesn't matter. As if Nate has sunk beneath the help of science, and she washes her hands of it. Paul the Fellow remains hopeful but the best he can say is, "We're in new territory." On good days Thea can feign a sense of adventure, while Allan proclaims Nate's regimen a model for other cancer children. Imagining Nate on an angiostatin tour with his heartwarming story, and himself (in his crazy euphoria) receiving an honorary MD, not that anyone has ever received such a thing. There are still good days. But it's hard to stay hopeful when she looks Nate in his yellow eyes. Is something wrong with his liver?

Allan and Thea have discussed what to tell Nate but have reached no conclusion. "If he thinks he's going to die, he'll give up," Allan will say, "and it will shut down his immune system," as if he thinks there's a chance that Nate is going to survive. For her, the world seems to have turned upside down. Instead of good things in store she sees nothing but horrors: pain and death, and no way to change it. An adult by Jewish law, Nate should know the gravity of his situation.

On the other hand, she admits to herself, she has an uneasy relationship to truth telling. Have she and Allan changed places? She has taken a family leave from work, six weeks during Nate's chemo. At home without blueprints to make, clients to woo, she empties the dishwasher, sweeps the floor, mows the lawn, alone, it seems, on the island of reality while Allan peter pans across the moon. One night when the air conditioner kicks off with its usual watery sigh, she wakes up wanting to tell him the whole story of her and Edward. Something new for them to grapple with.

One afternoon a few days before school ends, she drives the boys and Nate's friend Abbas to McDonald's. A treat. "Fuck the antioxidants," says Nate beside her, sidelong-glancing at her during the curse word. He is angry at God for allowing the recurrence, but his sense of humor is intact, and his appetite. He eats three cheeseburgers, one after the other, meat under an orange square of its mother's milk. "Go to hell, Yahweh!" Abbas looks pained. Dylan laughs raucously, perhaps exulting in Nate's rebellion, perhaps encouraging Nate. To her ears Nate's cursing sounds quaint—sweet—like Nate himself. On the way home, in the back seat beside Abbas, Nate can't stop talking. "You're so healthy. It's like you're filled with health," he says to his friend. "It's glowing off you."

"You're so *gay*," Abbas says, but Nate neither protests nor laughs. Abbas is from Iran, son of an American Peace Corps volunteer and a captain in the old shah's army. Older parents like Allan, they are conservative and strict with their son.

"I mean it," says Nate. "Your skin. It's shining."

Abbas looks down at his arm, Thea sees in the mirror. She pictures him ten years from now remembering. Missing Nate.

Nate graduates from middle school and is admitted to a top tier city high school. For the second year in a row he spends two weeks in a funded Jewish camp for children in treatment for or in remission from cancer. He calls it Camp Happiness, a loose translation of *osher.* Camp Osher Hanefesh, joy of the soul. Like last year, he returns Orthodox Jewish, a state that persists for a while, along with a radiant and tranquil joyousness. What do those Hassids do for him? At Osher Hanefesh he and his cancer pals penned beautiful Hebrew letters for a Torah scroll. They went to a Giants game, sat in box seats, received signed baseballs. He brought home a duffle full of high-end candy bars and shared them with Dylan.

A scan at the end of August will determine the efficacy of the new treatment regimen. The night after the day of the scan Thea and Allan go out to dinner all by themselves, Allan's idea. The boys' cousins have come by to hang out with them.

Thea orders wine at the restaurant in order to endure Allan's fantasy-infused pep talk or their anxious silence, but tonight her husband has something new to say. Without wanting to—wanting, in fact, not to—he has harkened ahead to the worst possible outcome, trying to find in it (he can't help it; it's his nature) something of value. God forbid, he says, but if worse comes to worst, their family will have become part of the community from which the fortune of birthplace and class has till now protected them. It's a grounding, although a tragic grounding. He speaks fervently, like a rabbi or a born-again. They have been lucky till now, protected, cut off, even, from the world of ordinary people. He got married and went to graduate school instead of joining the Peace Corps, while in sad, terrible places parents were losing children to hunger, cholera, typhus, malaria, to fanatics who cut off their hands or made them kill their parents as initiation into the rebel army. Now he must prepare to pay the dues of a world citizen and a father. He must be ready to take up this burden, as Jonah was obliged to take up his before he could be freed from the belly of the whale.

In the quiet of the restaurant Thea would very much like to get up from her seat, go out the door into the warm late summer night, and walk for a long time. Fight or flight? Flight, no contest. But she stays where she is. There used to be something about Allan that she couldn't grasp but loved and respected, and here it is again. What to say? You're amazing? She feels unworthy of Allan and dislikes the feeling. Embarrassing. She feels weak as if before Almighty God.

Just before dawn the following day Thea wakes in an empty bed. She finds Allan on the front porch, looking up and down the quiet street at the porch fronts of their tranquil neighbors, their children in happy dreamland. Thinking, perhaps, that he belongs in Rwanda or Haiti? She doesn't ask.

They're half dozing on the porch swing when the landline rings. Although no one of interest calls on the landline, they both run inside. Allan picks up. From the earpiece Thea can hear Dr. Elkin's flat voice. "Don't get too hopeful, Mr. Feinstein."

Allan leans on the kitchen counter, phone hard against his ear. Thea stands close behind him, hearing the doctor excuse herself for not following protocol. But there is some surprising good news, and the previous scan being so recent, there's no reason to make them come in again, especially since no new decisions have to be made at this time. The point is, against all expectation, Nate's tumors have shrunk.

Dr. Elkin provides details, numbers. Phone to his ear, Allan takes notes while Thea leans against the doorframe, awaiting the flood of relief. Wanting to hold out her arms and give her body to the onrush, to float on the waters of renewed hopefulness. But she is inside that whale, inside something that won't release her. Or even tell her the conditions for release.

VISION CONFIDENCE SCORE

Kimberly Blaeser

I always wake when the Joker's face changes to Trump's, when Dad's changes to Rusty's to Claude's. Sweat-damp and chilled, I grab a robe, check my phone—wait out the dark. But the tired sun spills no warmth, only imprisoned silhouette—and regret.

Just a dark shadow cast across a world of code, Claude showed up first at Hamburg in 2014. Another hacker body bent over his PC, fingers melded to keys. Even then his face was half hidden by glasses and hood. His monosyllables—*hey, check it out, later*—revealed little more, but his fierce eyes branded me.

I came on an official government dare—become a fake hacker to run surveillance on Chaos Computer Clubs. In the carnival atmosphere of the annual congress, amid the beamers and sensors, futuristic illuminated tunnel, robot statue built from boom boxes, and the endless snaking of internet connection cables, I channeled quiet geek. Black sweater, gray slacks, hair pulled back, little makeup—I should have slipped under his radar. I had had clear instructions on how to present myself. Always wear neutrals. Downplay everything else—your accent, your intellect, and your sex appeal. According to my superiors (and all popular films and comics) flamboyant hackers like Trinity or Skye never go undetected. I remained aloof while dark bodies gyrated in the giant dance bubble.

But Claude's eyebrows lifted a fraction, the corner of his mouth twitched a silent I *gotcha*. In that moment I knew he knew. As I turned away I fell deeper into the vat of deceit—does he know I know he knows? I was green and didn't realize then how many layers was the refractive espionage and counter espionage of a government mole's hellish world. Claude would teach me.

We met again at 32C3, did the same dance. He sat in the background wearing innocuous black jeans, a t-shirt sporting a bad binary joke— and the ever-present black hooded sweatshirt. I was with a group of hacktivists gathered at an open project space. We were tossing around pros and cons about the belated UK release of *The Interview.* Claude added a *humph* or other non-committal grunt while we talked motives for the Sony fiasco.

"Obama was right," I said. "You can't just cave to Kim Jong-un. Makes him think he's a power player."

Claude seemed to come to life. "Ever been doxxed, Winona?" he asked, never lifting his gaze from his keyboard. I didn't turn. I'd been trained in cool. But I felt my ears go hot even as I fed the conversation, squeezed lemon into my tea, laughed at pwning stories.

You see, my name isn't Winona—it's Dell. Winona's a nickname— used only by my single bureau indiscretion, my now missing—most likely dead—boyfriend Rusty. A shorthand reference to my Native identity. I crafted my operational security to keep that past past.

That night, in my tiny boutique hotel room, I paced, building my threat model. What does Claude know? Where the hell did he get his access? My slip up? And where was I vulnerable? How deep was the breach into the office? If Winona was out, who was at risk? Did that mean Rusty turned informer? He wouldn't. Ever. The sharp corners of the room prodded me. I wrote my questions, then tore up the phone pad. Pointless. So where did Claude get his info? And why? Why me, why now?

He showed up. I knew he would. And I was ready. No lip quiver, no shake to the hand that let him in, that buried itself next to the pistol in my sweatshirt pouch.

"You came. . . alone?" I ask glancing up and down the seemingly empty hallways before closing us in.

"Alone. Thought we should have a private talk. Mind?" He's checking things out, counting steps to the double window and every other escape route while seeming simply to inspect his reflection in the full length mirror. Our eyes meet there. His turn vacant almost immediately. Become marble. But I saw the movement. Glint of an old copper dish. Suddenly darkening, the fire stamped out.

My eyes have known the sharp flash of copper before. Exactly once. Suddenly, I know. "Oh, my god."

"My god, good?" With a learned nonchalance he runs his smooth hands over the stubble on his chin. "Like what you see? Looking for a patch to fix the missing boyfriend situation?"

I grab him then, and he doesn't resist. I push back the hood, lift the hair. "Open your mouth," I say all pretense of cool evaporated.

He does it again—the little eyebrow lift that singed me when we first met eight years ago, that singed me last year in Hamburg. I let the hood drop and sit down hard on the no-nonsense bed. No need to check the dental work. "You bastard. You stupid, stupid bastard. Why?"

"I had a little work done. New face. Tweak to the voice box. You know death is the only true exit from our job. Now you're in, I'm out. Perfect setup, don't you think?"

I stared. Couldn't catch up. This, this hooded, sable-eyed—yeah, okay sexy-voiced and presumably white hat hacker—was my Rusty? Too much ego for the Marcel Marceau faces some hackers sported, he had to hide in plain sight another way. Of course, given our business he had an in with the best forgers, the best surgeons. Hell, he could have made himself into an Elvis reincarnation, and the world would have bought it.

Now November is in the rear view mirror and the U.S. is tracking for disaster. Where I stand at the magazine rack in Barnes and Noble, every other cover reminds me ICE is unleashed and hunting. The wall promise looms over us like a boogeyman. Seems Rusty saw it coming or someone he is still protecting did. Who the hell does he even work for now? I pick up a bot magazine and then *Mother Jones* scanning for names of activist organizations. Can I even believe his smooth-faced talk? But the Hillary/Donald leaks, continuing legal battles, and post-election tweet wars are like truth serum in our drinks. Bad is brewing. We choose to face it together. We work fourteen hours, pentest one another for weak points in the off hours. To the world, I am still bureau; he is still dead. And I have taken up with French hacktivist Claude Brisbois.

Who, by the way, *Wired* makes mention of this month as a "misanthropic computer genius." Claude gets a kick out of this when I bring a copy home. He prides himself on his "genius" prestidigitation. Computer sleight of hand. He makes things appear and disappear using hacker hocuspocus. Titles, bank accounts, and of course—past identities. Tonight, I sit alongside him on a porch glider listening to its squeak, listening to the mimicking call of a cat bird. I hug my bare knees in the evening's cool air and watch his magic. "You used to live here, Winona? Can't have that address hanging around connecting you to trouble, can we?" He tweaks my cheek playfully. "Oh, look, no Big Timber Road in your 'known locations.'" For fun he fills his screen with photos of wild places, his face submerged in each one. His features a hidden picture in Yosemite Valley, Stonehenge, Owyhee Canyonlands. So hypnotically strange, but not malicious. At least while I watch.

I like to think of him as a now-a-day code talker. Touching story really. How I've fallen for him—again. But this time, I keep my secrets, too. You see I need his faces. Not the Rusty before, Claude after. Not the Marcel Marceau masks that hang on our apartment wall, that star on the hacker t-shirts we wear to Defcon. The goal now is to overload the algorithm. With eyes, eyes, eyes. To divert the gaze of facial recognition software. With noses and more noses, faces and hyperfaces. In the new invasive America, I am perfecting a formula in which facial confusion equals camouflage.

Because I'm Winona again—a Native first-born daughter. Presidential declarations have boomed like live ammo in the energy wars. In the new Indian wars. When Standing Rock captivated the world and gained support around the globe for #NoDAPL, the Trump empire was invested—literally. You saw the pictures. Vanessa Dundon's eye. Light gone forever. Sophia Wilansky's arm mangled by a concussion grenade. In the safety of our living room, I page through the accounts I've collected. They remind me why I play good at the bureau, why I can't give in when sleep wants to pull me deep into something people call normal.

I stood in the dark night, trapped, felt the water cannons. Thought of Rusty transforming to Claude. I left the Sacred Stone Camp empty. Dell was gone. I wore my clothes, my skin differently. Three hundred tribes and thousands of pipeline protesters made news. Their faces on CNN, in *Time*, and all over the internet. While you cheer, admin insiders laugh with manic glee—clones of Scrooge McDuck counting their lottery winnings.

I'm inside. I keep telling Claude—and I'm telling you—they are scanning faces at every protest, tracking movements, and building bogus files. The AIM leader who was found to have "terrorist activities records," the Dakota activist who was deported as an illegal immigrant—not fluke "discoveries" as the press reported.

"Trumped up?" Claude asks when we hear it on the news. I groan, and he laughs. "A little humor to lighten your day."

"Very little." We are tangled together under a puffy comforter covered with stars. This tiny safe sky a replica of nothing.

"We have to get the word out faster." We both know tribal resistance groups are in the crosshairs. Shutting down the Dakota Access and Keystone XL pipeline protests was just warm up. Reviving coal. Challenging all the rulings against copper mines. Reactivating nuclear plants and transporting the waste from sea to shining sea. Somehow inside Trump's twisted logic this is making America great.

Among those opposed—Indigenous people, protectors for more than eighty percent of the world's biodiversity. Winnibigoshish Lake looking like a garden giving her harvest of fish and wild rice. Our water poured from the blue belly of the Mississippi, the Missouri. Here among resources like ours, protection means resistance. And resistance will be shut down. Unless we find a way to protect the protestors—not from guns and water cannons, but from intrusive technologies. *Keep your head down, Winona. Your hands gloved.* All the old hauntings tell me captured features will be criminalized—or now, painted as terrorists. I long for the skies of my childhood, the northern lights spilling color, our small brown bodies anonymous—secure.

"They have networks—the same ones you have. Can't you use them or at least track them? You are literally walking by their secrets every day, Winona. Get your hands a little dirty." Claude has thrown off the comforter, stands to challenge me.

"An evil maid attack? So damn risky." I pull the stars closer. "No, we have to lay low for now." Or hide in fake multitudes—that's my plan. Fuck with the algorithms. "I need a little more time."

"We don't have time." The now familiar bass Claude voice growls in anger. I long for the old soothing tones. My grandpa's songs, my dad's hand drum a wave of background rhythm. "What's the point of having access if you don't use it?" He turns off the TV and spits this last question at me. We have this argument every few days. Any patience he had gets a little more frayed each time another activist gets arrested, another EPA office is locked down.

In the car mirror, I watch my own transformation, eyes sinking deeper each day. Moon craters. What am I waiting for? Another fascist regime? Trump to perfect his PR about who is a terrorist, who is a danger to national security, who is standing in the way of American prosperity? No white arm band, no star of David this time. We have lip curvature and other facial landmark geometry to tell the same racist stories. This is phrenology and Francis Galton's eugenics all over again. You want to know what the contour of an eye socket really tells you? How deeply fucked up is our system. How dangerous.

As I park the Volvo, the fisheye lens of my backup camera is beeping. About obstacles. Ditto my now turbocharged innate computer. I measure escape distances every day. Remember the story of Marcel Marceau and the holocaust orphans he saved with his sleight of hand? This time when we go underground we have to do it as illusionists. I need Claude's anti-surveillance textiles. I print and morph, then print the patterns again until my eyes look as hollow as the spooks on the computer generated designs. Claude's aristocratic nose, my almond eyes, Claude's square jaw, the exaggerated clown turn of each. We have become more faces than lives.

Today I've picked up a bolt of the latest prototype fabric. I want to spread it out, modify the ground, and then check the computer vision confidence score. My arms quiver under the weight—another sign of my exhaustion. I try to catch the door with my foot, but miss. The house echoes around me when it slams. The thud says *do it, it, it. . .* "Claude? Hey, hey, hey, look what I have?" I inject extra enthusiasm to cover my sudden wave of uneasiness. I can't find him in the kitchen where he is supposed to be making lasagna, so I check down in the basement. "Oh, man." He has projected himself all over our lab walls. The bent C hooded heads repeated, repeated. The half-moon of face beneath is covered with ones and zeros. He could be one of them. I lose myself in the flickering 3-D images.

"Find me, babe." he taunts. "Sign in."

"I. . . this is creeping me out. Claude?" I look for him, feel my hand miss, touch one flat surface after another. My stomach says I have been here before. Was it training? A dream? Why can't I remember? "Shut it down, Claude. I'm not playing." I turn, leave him all over the walls, laughing at me, as I walk out the door I came in.

I pack and go—no fake death, but no goodbye either.

In this loop of fate, the dreams start. The Joker's face changing to Trump's, Dad's to Rusty's to Claude's to the last flashing mob of detention. All day I see the real, only at night the horror replays. We have gathered for a peaceful march. I am still bureau by day, Marcel Marceau in the off hours. Oh, we have all taken to wearing the MM masques for rallies and the camouflage hyperface clothes. Hooded hyperface, naturally.

This is the big unveil. Like the Women's March and Native Nations Rise before us, Water First activists have come to Pennsylvania Avenue chanting for change, our signs and banners spelling out resistance: *Make Water Safe Again! Pack up the Pipelines. Defend the Sacred. Keep it in the Ground. Water is Life.* But this time our privacy will be protected. No one will collect identities. Trailers carry little kids and anybody who can't walk. Picture it. They are all hyperface carpet and awnings. The huddled hyper masses baffle surveillance cameras, oversaturating them with thousands of faces. The walkers too create waves of computer-generated hollow, blinking eyes, smiles and straight-line mouths. Who do you see now, Washington? Can you find us in your database?

As we march time drifts. I keep checking my phone's digital reality. I count down to high noon, to when hacktivists have programmed the city water service to fail for one hour. A short but dry reminder of what head-in-the-sand energy policies might bring. My nerves stretched like manic yogis, I jump when I see the flash of metal beneath the curtain of false faces on a marcher's coat. No guns. We said no weapons. I see huddled security officers. Summon my agent cool. Remember to breath. They have no grounds to interfere. None.

Metal equals phone, equals tablet. No worries, I tell myself. So far, flawless. I think of what anonymity will mean. If The Fox could plug sewer outlets and dump buckets of dead fish in a Chicago company's executive offices, imagine what daring escapades the camouflage will inspire. We are the new Everyman. I see the infrared illuminators mounted surreptitiously along our path. Hello Homeland Security. Go ahead, use your invisible power. We have our own now.

Then I start seeing Claude on the video screens we've posted along the route. Screens meant to confound with more eyes eyes eyes— eyes watching, moving across the thousands of gas-filled cells and refusing to be captured. But I see Claude images. Claude kneeling, saying, "Please." Saying, "Please no, no more." At first I think I am hallucinating again, or experiencing a planted memory.

But then one of the marchers stops and screams, "What are they doing to him? Isn't that Brisbois?" Then I know someone has hacked our botnet.

"Who has him? Where are they holding him?" another marcher asks. Or maybe it's me. I've come unglued in the faces. Maybe I am mere computer, too. Sabotaged.

Again.

No one ever told me not to look. They forgot the first time, too, when my Dad was taken from our house. His long grey hair spilling from the strands of his braid, he turned his face back to find us over his shoulder. I saw his fear become hopelessness. For a week his sad eyes stared at me from every newspaper in the village store. They followed me and followed me until I arrived here. I always knew I would see them again. They said, "Please." Or maybe all the eyes say that at the end.

THE TEN OF WANDS

Sarah Elizabeth Schantz

As a boy Jack was afraid of the sunflowers his grandmother grew.
Every year from July to September, the sunflowers edged the western
side of the house before marching through the backyard toward the
river like a fence. Running parallel to the row of sunflowers, but only
a quarter of their length, the clothesline stood on the other side of
the yard where their long underwear would hang the shapes of their
bodies come winter.

He was three the day he watched his granddaddy till the
stretch of yard where the sunflowers would be planted—three-years-
old when first he saw the earth ripped open.

Once the soil was ready, his grandmother had followed the
long row. She'd worn her hair in the same no-nonsense bun she wore
whenever she worked which meant she almost always had that thick
coil of salt-and-pepper knotted tight at the back of her skull. Like a
machine she squatted every few feet to tuck the seeds into the black
dirt, standing only to move forward enough to squat back down and
fold more potential life into the furrowed ground.

When she finished planting, she watered the row. Pulling the
garden hose to its limits, she wasn't able to reach the last ten feet so
she'd filled the watering can, and for this last bit she called Jack over
to help. The watering can was heavy so she spotted him as he lugged
it down the line, dousing that last section of the earth where the
sunflowers would later surface, the water spilling from the large
fountainhead like a small rainstorm, like he was some kind of
small god.

Eventually the sunflowers grew themselves and his granddaddy
called them, "Volunteers."

By August the sunflowers got so big they'd be a towering eight
to ten feet tall, and when he was eight, nine, and ten-years-old, he'd
find himself running past them just to get to the river. He'd shrink away
from their looming yellow faces so large the weight of their heads

sometimes caused their own necks to snap. The remaining flowers which turned to follow the sun's journey across the sky also turned to watch him run, and he only ever slowed down once the yard sloped enough the dock would then rise into view—a wooden shrine offering water; offering freedom; offering a river that could carry him away.

The sunflowers were there to watch him go to all the places he wasn't allowed to, especially not alone in the boat on the river with no one knowing. By the time he was allowed to take the boat out on his own, he was thirteen and no longer as interested in the river anymore. Instead he loitered at the arcade in town where the pinball machines tried to compete with the electronic glory of Ms. Pac Man and Donkey Kong, or he'd go to the new indoor shopping mall along the highway where the girls with the big hair all congregated around the fountain by the food court. Underneath the neon signs advertising Orange Julius and Chick-fil-a, these girls cracked their gum to punctuate the very little or awful lot they had to say, and eventually they'd smoke Marlboro Lights and French inhale their question marks instead; these girls who wore tight jeans like second skin and lipstick so red their smiles were open wounds.

This was a new way for Jack to escape his grandparent's house by the river where he and his parents had lived in the basement ever since he'd been conceived—a story his father loved to tell especially if he'd been drinking. Later, Jack would come to see how the story was meant to be a cautionary tale full of American motifs like the backseat of a 1953 Mercury and a make-out place called The End of the World because of the way the parking lot overlooks the old quarry in the woods just north of town. A place Jack would haunt himself once he was older once his best friend Tuck had his own set of wheels.

While Jack never had a girl to make out with, not back then, he'd sit at the edge of the quarry so Tuck and Charity could practice being married in the back of the Nova, the steamed-up windows their only privacy. At first Jack refused to look down, watching only the eternal drama of the stars above but eventually he'd make himself peer down into the other darkness where he tried to scry the pitch black below for answers to the questions he found himself always asking.

He was either trying to escape the two-story brick house on

the corner of Third and Oak or trying to make it feel like home. That house where his aunt still lives. Where she will likely always live unless she gives him reason to put her in a home in which case he'd have to sell the place to cover the cost of assisted living. That same house where his three uncles came and went depending on their employment and marriage status.

That house with the piano crammed into the corner of the already too small living room where they'd gather to sing "How Great Thou Art" and "Just a Closer Walk with Thee." Where they took turns playing that row of black-and-white keys, but when his daddy played and Aunt Marilyn sang, everyone just listened, and if they did join in, it was only ever for the chorus and only because Aunt Marilyn would have insisted.

That house with the basement his granddaddy, daddy, and uncles dug out themselves when Jack was just a baby—the basement where his parents' two-bedroom apartment took shape and came to crouch beneath the two stories above. Where they almost had all the rooms a family needs to be a proper family, only another kitchen was too expensive so they used the one upstairs.

That house on the corner of Third and Oak by the old stone bridge that washed away in the flood of '81. The flood that almost swallowed his bedroom. The flood that left a wedding veil tangled in their apple tree, the white lace spun amidst the branches like a spider's web.

That house with the closed-up well out front where his grandmother planted pink geraniums for summer and marigolds come fall. Where his aunt now grows purple-black pansies and arranges the Jack-O-Lanterns she carves from the pumpkins she grows along the riverbank, the ones she called "Cinderella's Carriages" last he called her up to talk.

Jack was eleven when he learned what happened to the sunflowers once they were spent, their heads so heavy post-bloom they'd bend all the way to the ground, a row of prostrating monks for the crows to feed upon. Trying to catch his daddy's attention, Jack had been in the yard tossing a baseball in the air hoping he'd lure the man out for a game of catch. But when the door did open it was just his grandmother leaving for the butcher's to buy a Sunday ham. His granddaddy had followed to wave goodbye from the driveway where he'd stood until she turned right on Maple and her Crown Victoria had disappeared.

Rather than going back inside, the old man headed for the shed and came out with a scythe. It didn't take him long to cut down the long row of dead sunflowers, the stainless steel smiling as it caught the shimmer of the late September sun. When he was done, his granddaddy carried their bodies to the river's edge the way a groom carries his bride, only he dumped each load beside the burn pile he'd been building all month, and then he called for Jack like he'd known the boy had been watching.

He taught Jack how to light a strike-anywhere match on the hardness of his own thumbnail and was patient when it took Jack several tries to get the trick to work. His nail was still soft with youth but finally the match caught and the blue fed the orange feather of fire up top. When his grandfather nodded, Jack tossed the flame, and turned the nest of yard waste into a funeral pyre.

Together they sat on cinderblocks to both watch the fire burn and tend to it. The heat consumed the sunflowers almost instantly whereas the branches from the catalpa tree Jack's father had chopped down took longer, and the treated wood from the busted chifforobe had hissed at them like a dying snake. The old man liked to keep a flask of whiskey in the back pocket of his coveralls so he could reward himself while he worked, and this time when he took it out, he'd passed the liquor to Jack who'd taken his first drink that afternoon as he watched the black smoke curl up into the blue.

That house which had always been too small grew even smaller when the GM plant shut down and the men didn't know what to do with themselves, and it wasn't just at home that everything got to be too much, but everywhere in town. The bars filled with all the men who'd been laid off and Jack's momma took to saying—"It's all just too much," and his father didn't like her saying this so much and commanded that she cut it out, or else.

And she had managed to stop until one night when she said it again by accident.

She'd been washing the dishes while his father leaned against the counter next to her, nursing his usual bottle of Miller High Life and smoking a Pall Mall. They were performing the same ritual they performed together most every night. She'd just told him about

Betsy's breast cancer, the thirty-two-year-old woman she sometimes sold Avon with, and his father had responded by telling her all about the Polanski boy who'd been paralyzed in a freak accident at the cement factory over in Detroit that week, and that's when she slipped—"It's all just too much," she said. She tried to cover her mouth as if to push the words back but his father slapped her before she could even get her fingers to her lips.

Jack was still eleven, only fall had turned to winter, and when he remembers that December, he remembers it being the hardest and most bitter December he's ever known. He'd woken up cold again and had gone upstairs to warm some milk on the stove, but when he heard his parent's voices he stepped into the shadows of the dining room where he could hide and perform a ritual of his own. While his parents talked like this most every night as his mother cleaned up, it wasn't often the two of them could be alone together because privacy was hard to find in that house, and Jack liked to watch them when they thought they were alone because they could be tender with each other, even if tender was just a quiet tally of tragedies, big and small.

But tender turned sour and Jack watched as his mother sat down, the way she touched her cheek which must have still been hot from the sting of his father's hand, and then he watched his old man collapse to his knees like he was planning to pray.

"You got to stop reminding me," his father said, and the man buried his face in the woman's aproned lap that was likely still damp from the dishes, and after he'd cried for what felt like forever, he volunteered to tell her why he'd been weeping.

"I just hate to have to hurt you like I sometimes do," he said.

Jack's mother looked out the window rather than at the man kneeling before her, and she must have been looking at herself because the night outside had collided with the lights inside to turn the glass into a mirror. Even though he'd known such a detail in such a reflection would have been impossible, Jack still had the strangest thought his momma was watching the warning flare of her reddened cheek go off.

Eventually it did get to be too much only Jack's granddaddy was the one to break instead. Jack was fourteen when it happened, running laps around the football field at school while Coach Reardon blew his whistle to keep the boys from faltering.

According to the story his momma told them later, Jack's grand mother had gone to the butcher to pick up a nice pork roast for supper and his aunt was at the library where she volunteered in the children's section, likely reading *The Story of Ferdinand* to another circle of snot-nosed toddlers, and the men had all been out too which means they were at the bar, so his momma was the only one home when the family patriarch came downstairs.

She'd been drinking coffee and clipping coupons at the kitchen table, listening to a religious show on the radio when she saw the man take his shotgun down from the rack above the back door. He stepped outside, and after he pulled the door shut, she heard him start his pickup. Through the window of the Dutch door, she'd seen him head east on the leaf-littered street because another autumn had rolled back around again because the test of yet another impossible winter was quickly approaching.

"He was driving real slow," his mother reported but everyone knew the man tended to drive way below the speed limit, had even gotten a ticket or two for doing so, and this was how they'd known she was trying to get to what was odd, and what was odd was the way he'd used his turn signal. "It'd been blinking like he'd been planning on going left," she'd said, "but then he went right instead."

"I thought he was going to sell the gun," she'd explained, and they all nodded because the old man had pawned the chainsaw and his father's pocket watch the week before, and the week before that it'd been his mother's silver, and his hunting knife with the antler handle the previous week. Plus turning right would have been the direction to go if the pawnshop was where he'd been headed which means he must have taken the long way to the quarry like maybe he was giving himself time to change his mind.

The working theory was he'd been going to the quarry for weeks to stand at the lip of the chasm, throwing all those things he'd told them he'd sold into the water the way Pharaohs filled their tombs with caches of goods for the afterlife before they died.

The recently fired shotgun was found at the edge of the quarry where he must have dropped it once he'd used the blast as the final push he'd apparently needed. When the divers recovered his body one of them surfaced with the Husqvarna 460 like it was worth saving.

When his momma told them where she assumed the old man

had been headed, she wasn't just speaking to the family but to the sheriff who was sitting with them at the kitchen table with his hat in his lap. She'd just served him coffee, which he'd taken black with three lumps of sugar, and she hadn't yet cried.

She didn't cry until after they'd all showed the sheriff out like he wouldn't be able to find the door otherwise, thanking him the whole way because that's what Midwesterners do—they thank anyone and everyone for anything and everything even if they're thanking a person for bringing them a shit sandwich, and once she did start crying, she couldn't stop.

Couldn't stop crying, she also couldn't stop begging her mother-in-law to forgive her. "I didn't realize what it was he was aiming to do," she kept saying until she started saying, "I should have stopped him, I should have known," and this was the only time Jack had ever seen his daddy not get mad when his mother took to repeating herself the way she sometimes did. Instead, his father had gone and wrapped her in his arms and he'd held her like he was never going to let go.

Extra awkward from a recent growth spurt, Jack stood there not knowing what to do. His uncles had followed the sheriff out, using it as an excuse to escape. Jack saw them through the picture window standing by the well, smoking, and staring at their feet.

Jack wanted to go to his grandmother the way his father had his mother, but when she wiped the tears from her face using the backs of her hands he found he couldn't move.

Then she pushed herself up from the davenport where she'd only just sat down. He hadn't known how much he'd needed someone to come to him until it seemed like that was what she was doing but instead she walked right past him. Using the back door she slipped outside and she'd gone down to the river where she would sit all night and most of the morning too.

***

Now Jack is a man with a family of his own, two daughters three years apart, but nothing adds up anymore, not since the oldest died in April from a faulty heart the doctors said no one could have ever known about like this would keep them from blaming themselves.

His daughter who was performing her poetry at an open mic in Pittsburg when she allegedly paused somewhere in the middle of a rant about domestic violence to take a deep breath. Who then looked at every single person seated in the crescent audience around the small stage like she knew them all and meant to say goodbye. Who then, according to her girlfriend Taylor, seized, and that was that, their little girl, a month shy of nineteen.

Their daughter who they'd only been able to bring home for Christmas because they couldn't afford Thanksgiving too, who they had to have cremated in Pennsylvania because it was easier that way, and less expensive, so that's what they did once the autopsy was complete. Then they'd flown home with her inside a plastic bag inside a black plastic box similar to what she'd weighed as a newborn, but entirely the wrong shape.

This box his wife kept clutched to her chest the whole trip home, and on the plane she'd kept her eyes closed like maybe she was somewhere else, maybe even tucked inside the memory of the day they'd found out they were finally pregnant—that pink plus sign a glowing crossroads where their already happy life had gotten even happier.

His wife who can't sleep anymore, especially not at night.

Who has a recurring nightmare where she finds their dead daughter in the house, and the girl's ghost is licking all the photographs they have of her, licking the pictures but not responding to her mother when she tries to talk to her. Licking the pictures inside the photo albums in the den, but especially the ones they framed which hang on the wall that climbs the stairs up to where the bedrooms are.

These pictures that document her too short life from the baby bump his wife so proudly sported to the day she graduated valedictorian, and they'd been meaning to print the pictures they'd taken when they dropped her off at college—to get one framed while they'd use the others to start a whole new album—but there'd been that gaping hole in the roof to fix, especially with winter coming, and then they had to evict the family of raccoons that had moved into the attic as a result.

"But we did *take* the pictures," Jack kept telling his wife because he knew she fretted as much as he did over how sloppy they'd gotten since they'd abandoned the disposable cameras of yesterday for the ones their smart phones offered. So she'd put Jack in charge of getting them developed. Using the first online service that appeared when he googled, "Print pictures from my phone," he'd scrolled through the digital images on his laptop while he sat in the home office he shared with his wife.

In the past, he never would have chosen to print them all, but he found himself clicking yes for every single picture, including the multiples and the ones where the composition was wrong or the lens had been out of focus.

Their oldest daughter standing in front of the English building because that was her major; then she's turning cartwheels outside the Rainbow Alliance where she volunteered answering phone calls for the suicide hotline; and then the series they'd shot of her in the stacks at the university library where she kept joking she was really going to live, and she'd put air quotes around the word "live" because she meant to be ironic about what home meant to her, but now Jack wonders if she'd known she'd be dying soon and meant to be ironic about that instead.

When the stiff white envelope arrived in the mail a week later containing the prints, neither he nor his wife could actually open it, so they'd left it on the credenza in the vestibule where they put their keys in a ceramic tray one of the kids had made one of them for either Mother's Day or Father's Day back when both girls were little. Smothered in a lumpy glaze of cobalt blue, the tray reveals the starfish imprint of one of their daughter's tiny hands, but which girl pressed her palm into the clay Jack can't recall no matter how hard he tries.

Sometimes when he sees the envelope, he'll pick it up, and tempted to disobey the instructions *Do Not Bend*, he imagines himself folding the envelope again and again like origami until it can't be folded anymore.

"She licks the pictures like she's starving," his wife says whenever she describes the nightmare. "She licks them until her image disappears," she says.

He too has a terrible dream of his own but he only ever tells his wife whereas she tells their therapist about her dream at every single session like it's brand new information, and then she insists on telling the few friends left they haven't yet scared away.

The other daughter who was supposed to start her senior year of high school is now downstairs in the den on the sofa bed that folds out. Instead of overseeing try-outs for cheerleading because it's finally her turn to be captain, she's all doped up on painkillers and benzodiazepines, her immune system wrecked from the onslaught of intravenous and now oral antibiotics she's had to take because of the risk of infection to her bone.

This daughter whose left leg is a white cocoon of bandages, suspended in the air by way of a special sling a volunteer from the hospital brought them from a place that loans these things out. Things like the bench in the downstairs shower and the wheelchair folded up in the vestibule. This daughter who's only just home from the hospital, whose doctors all keep using the phrase: "A long road ahead" even when he hasn't asked them for a prognosis.

Their little girl who's home after almost a week following that midnight phone call from the nurse that made Jack jump awake like he'd done when the nurse from UPMC Mercy called from Pennsylvania when their oldest daughter died.

Almost a week since an ambulance rushed this daughter to the ER when he and his wife hadn't even known she was still out because they'd fallen asleep after another failed attempt at making love. And even though he'd gone soft again, they'd both slept as if they'd fucked for hours. And because they'd finally slept, they hadn't known this daughter was not only still out past curfew but seriously wounded and being assessed by paramedics. Finally asleep while their only living daughter had been bleeding, bleeding, bleeding.

Almost a week since the 1:00 a.m. emergency operation where the doctors took three hours to repair the lacerations this daughter had gotten from grief-riding out by the water tower on the edge of town at night where the road is a dangerous washboard. This road where he'd taught her how to drive, where he'd told her again and again to be careful, to slow down. Where more than once he'd said even twenty-five miles per hour can be way too fast. Where he'd taken her sister to learn as well because he knows that road is where all the kids go to make out or race their parent's cars. Where the turn-around by the trailhead is littered with used rubbers and broken beer bottles. Where the state trooper told his wife the kids all go drifting now, some terrible game where they speed up to then pull on the emergency brake.

This place he's heard both girls call The End of the Rainbow. Where the gigantic water tower stands out there amidst the tumbleweed and cattle like a leftover pillar from an ancient ruin. The water tower with the faded rainbow painted on the side that bears witness again and again to the rise and fall of both the sun and the moon.

This place where their only living daughter didn't go to drift, but where she did drive way too fast because she's been running ever since her only sister died.

This place where this daughter slipped on the gravel and hit the ditch, flipping the family station wagon—where the seatbelt held her in place as she hung there upside down like the Hanged Man from the Tarot cards his wife shuffles through the nights now that she can't sleep.

Where the windshield shattered and the girl's leg flew into the sky to get sliced open on a sickle moon hanging too close to earth because Heaven is just another predator in wait.

Forty-three staples on the outside, the surgeon didn't try to count the hundreds of inside stitches that will dissolve the way Jack wishes his daughter's new boyfriend would. The boyfriend who posted pictures on Instagram with a caption that read: *Girlfriend gets into fight with shark and wins.* Like it's all a big joke. The boyfriend he never liked with the bumper sticker on the back of his jacked-up truck that reads: *Buckle Up I'm Going to Try Something.*

The one who manifested a month after the other daughter died, who showed up the day after his wife swears she pulled The Devil card.

When Jack last checked on this daughter, she was still asleep, a rerun of *Buffy* on T.V., he'd stood there long enough to recognize the episode where Dawn is suddenly Buffy's little sister, and none of the characters question where she's come from because of some spell that was cast, and he remembers both daughters being confused when they'd watched the show as a family even though he'd insisted it was a brilliant move for Joss Whedon to make.

Now he's standing at the kitchen window watching his wife in the garden, thinking, We've all lost control.

He wishes his wife would have kept her hair long instead of cutting it so short but he would never tell her this. The crow's feet pull hard at the corners of her eyes and she bruises too easily these days. While she's thin from not eating enough, the estrogen keeps pooling into the pouch that is her belly. She might curse this perimenopause, but he blesses these hormones that form this soft pillow where he likes to lay his head. Where sometimes he lays wishing he'd sink into her once and for all, absorbed by the space where she grew his seed.

She's standing in the yard, still wearing her nightgown even though it's well past noon, maybe even past one o'clock. But she's always done this, especially in the summer when it's too hot for normal clothes, yet anyone else would likely try to blame it on the grief.

The white cotton billows around her body, and through the fabric he can see the nest of black between her legs. She's holding the green garden snake of a hose with both her hands as if she's just had to fight it, and it's not the first time he's come upon her in such a way where he's had to wonder what battles she's forced to fight alone when he isn't there to help. While she doesn't need a hero, he still wishes he could save her from all this suffering.

She planted the seeds back in May in the bed of ash and dirt they'd framed together using chunks of rose quartz and other pretty rock, but in the last week since they've been home she's been trying to coax the sunflowers into blooming by watering them three times a day. Not yet open, there are ten green stalks his wife likens to the Ten of Wands, a card he found sad even when she insisted it was full of hope.

He looks at the row of sunflower stalks with their green crowns and thinks of Ginsberg's sutra, how the poet also personified this flower.

The sunflowers are taller than he is, their leaves waving at him again, their shadows reaching. He wonders if they are strong enough to pick all three of them up—his wife, his daughter, himself—to carry them to safety. There are no nearby rivers in this place where he's come to live, where his wife is from, and his daughters too, and even the farmer's ditch has been sucked dry by the drought, and while he would never run away, not now, when he looks around he sees only the prairie, only the sky, and then only the nearly insurmountable wall of mountain to the west.

THE MAN WHO BORROWED BLACK SHOES

Stewe Claeson, translated by Daniel Barnun-Swett

> Is it strange that
> each person is alone?
> *Vilhelm Ekelund*

After the long season of slush and gray days, he wrote a letter in March to report that he had bought a lamp. The kind that stood on the floor and split into three parts, each ending in its own shade. His mother wrote back and asked whether Mrs. Berg, his landlady, was supposed to provide lighting. "Why would you buy a lamp with green shades?" she wrote, "you can't stand green."

That night, Mrs. Berg knocked and asked if he wanted a cup of tea. "Such a peculiar thing, that lamp," she said.

He figured she didn't like it either, but said nothing. They sat in the kitchen and drank tea. It was hard for either of them to find anything to say. He tried not to look at her, and she eventually stopped talking, lacking any response from him.

"These gray days are so depressing," she said. He nodded toward the cup. "But," she continued, "you always know they'll be over." She added, a little later: "That makes it easier."

The sky brightened, but the days stayed cold. A guy who worked at the warehouse, who they all called "Southie" since he came from Skåne, told him he might as well move up north. "It's all Arctic to me."

He didn't get it, Gothenburg being so far from Lappland.

"What are your friends like?" wrote his mother.

He thought a while about how to respond, then wrote that his coworkers were all fine. That they teased him because he was quiet. "I guess they call me The Wall," he wrote. He couldn't write about any other friends. He didn't hang out with anybody. He sat and stared into the grain of his rolltop desk for an hour: he wrote on scrap paper and when he glanced up, he saw its upper shelf of cubbies, their strange shapes and long lines like doors, each one with dark brown knobs like the knots in the wood.

He was lost in thought. He didn't notice that Mrs. Berg had opened the door and asked if he'd like to have some tea. He folded up the letter, then opened it again and wrote his name under the last line. He saw that he hadn't used the whole page. Something about it looked a little off. Almost sad.

Weekends, he liked to go for walks through Slottskogen, the park on the old grounds of the royal forest. He didn't know what else to do with himself. He'd heard his coworkers talk about going to parties, and since the start of spring, soccer became the major topic for everyone at the warehouse. The guys got into all kinds of sports, even handball, but they never asked him to join. They would get quiet whenever they noticed he'd heard them talking. *No need!* he wanted to tell them. He wouldn't have gone with them anyways. He wouldn't even know what to wear.

Once, Southie had asked him: "You like soccer?" and, of course, he'd answered that he did. "The Comrades?!" Southie went on, excited about their home team. "Sure, sure, them too," he'd replied. The rest of the guys at the table wondered what the hell he meant by "*too.*"

That early in the spring, there were never many people around the forest. He liked most walking past the still closed open-air café, then walking up the hill until he came to a flock of thick-maned sheep, looking out of time and place. Sometimes, he'd find a moose standing near the fence when he came—a true honor. There was one time when he saw a dead cat on the trail. Someone had impaled it on a fence-rail, and there were goats gathered underneath that cat-corpse glaring at it, just out of their reach.

Mrs. Berg asked if he'd been feeling well. "Gothenburg can be such a beautiful city," she said. She spoke warmly out of nowhere about the city's planner, or whoever had the job, "some master gardener, or whatever they're called now," saying that they were so skillful. "That's why we have so many parks. And all the crocuses!" Hadn't he noticed them?

In the beginning of April, Elsa from the office died. She wasn't that old, but afterward, everybody said that she had seemed different in her final days. And then she'd died. Her brother had found her in front of the door of the apartment. She was fully dressed. It was likely that she had been on her way to work as usual. Maybe it was her heart. Southie and another guy from the warehouse, Erik, who was a little bit older, both said there'd been something special about Elsa.

He wrote home and explained that he'd been invited to the funeral. His mother wrote back that he hadn't really been invited—only out of politeness—and that he didn't have any clothes to wear anyway.

Mrs. Berg noticed he was anxious, so he told her why. She paused to think, then went out from the kitchen and returned with a pair of black shoes in her hands. Shyly, she asked if maybe they wore the same size shoe, he and her late husband. She said she'd kept her husband's clothes. She'd cleaned the shoes—they smelled strongly of polish. He felt strange trying them on while she stood next to him and watched.

That night, he woke himself screaming. Covered in sweat and unable to fall back asleep, he lay in bed and listened to the slow silence.

The burial place lay out in the eastern part of the city. He had to take the trolley a considerable distance and then walk a bit farther still. It was an unusually beautiful day, a Saturday. It felt like summer again. Strange to think of death on a day like this, to think of Elsa dead, to be reminded that everyone would die. Inside the gate, he paused, and an older couple who passed by peered at him. After a few steps, the woman turned and asked if he was on the way to Elsa Moréus's funeral, and when he nodded they invited him to come with them. They mentioned that they didn't recognize him. *Of course they're wondering who I am.*

He explained, "we were coworkers."

Still, the woman was curious, and stole several glances at him before they arrived at the chapel, where the casket was set up at the front by the altar and what passed for a lectern. He saw that Southie was there, along with several of the girls from the office and Erik. It was completely quiet. Other than when someone entered the room or moved in their seats, shuffling shoes against the floor, everything was silent. Then, the sound of someone clearing their throat. Or whispers.

He stepped into one of the pew rows and sat down, surveying his surroundings. On one side of the chapel, there was a recess in the wall where a cross stood flanked with votive candles. It was moving, beautiful. All those flowers. They covered the lid, and wreaths leaned against the casket. That was touching too.

A man's voice began to sing *I am a stranger* somewhere behind them, but he would not turn around to see where the singer stood. It sounded bleak and tragic: he breathed deeply several times, and still his nose tingled as if he were about to start crying. Some folks sat two by two around him, looking sad.

An elderly priest spoke. It was hard to make out what he said, only that he seemed to have known Elsa fairly well, that she had struggled in silence, that there was, in her silent suffering, something great and human. The idea captivated him; he sank back into his grief. There was something else, something awful about the fact that she'd never spoken up, he thought. An older man, who sat in the row before him, nodded the whole time, approvingly. Or was it just hard for him to keep still?

The mourners all rose to file around the casket. Some said "Goodbye," and "Thanks, Elsa," or just nodded. He didn't know what he should do, if one was expected to go with them or if he should stay seated. He sat. He looked at his shoes. They passed muster, but their black color felt gloomy, too mournful. They reminded him of mud, like back at home. The black of mudpies, of all things. His father would come up from the fields and take off his muddy gumboots in the hall. Again and again, his mother would sit there and brush them. Big, heavy boots. She always brought those mud-covered boots back to black. Their glossy shine. Suffering in silence.

It was hard to think about. He felt his throat catch and couldn't hold back a sniffle.

That was how it was with Elsa: *the silence* was the worst of it. She could have said something at any time. Suddenly, he wept. Amid the solemn silence, he cried. He tried to dry his eyes without being noticed, but the older man in front of him turned and regarded him through thick, nearly cubic glasses.

Crying was ridiculous. He hardly knew her. What would she have said to him? About her pain?

He wept openly. He cried, first trying to stay quiet—but the room's silence could no longer contain him. He bent forward and let the tears form and fall. It's just too wretched, he thought grimly, but he couldn't stop. He thought the organ music was more muffled now. *Nobody better start singing now,* he thought—*just no singing!*

One of the women on the other side of the aisle came over and laid her arm on his shoulders. She patted his arm, nearly startled him. Then he leaned against her. If only the organ would stop. If it would only stop, he would be able to catch his breath–to take some deep breaths and stop crying. She whispered that everything was alright, "it's all okay now, it's all okay," she said. It sounded cliché, as if she had nothing else to say. It didn't seem like she thought he should feel embarrassed. "Do you have a handkerchief?" she asked, but he didn't. He dried his eyes with a thin one from her, then finally looked up. Everybody was back sitting in their seats. The older man was turned around entirely and staring right at him through those monstrous glasses. He seemed alarmed.

But it was time to leave. A few people stayed to carry the casket. It was that kind of funeral.

"Will you be joining us at the graveside?" asked the woman. She looked uncertain. "Did you know Elsa well?"

Hearing Elsa's name caught him off-guard and he began crying once more. She leaned his head against her shoulder, and so they stood in the church's aisle.

"I'm so glad it was you–" he heard her whisper.

"Yes," he began, but what else could he say?

They walked out. In the fresh air, it felt like it was all over. Only a few steps from the chapel everything was normal again. He followed along, feeling a little foolish. He'd lost interest. When everybody threw flowers on top of the coffin lowered into the grave, he stood at a slight distance from the crowd. When it was all finished, he hurried to leave. The woman caught up with him by the fence and asked didn't he want to follow them to the reception.

He mumbled he thought he better get going and she nodded. For a moment it seemed as if she was about to say she understood, but she didn't.

A strange day. He had a hard time getting a hold of himself. That afternoon after the funeral, he sat in his room without changing clothes. Even left on his shoes. The emptiness around him was palpable, and the shapeless sense of something missing gripped him. He sensed it like something old and familiar, yet strange and unbidden. He lit the lamp with the green shades and stared at it for a spell. It didn't help, just left him still feeling off. Finally, he unlaced the black shoes and walked out into the hallway with them. Mrs. Berg was home. He heard her puttering about in the kitchen. When he set the shoes in the hall, she came out and asked how it had gone. "And the shoes, did they work out or what?" she asked. He answered that it was kind of her to lend them.

It was a good time to write letters, but he just remained sitting. It was getting darker out, though not as early as it had the weeks prior. Outside, the leaves on the trees were already growing large.

When he lay down in the dark and tried to fall asleep, he felt something was missing, that there was a lack. Whether it was someone or something, he couldn't figure out. It made him uneasy, like he'd forgotten something important. He was certain he'd never sensed that lack before, though how could he be sure? *Who can remember how the past felt?* he thought, lying still. In the dark, he became aware of his heart beating and hammering. He lay completely still and let it transfix him.

Sunday came and went. Same with the workweek.

"Now, when summer comes, we're counting on seeing you here at home," wrote his mother. "Klara and Göran are getting married the first week of June."

Mrs. Berg nodded in a friendly manner to him when they met. She didn't talk as much now that he was grieving.

Everyone down at the warehouse planned to go to Ullevi Stadium. "Those guys win enough already, damnit—one to six, eight to nothing," droned Southie, but he didn't know what they were talking about, or what it would cost. He said he didn't have time. They sat in the lunchroom and an old Gothenburg Post lay open in front of them. There was a clip about Elsa. An obituary. A burial service took place, it stated, a solemn occasion. Under other announcements it continued: it was held someplace or other, wherever. One line suggested wiring donations. It was unsettling to see.

By that weekend, it felt like spring, or at least that it would be soon. When the wind kicked up it was a little chilly, but everyone just wore a jacket. Cafés on Main Street had set out tables and chairs on the sidewalk, and even if no one was sitting outside, it still looked cozy. Like a postcard of a city scene. The days were finally warming up.

"Now you've just got to go for a long, glorious walk. Get to know the city!" nodded Mrs. Berg. It was Saturday, but where would he go? At last, he took an eastbound trolley, same as he had taken the Saturday before, the day of the funeral. Going back there again, he found the whole place was still beautiful: peaceful, filled with flowers.

Some people stood and waited at the gate, and one couple asked him if he knew how to get to the chapel. It made him lighthearted that they would ask him. He smiled and nodded. They followed him, somewhat taken aback, and asked aloud if he really was going to Erik's funeral. Surprising himself, he answered yes.

They walked beside each other now: the woman with short steps in her black high heel shoes, the man occasionally sneaking sidelong glances at him, probably wondering just who he was. He'd answered yes. Now he had to sell it.

"We didn't know each other well," said the man. "It was actually my brother who knew Erik. But he—sorry, let me explain: not Erik, but rather Lasse, that is my brother—he's in Stockholm this weekend, and I said that Eva and I, that we could always go in his stead."

He nodded affably at the man and answered that Erik would have wanted it that way.

The woman had already discerned that he wasn't dressed for a funeral, but said nothing. She was rather discreet. She said, soberly, that since he knew Erik, wouldn't he have a problem with someone faking sympathy? Catching sight of his shoes, he was filled with regret: what if she thought that their black clothes were a mistake, seeing him dressed so casually? He lied, saying that he'd first planned to wear black shoes, then decided against it. The man listened without saying anything.

They arrived.

He sat a bit behind the others. This was a different sort of funeral. Not the flowers, or the casket, or the organ music—those were all nearly the same. The priest was new, and a completely different sort of person. Far in the front sat two little girls who cried the whole time, and next to them, there was a broad-shouldered woman with red hair beneath a black hat. She was crying so much she couldn't catch her breath. The priest walked over to her several times and comforted her, or tried to. It didn't really help.

He should have known that talking wouldn't help!

It was a more sorrowful funeral, but much more beautiful than when Elsa was buried. There was different music, heavier, more final, he thought. It felt hard not to give in to it. He noticed how the music affected him, how it struck through him, ringing over his own heartbeat. When he couldn't manage to resist the feelings any longer, he surrendered. Something within him burst; he had to cry. He couldn't hold back, and he realized he didn't want to either. Astonished, he remembered that this was how it had been before. This was how he had felt.

It felt warm, gentle.

Since everyone greeted the person crying in front and mumbled something to her, he did too, riven with tears. He pressed her hand and said something, but didn't hear his own words. Not long after, when he sat in his row and screwed up his face to stop the tears, he noticed that the woman from the couple he'd walked over with earlier was staring at him, shocked.

Outside in the fresh air, he stood beside that man who had come in his brother's stead with his wife. They saw that he had been crying, that he was especially sensitive. "You were such good friends," the woman said, and took hold of the sleeves of his jacket. When she touched him, it was all over again. He could not hold back his sniffles, so only nodded. She said she understood, and her husband looked in their direction, like he understood too. When she tried to comfort him, he walked away. Just left. He knew that they would talk about him now, wondering who he was. Some mysterious stranger who appeared out of thin air. Then gone. He'd certainly given them something to talk about.

On the trolley, it all abated: the tension, the tears, all of it. He leaned against the backrest and felt calm and relaxed.

Back home, just like the last Saturday, he sat still for a long time in his room. He heard Mrs. Berg busying herself with something somewhere in the apartment. He looked at his things: the endless coils of the woven wall hanging, the random lithograph above the writing desk, the bed all made up, the lamp with the green shades.

Now all was calm, and he could rest. What was it he was missing, exactly? Maybe what he felt was just hunger. He turned his head and looked out the window.

Saturday and Sunday passed. He returned to work on Monday. He kept to himself. The next day came, then on Wednesday, Southie and the foreman had an argument, about who knows what. When Southie saw people standing around watching the kerfuffle, he yelled that they should take a side. "Y'all could get shit on and you'd just say thanks." They talked about it for a few days around the warehouse, as did the women in the office. But as outsiders, not knowing what had happened.

His mother wrote: "You could come this weekend." But he put the letter on the dresser's writing-board and let it be. He couldn't keep focused enough to write letters. Instead, he sent a postcard on that Friday: "Spring's here." He was so distracted, he forgot to sign it. After work, he only wanted to wander through the streets. It was spring; there was that light: pink, warm, glowing fantastic over the houses that looked new and full of promise. Everyone was talking to each other. Spring—he felt it in his bones. The weather was already so mild, and it would soon be summer again. He had never been in the city during summer. A few short visits, but not really, not like now.

But his worry—that peculiar longing, whatever you called it—wouldn't budge. He brought it home with him from work. He went to bed with it. It stood at his bedside when he woke up. *And he knew!*

"What an outstanding day," said Mrs. Berg while he read the announcements in that morning's Gothenburg Post and dipped a sandwich into tepid coffee. She said that it had been spring when she became a widow. He nodded, then asked if he might borrow the black shoes again. He had to tell it like it was: a friend had passed away. She nodded gravely.

"Two friends. And in spring," she said at last. She stooped forward and clasped him by the hands and he immediately felt his chest tighten. Desire spread through his body like a hot breeze. "And you're all so young," she said. "In such a short time—how you'll remember your early days in the city, one can only wonder."

While he was getting dressed, a warm ache spread up from below his waist when he bent to lace up the black shoes.

He tried to remember: the Western Cemetery, the names, the right times.

When he stepped in through the high gates, he met a plump little old man carrying a watering can and a large floral wreath. Its ribbons twirled slowly in the nearly non-existent morning wind. He nodded several times and then said he was surprised to see there were no funerals scheduled before 1:00. "Yes, the chapel's over there," he pointed. "But you're awfully early."

"I know," he answered and looked straight at the short man. "But I just couldn't wait."

"Is it Willhelmsson's funeral or is that other one, old what's her name, Berglund. Yeah, Berglund. A lady."

He couldn't answer straightaway. He had to pace his breathing against an unprecedented feeling of expectation. Joy, near jubilation. He nodded to the sexton, who nodded back, stunned.

"Yeah, so... both?"

He nodded.

It was so beautiful now back at the cemetery. He looked over his shoulder at the sexton.

"Yeah... so, that's two funerals?"

He said it was so.

Disturbed, the man turned away and walked off with the wreath and can. Still within earshot, he mumbled something about some poor devil.

Even so. The whole morning stretched out before him.

Between the untold graves.

THE GAUNTLET

Barry Kitterman

Preston Booth, a distant relation to John Wilkes Booth (it was a connection which brought him a deep and abiding shame) pulled his ancient El Dorado (*timeless* El Dorado, Preston liked to say) into the parking lot of the Bitterroot Tavern. Stepping through the door in the early afternoon, he found the place already filled to capacity. A hard crowd, men and women in Levi jackets and work boots, spilled from the booths near the juke box. They looked at home in the tavern, unlike Preston, and unlike the group of men who walked in behind Preston, an odd collection of nervous men in black tuxedos. They hovered a moment near the pool tables, at least thirty of those tuxedoed men, blinking their eyes in the dim light before they moved to the bar. Listening to their give and take with the bartender, Preston understood them to be some kind of men's choir from Missoula. Little bits of song passed between them, the way other people would simply talk to each other. These singing men had washed ashore, stranded (aren't we all, thought Preston) when their bus broke down outside the supermarket next door.

The clock behind the bar said it was half past three, and Preston had already stopped in at two other taverns. He wasn't used to drinking this early in the day, but he had asked for a beer in each of those taverns, sipped at it, paid for it, abandoned it. The men in their tuxedos were drinking too, less tentatively than Preston. They had loosened their ties. They told the bartender they were on their way to a concert in Stevensville when their bus gave up the ghost.

Timing belt, said one of them. Preston supposed he was a tenor.

Timing *chain*, said another.

Threw a rod, said a man with an unbelievably deep voice.

The whole group of them stared out the window at Preston's El Dorado.

Is that your car? asked the tenor.

It is, said Preston.

160

Ah, said the tenor, then you have a means of escape. I am coveting your means of escape from this dim and hopeless tavern.

In the corner next to a wood stove, a man in a cream colored hat (the bartender called him Val, as in, Val, give us a song) pulled a guitar from its case. He picked up a stool and moved it to the center of a small stage. Val looked like he might once have been a ranch hand, like he might have kept at it a few years longer than a man ought to do that sort of work.

Oh, said the deep-voiced man of the men's choir, eyeing Val and his guitar. Oh no, he said.

The man's obvious dismay, his total lack of concern for another's feelings, heartened Preston. He had left home with a plan, one he was doing his best to carry out, and the plan felt easier to him now, in an unkind world. Possible.

That's your beat-up Caddy out in the lot? said the barmaid, the pretty one circling the tables. She stared at it a moment through the window. Too bad, she said. She pulled a feather from Preston's sleeve.

Down jacket, he told her, but she wrinkled her nose.

I don't think so, she said.

He'd left the car running while he came into the bar to fortify himself. He hardly bothered to keep an eye on it through the window. He wasn't worried that anyone would steal the El Dorado, even with the key in the ignition, the engine running. Theft of the car might actually solve several of his problems. It was a lousy car, smelling of bread crumbs and chicken manure. It was absurd to think anybody would want it.

Coveting, said the man with the deep voice. I am coveting your car.

Preston had thought he was desperate when he came into the tavern, but these men in tuxedos were cheering him up. No matter how sad his life might appear to be, no matter that his wife and daughter weren't going to be speaking to him when he returned home, no matter that he was holed up in a tavern on the highway with Jeannie C. Riley on the jukebox and a cold woodstove in the corner telling him to rethink his life and all of its misdirections. (Was the stove not talking to him? Were these men not looking at him? The man named Val, with the guitar, wasn't he smiling this way?) None of it mattered so much now, as long as he himself was not being forced to wear a tuxedo.

We'll give you a hundred dollars to take us away from here, said the man with the deep voice. We'll give you all the money we have between us.

The man's friends stood by his side. They had the unmistakable aura of second tenors. Small failures. Also-rans.

I don't need your money, said Preston.

The men of the choir gazed out the window at Preston's car, unconvinced. Preston didn't care. He didn't care what any of the people in the bar thought of him.

If they had seen all the things he was good at, if they'd even once seen him in the classroom teaching Proust or Joyce, seen him sit across his desk from the young students who came to him off farms in Eastern Montana, even a couple of kids, two cousins, from the reservation over by Havre, if they'd listened to him guide young people through the writing of a single thought, and from there to the linking together of their random half-baked thoughts into one glorious idea, then those men who were staring at him and smiling and turning away from him in this bar would know what he was capable of.

He would show them what he was made of. Consuelo was waiting for him in the parking lot. He had to take care of Consuelo. He would throw caution out the window of his car, and he would carry out his well-conceived plan.

Whoever's with me, he said, let's go.

And he heard them cheer as he walked out the door and crossed the lot to the El Dorado. He didn't know how many of the overdressed men had followed him. Eight? Ten? Fifteen? A large portion of the Missoula Men's Choir had every intention of crowding into his car. Consuelo moved over, squeezed into an even smaller version of herself than before. More men, more black suits had followed him from the tavern than could fit in one car, even a car as spacious as a Cadillac. The ones who couldn't get in his car had managed to commandeer another ride. (Was that Val with them? Were they really carrying Val on their shoulders?)

We're following you, said a man who might have passed for Val's brother.

162

Lead on, my captain, said a white-beard in an ancient tuxedo. His aged jacket had turned an odd shade of green.

Well, let them try to follow, thought Preston. They'll have to do their best to keep up.

If he'd had any sense, he would have stuck with the things he already knew how to do; fly fishing, a little woodworking (he was well-rounded), things even the magi of the Bitterroot Tavern might not know how do to do. Or how to do well. He should not have tried raising chickens.

The chickens were for his daughter. He wanted to give her some way to touch the earth. She needed to know where the food they ate came from, and after the city of Missoula decided it was okay after all, safe even, for people to raise chickens in their back yards, then chickens began to make a kind of sense to Preston. Less sense when the Rottweiler next door crossed the yard and tore into the henhouse he had built for them. The dog killed most of the chickens before they laid a single egg.

He'd thought about getting more chicks and starting up again, but there were still six of the bigger ones left, and he didn't know if it was a good idea to mix a new batch of babies with the older chickens, the survivors. The older ones were awkward and sullen. Teenagers. Preston put off ordering replacements, decided to wait and see how the remaining six fared, and it was touch and go for a while. One chicken died from a wound the dog had given her, and another died for no reason at all. The young hen looked at Preston one evening, as if she was summing him up and finding him wanting. In the morning she lay on her side in the dirt.

His wife had not said anything about chickens out loud. Beverly was long suffering. She'd taken up water skiing when it was something Preston wanted to try, and she'd taken up drinking gin when he wanted to drink gin. But she refused to feed the chickens. Once they decided to lay, she didn't like to see where they hid their eggs. The hens were forever getting out of the coop, although he thought that might have been his daughter's doing. When there were only four of them left, his daughter Tess decided to name the chickens. Aurora, Califax, Bert and Ernie. Prescott wondered about the names, which he could never keep straight, but as long as Tess

163

didn't bring the chickens into the house (the people house, not the hen house), Beverly let the names go.

Bert was carried off by a fox, or maybe it was a raccoon. Preston's daughter saw it happen, but Tess was too upset to identify such a dangerous animal exactly, something with teeth and with ears. His wife said he should stop trying to pry it out of her.

She's just a child, said his wife, and the child Tess looked at her father in a way that told him she had received a wound, and she would blame him for the wound, one of many wounds that would stay with her for her entire life.

Tess could no longer go out to collect the eggs. Preston had to do it, twice a day. The thing was, nobody in his family cared for the eggs. He ate a couple every Friday, but his daughter insisted she was a vegetarian or a vegan or allergic to eggs, something. His wife ate eggs. She bought hers at the store.

It had been his wife who first said it. He was reinforcing the coop against the neighbor's goddamn Rottweiler, who acted like a nice dog, sure, but was obviously capable of killing innocent chickens. One night, and it would serve his neighbors right, the dog was going to turn on them in their sleep. Let it happen. They were lousy neighbors.

Preston prided himself on being a good neighbor, not once causing offense to Simpkins on the left side or Petree on his other side. Petree complained about the smell from the henhouse. Petree could shove it. Petree was lucky there were only four survivors, and even luckier when Bert and Ernie died. The thing about Ernie bothered Preston. It was the other chickens who killed Ernie. The vet told him it happened a lot: Ernie probably had a sore place on her back and the others pecked at it, not meaning anything by what they were doing.

They're just chickens, said the vet, who seemed put-out that Preston had brought a dead one to the woman's office.

You can't help me out? said Preston.

What, said the vet, like a resurrection?

But what Preston meant was, can't you do anything with this animal body now that the life has gone out of it? What was Preston supposed to do with a dead chicken?

And that's when his wife said, well what do you plan to do with the other two when they die? We're not eating Clackamas, or whatever that white one is named.

And his daughter cried some more, which she'd been crying all morning anyway, since they discovered dead Ernie.

He watched the hens carefully after that; he meant to keep them alive, yet he was horrified by the fact that every day they were still alive. They laid eggs through the summer and then they stopped. Preston went to the vet again, who told him to look up the word *chicken* in an encyclopedia or something, she had other things she had to do, like take care of somebody's quarter horse.

You think you got problems, said the vet. What do you think I'm going to do with a dead horse?

But he couldn't think about the vet's problems with a horse.

He started letting the chickens out in the yard, sometimes forgetting to close the door to their coop. He tried to make amends with Greta the Rottweiler, thinking the dog could be of use to him after all, but Greta had to go and bite Petree's old mother, and then Greta the Rottweiler had to go and live on a big farm. That's what Preston told his daughter Tess, who (and he never realized this before) cared deeply about the neighbor's dog.

So what the hell, he left the door open to the chicken coop. The hens outsmarted him. One of them, he was pretty sure it was the red one, who was that? Imelda? Consuelo? She learned how to close the door of the chicken coop at night. He saw her do it. She flapped her wings and rushed up against the door and the door closed and the latch clicked and Imelda Consuelo, whatever that bird's name was, climbed up on her perch and clucked once and went to sleep. He had been surprised the first time he saw them sleep. He couldn't say why. He thought chickens would stay awake a lot more than these did.

Then the other red one, the one who was not Consuelo, disappeared, just wandered off and never came back. Well good for her. Maybe she was adopted by another family. Another family would probably let her in the house and feed her special food. He was down to his last chicken, whose name *was* Consuelo, he was sure of it, or her name might have been Bryan, some kind of man's name. His daughter Tess didn't understand the principle of gender when it came to names. When it came to chickens' names.

A workman came to the house to fix a leak in the roof, a leak right over Preston's desk that resulted in a set of lecture notes on Proust getting thoroughly soaked although it didn't seem to bother the roof repair guy. (Weeks later, in the Bitterroot Tavern, Preston thought one of the men at a corner table looked familiar. Maybe he was the roof man? No, Preston wouldn't believe that was true. That would be far too much of a coincidence. Nobody would believe him if he told them that.)

The roof man asked what he was going to do with the one chicken he had left, and Preston said he'd be happy to give it away, and the roof man would have taken Bryan or Consuelo home with him, but she was nowhere to be found. It was as if this Consuelo knew what was what. And was that even possible? Anyway, the roof man drove away without a hen, and that night when Consuelo showed up again, she looked around like she'd been caught out with the wrong rooster before she walked into the coop and climbed up on her roost, her perch, her loft. Whatever it was she slept on at night.

That was the week Preston's daughter began to write stories about Consuelo, stories in which the chicken fought off intruders or saved small children who were threatened in some way. By a house fire. By a flood. By deportation. Tess tried to bring Consuelo into the house, which was only the second time his wife Beverly had ever considered leaving the family; Beverly found the bird's droppings on the dining room table.

Daddy, can we assure Consuelo? asked his daughter.

Do what? said Preston.

She means *insure*, said his wife. Like life insurance. She's worried something will happen to her chicken.

He tried to imagine the difficult route a conversation about Consuelo's insurance must have taken.

No, honey, he told his daughter, you can't get coverage on a chicken.

You didn't even try, said Tess.

I did, I did, he said, I did try.

It's time, said his wife.

Time for what? said Preston, but he knew he was stalling.

Time to do your farmer's duty, said his wife. She nodded out the back window to where Consuelo was lurking in the chicken coop.

Preston had pulled the family car, a Honda van, into the backyard and he'd opened the side door, the one with the electric sliding mechanism, and he had sprinkled a line of bread crumbs from the coop to the van, throwing some right in on the carpet, waiting for Consuelo to take the bait, which she did quickly enough. The bird walked right up to the open electric door then turned and walked away. Preston tried again every day for a week, and he lied to his daughter, telling her he was airing out the van and keeping Consuelo company at the same time.

Maybe she hates the van, said his wife.

How can a chicken hate a van? said Preston. That's sort of strange.

Not as strange as some of the other shit that's going on around here, said his wife.

That's when Preston knew his wife had about had all she could take. Beverly didn't like him to swear around their daughter.

Maybe the chicken's holding out for a ride in the fucking El Dorado, said his wife.

It's how desperate he was. He pulled the Caddy around to the side of the house and made a path of bread crumbs across the yard. He'd recently been to a wedding where the flower girls spread rose petals for the bride to walk on. It was a lot like that, only with bread crumbs. The El Dorado had been a beautiful car once. Even now, it was one of the hardest things he'd ever done, throwing some of those crumbs right up onto the back seat.

He only hoped his wife was right; she was always right.

And he hoped his daughter wouldn't catch on to what he was doing, and maybe she wouldn't, but only because it was also the week of Tess's dance recital, and the girl was preoccupied with her dress and her shoes and the size of the audience, and whether she should bow at the end with the other girls or save it all up for her very own bow.

I wish Consuelo could come to my recital, said his daughter.

And Preston told her it didn't seem likely since Consuelo hated riding in a car, even on trips other than those trips they had taken together to the vet.

What are you going to do when you get the damn chicken in the car? asked his wife.

I don't know, he admitted.

He had been thinking about Greta the Rottweiler and the beautiful farm, and he asked his neighbor Bud Petree about it, who looked at Preston like he was a little child.

I expected your daughter would fall for that line, said Petree, but not you. Christ sakes, will you grow up?

He had to work at it, but the day came, a small miracle, when his fortune changed. He parked the El Dorado in the yard and killed the engine and walked away. He left the radio on to play something smooth, and he let the heater keep running too. It was a cold afternoon. It looked like the darkening sky might bring the first snow of autumn, and he thought a chicken would be encouraged to climb into the car if he kept it warm.

If you leave the heater running, you'll kill the battery, said his wife, shouting at him from the back door.

He shrugged her off, but after a few minutes he considered how hard it would be to get a second vehicle up in the yard alongside the first one in order to jump a dead battery, and he hurried over to turn the engine on again, surprised to see Consuelo sitting on the floorboard in the back. The bird looked at him, and he would have called her look a sheepish look, but he was sure that was some kind of mixed metaphor. Consuelo made a break for it, and Preston did an uncharacteristically brave thing. He blocked the door with his body and blocked it again until he could get the car door closed, watching Consuelo clamber in reverse onto the back seat.

The men of the men's chorus had crowded into his car.

Jesus Christ, said one of the tenors, who must have sat in something Consuelo had left behind.

It will wash, said another man.

I'm going to wash that man right out of my hair, sang a redheaded fellow who had taken off his cummerbund.

Oh lordy, said the familiar bass voice.

Preston drove the car across the parking lot and onto the highway. He knew exactly where he was going.

This is not the way to Stevensville, said the chicken-beshat man, as Preston turned off the main highway and picked up elevation.

Road trip, road trip, said the redhead, but he must not have known a song about road trips, for he grew silent as Preston drove toward the forest ahead.

He realized he had probably missed the dance recital. Preston tried to imagine Tess and his wife waiting for him at home, waiting up until the very last minute. But he knew he couldn't do anything about that now. He was caught up in something a lot bigger than dance recitals. He was doing what he should have done months ago. He was setting the chickens free, or he would have been setting the chickens free, but there was only one left, and so he was setting the chicken free. Consuelo would live out her last days in the woods.

It would have been better if there had been a friend for her, but Consuelo had not made friends easily. Preston had a quick mental image of his daughter Tess and the chicken building a small hut in the forest, gathering supplies for the long winter before them. He shook his head and drove on toward the National Forest. A snowflake fell. Snow was somehow falling inside the car, and then he realized it wasn't snow, just some wispy feather from Consuelo that the heater had caught up, floating around inside the car, landing here and there. He swatted at it and almost lost control of the steering wheel and decided not to do that again.

There was a logging road he remembered: he had skied down the road just the winter before, his skis fitting perfectly in the tracks another skier had left behind. Or maybe it was two winters, he couldn't remember. When had he last come up here to ski, or brought his daughter so she could sled? She had a purple sled in the garage, with a yellow rope for a handle. He turned onto the logging road, driving a little slower now, looking for the perfect place to stop: a wide place in the narrow road, someplace far off the highway with room for all these singing men to get out, a place he could think back on later and convince himself that he'd done the right thing, the decent thing.

He took a turn a little too fast and whispered to himself to calm down, and he drove sensibly after that into the last of the afternoon light and the cold, stopping finally when he came to a place where a tree had fallen across the road. He turned off the engine, surprised at the silence. His ears were ringing. In the quiet, the ringing grew louder and louder. Preston got out of the car with his choir friends, who insisted on opening all the doors, even the door to the trunk though he couldn't say why. Had someone been riding in the trunk? In the distance he heard the first tentative yips, then the howl of a coyote.

The second car pulled up behind them. The men in that car were treating Val as if he was their hero. They were singing a song for him, a song without words. It sounded like Wagner. Preston let the El Dorado's heater run for a few moments with the engine turned off, because, as his wife would say later, some people simply never do learn. The battery, weakened by the events of the long afternoon, quickly played out.

I'll take a look at it for you, said the man with the deep voice.

He raised the hood to the engine and took the black caps off the battery.

This battery, it's a million years old, he said. It's dry. Do we have any water?

Pour beer into it, said the redheaded tenor.

Do we have any beer? said another man.

Get Billy to piss in it. That's mostly beer.

Preston gathered Consuelo into his arms and walked slowly through the men of the choir. The basses and the baritones. Val, who looked a little lost without his guitar. But Val was game, happy to find a place among the tenors. Billy climbed up on the bumper and he was pissing into the battery, but then he wasn't. They pulled him into line with the rest of them.

They had taken a moment to straighten their ties and button up their jackets. Val tucked in his shirt. The ones who had been smoking put out their cigarettes. They had lined up in two rows. One of them took a small round pitch pipe from his pocket and blew a wobbly note.

Drink with me ... he began, and the others filled in behind him ... *to days ... gone by....*

Preston turned and walked away from them, all those men, all those tuxedos. Under his fingers, he could feel Consuelo's heartbeat. She looked around, taking in the valley below, and he wondered if she could realize this would be the last time she would ride in a Cadillac, the last time she would hear an entire men's choir sing in her honor. He bowed his head and waited for them to finish. The music was beautiful; the men were beautiful. Preston held Consuelo aloft in both hands, and considered whether he should set her down, or gently toss her into the air and watch her fly away, as best she could.

The men started a new song. He recognized this one, remembered it from watching a famous movie with this song in it, remembered dancing in his living room with Tess.

To life ... to life ... l'chaim ....

He held Consuelo close to his chest, felt her heart beating next to his own. Felt her glory.

I can't do it to you, old girl, he said.

He looked back at the crowd of men. They had formed a sort of gauntlet between him and the car, but it wasn't threatening. It was a gauntlet of love.

We'll find another way, he whispered to her. We'll stop at every bar on the way home. You and me. And these guys, if they want to come. You and me, he said again to Consuelo. You and me forever.

He heard the coyotes howling in the distance, a sad sound. It was a disappointed sound, but he didn't care.

L'chaim .... l'chaim .... the men sang ... to life.

HUNTED

Sarah Kaminski

Crisp.

That was the only word for it. Crisp. Not quite the balmy warm days of spring, when the threat of tornadoes looms heavy over every day. When storms roll in and uproot, destroy, and change. But also not quite the cold, icy days of winter, with temperatures plunging below zero. With it, the feeling of being trapped inside, anxious to go outside. The hiding, like a rabbit in its burrow, and the waiting.

It was somewhere in between. At times, pleasantly warm. In the sunlight, when the wind died down, people in the crowd stopped and turned their faces upward, like sunflowers turning toward the sun. When the wind picked up, it felt cool, but not bitterly so. In the shade, she regretted leaving her jacket in the car and pressed against her father's side for warmth. He was a large man of few words, whose facial expressions revealed nothing, hidden as they were beneath a burly beard, already turning grey. He could be counted on for an arm around the shoulder or a gruff kiss on the head. He had intended to raise boys but had been saddled with only girls instead.

When the wind blew hard, the hem of her skirt danced around her legs, revealing thighs still stark white from a winter spent indoors. Her father watched with a blank expression as she struggled to smooth it down. She wore make up, badly done. Too much of it, applied all wrong. Unnatural. She wore newfound femininity like a dress, pressed flat, not yet faded or torn from overuse, not yet dirtied. Her womanhood was newly discovered and tried on, and she twisted and turned in the mirror, smiling and batting eyelashes, and practicing coquettishness. She hadn't used to do that. He hated the skirt the most.

For fifteen years, she had been a tomboy. His tomboy, almost a real son. She had scraped her knees raw every summer. She had played third base for the softball team, and she could bat on both sides of the plate. She knew how to fish, and she wasn't squeamish about gutting the trout. She could hunt. She could sit and wait in the early hours of the morning, before the sun had even peaked over the horizon, and she could spot a buck from a mile away. She knew how to lure him with deer urine; she never once complained about the smell. The two of them, father and not-quite son, climbed trees together, downwind, and watched through the scope. She knew how to shoot a gun. She knew how to kill, to harvest the meat, and to avoid waste.

But she had changed this winter. The moment deer season ended. She had changed. She had become a woman.

—#—

She first noticed the boy while they stood in line for tickets. He was alone. Going stag. Strange to see someone alone, stranded in a sea of families, her own included. He reached the counter before she did, and she heard him say:

"One, please."

His voice rang round and deep like her father's. He wore a dark green hoodie with Greek letters embroidered into the front. When he turned from the counter, she caught his eyes. Brown.

They passed each other a dozen times that day in the way people do in shared spaces, where the path is not demanded, merely suggested. People go along together without purpose, like animals. Herd mentality. At the polar bear exhibit, he stumbled over a rock and looked up sharply with embarrassment. She feigned looking the other way. At the lions, he sat on the bench and smiled when she glanced in his direction. He had a dimple in his left cheek that reminded her of her younger sister.

At the tigers, he stood next to her and watched through the glass, offering up only a single word:

"Hey."

It might have been spoken to anyone, or even to the tiger, which looked up at them with hate-filled eyes, but she felt he had spoken to her. When she turned to respond, he had disappeared.

She ate a packed lunch with her family on the veranda just outside the reptile house. She watched him devour an ice cream cone in only a few large bites before pulling a pack of cigarettes from his back pocket. He winked at her as he lit one, and she blushed and turned away. The wind shifted and she could smell burning tobacco in the air. Nicotine and tar.

—#—

The rains began mid-afternoon. The thawing of winter and the welcome of spring. She stood outside the antelope run and listened while her father read facts from the metal plaque affixed to the fence. The beasts meant nothing to her, only deer in another form. She imagined herself lining up the shot, holding her breath as she squeezed the trigger. She imagined the animals falling before her, mindless creatures made only for her consumption. She imagined the boy wading through the tall grass with the animals, racing when he heard the gunshot, running for cover. She timed it perfectly, leading with her gun, then squeezed again.

And down he fell.

The first drops of rain landed softly on their heads, carrying with them the promise of torrential downpour. They cowered under an awning - her father, her sisters, and her. And the boy. He pressed close to her. He radiated warmth. She shivered.

"Home," her father said, leaving no room for argument.

When the rain let up, they ventured toward the exits, stepping gingerly around puddles. Her skirt, damp, clung to her legs; the thin cotton had turned translucent. She felt his eyes on her bottom as she walked away, but she didn't turn around to verify. She flushed with shame and desire, excitement and fear.

She made up an excuse to separate, a sudden stomach ache. "I'll be quick. I promise."

She turned and ran, weaving through the crowd, a salmon against the river of people making their exodus, before the real storm hit. Those spring storms can be tricky. Warm front meets cold front, and the sky turns over. It can happen in a second.

She found him sitting alone with the sea lions. Rain droplets danced on the water's surface. His hair had turned dark with the rain; he hadn't pulled his hood up. Thunder cracked overhead, and in the second that she looked up, he closed the distance between them.

"We should take cover." He didn't wait for a response. He took her hand and made for shelter.

They stood alone, awkward, just inside the glass doors of the ape house. She wrung water from her skirt.

"I'm Kevin," he said.

"Cara."

They smiled and looked away. She admired again the boyish

dimple on his cheek. A remnant of childhood that could never
be shaken.

"We're stuck until it's over."

"I guess."

They sat together on a bench. She kept her eyes trained on an
empty gorilla exhibit. The animals had all sought their own cover. She
wondered where they had gone. She glanced his direction every few
seconds, ever aware of his presence, but he didn't move. He watched
the rain beat the grass down and form miniature rivers of mud and
leaves. When her teeth chattered, he rubbed her arms. When they
stopped, he kissed her. She shivered again but not from cold.
Thunder crashed. The lights flickered.

"Are you scared?" he asked.

"Should I be?"

—#—

They walked together through the exhibits. All empty. They
stopped by the chimpanzees, and he read aloud from the plaque, like
her father might have: "Chimps are more closely related to humans
than any other animal." He paused and shrugged. "They share 99% of
our DNA."

"Really?"

"That's what it says."

She moved away, crossing the room. She could hear her heart
pounding in her ears. "What else does it say?"

"That they sometimes kill their own young."

Perhaps he expected her to show girlish unease at the idea,
but she only blinked. "That's nature for you."

She leaned back against the wall and lured him to her. Her
prey. He walked toward her with slow, deliberate steps and pressed
against her, warming her with his nearness. He kissed her again.
More. He tasted like the rain and cigarettes. The lights flickered again,
and went out, and he pressed her harder. He twisted fingers into her
hair. He pulled her to the floor and climbed over her. Emergency lights
came on, tinting the world red. Red against the glass, red against the
walls. His skin glowed red, like fire, and she shrank away.

"We should go."

He shook his head. "We're safe here."

He kissed her again, but she turned her face away. He moved

175

to her neck. He lifted her skirt. She froze, like a deer catching a hunter's scent. Preparing to leap away at any sound. The world froze. Her lip trembled. From the cold, or from something else, she couldn't be sure. The red lights blinked, like eyes. Watching her.

He pushed inside her, and she shook. She lifted her eyes to the exhibit glass, where a lone chimpanzee, only a few years old, watched. He thrust into her again, animal-like in his need. She felt her breath come in short, whimpering gasps. She closed her eyes and counted, attempting to slow her breath to a stop. She waited.

When he finished, he stood and looked away. "The storm's over."

"Yeah," she agreed, trying and failing to smooth her sticky, wet skirt around her nakedness.

"You think your dad'll be worried?"

"Probably."

He gave her a wry smile, the dimple popping out again, a black hole on his narrow face. "I guess you should get going then."

She nodded and ran.

—#—

She found her father calling her name into the women's restroom.

"Here I am," she said, breathless from running.

His eyes swept over her, detecting change.

"Good," he said. "You're safe."

THEIR NAMES, YOUR MOUTH

Sara Levine

Selena Mills and her son appeared in Margate Park that spring like a pair of astronauts just landed on the moon. They had a queer, marooned look about them, and as they stood outside the park, holding hands and watching the boys squirt water guns, it seemed that maybe, after all, they would not come in. Then Selena unlatched the gate and Lucas zigzagged over to the sand box, clutching a plush toy.

"I like your anteater," said Derek who's three; he's my oldest.

"Actually it's an aardvark," Selena said, and I was put off by the brisk manner in which she enlightened him. It sounds silly now, but she was very beautiful. Wide-planed face, long hair, green eyes I'm sure her whole life she was told were mesmerizing. She wore a short white dress and was probably thirty, but she had the body of a younger woman. And it seems to me that if you are that beautiful, you ought to take precautions with people.

The Mills had just moved to Chicago from North Carolina.

There was a husband too; his name was Mark Mills; they had moved for his job. Lucas, who was three, called him Poppy.

Selena and Lucas began to show up at the playground every day. After urging Lucas towards the other children, Selena would sail over to the knot of mothers on the park bench, as if she had arranged to meet us and were only a little late. Her ease had something amplified and hearty about it, a willed, nervous sort of confidence. She always wore dresses, and she would fold her skirts beneath her and say, "You all, hi!"

She had a bright, relentless way of talking.

Frequently she interrupted other people, jabbing at them with irrelevant questions and declaring, with disarming ease, that she didn't follow the story—as if it were important they know what a simple person they were dealing with. "I don't know that word," she might say, and you would have to define the word ("affect," or "toney") and start again, or else convince her that it didn't matter. Once Lisa was spouting off about her mother-in-law who had a talent for remarks that peeled the paint off Lisa's confidence. We sprawled on the park bench, laughing and nodding with bitter recognition. Selena sat gravely, her hands folded in her lap.

"I don't get it," she said. "I don't get it. You'll have to tell me again."

Lisa shook Selena's hand off her sleeve. "Don't worry, Selena. There isn't going to be an exam on this one."

When it was Selena's turn to talk, she asked how much fruit we gave our children and what were our rules about TV and did we think she ought to let Lucas have a toy gun. She spoke as if she laid awake nights worrying about such things. When she wasn't talking about the management of Lucas, she talked about Mark. Mark was where her deepest enthusiasm lay.

"Mark is from Chapel Hill, he's miserable here. He misses the music scene. He misses the climate. It's so hard for him..."

None of us had much to say to that. The Mills lived in a greystone close to the lake; Mark worked in advertising; Selena showed up at the park every day in a different dress. We had limited pity for minor afflictions such as regional adjustment disorder. "If you don't like the Midwest, get out!" Tria hissed when Selena went to spot Lucas on the monkey bars.

But Selena talked. On and on like a river she talked. I must have fallen under her spell a little because I found it a pleasure to look at her, even if I didn't listen, and I waited with interest to see all of her spring outfits. She was the best-dressed mother by far, although Lisa, who ran a feminist book group, would have killed me if she heard me say it. Lisa told her daughters beauty was inside them and clothing designed only to ward off weather.

"Selena's all right," I said. "It's probably just her getting used to the place. And her husband not being around much."

But at times it struck me as strange the way Selena spoke of her husband. She repeated his little comments as if Mark were a movie star and she a tabloid reporter. "Guess what Mark did this week!" she might begin, and then she would tell a story—in which Mark dressed down a waiter in a restaurant, Mark performed a perfect mimicry of Chicago accents, Mark refused to eat the lasagna she had made because he'd decided, that day at noon, to be vegan. She might tell five anecdotes in which her husband came off as a top-drawer asshole, and always she ended the encounter by clutching our sleeves with her bony hand and saying, "I can't wait for you to meet him!" She spoke with the fervor of a girl with a new boyfriend.

"*How* long have you guys been married?" Lisa asked.

"Six years," Selena said. Later Lisa said it probably only equaled two, given how little they saw each other. You had to compute marriage years as you did dog years, and Lisa had complex equations, based on how many hours a week the man and the woman worked. She factored in too whether the couple ate meals together. Lisa's husband, a professor in the American Studies department at Northwestern, worked from home, and often came home for lunch on the days he was teaching. She said it felt like they had been married forty-five years already.

"Divorce material," Jane said later when we walked home. "I give them two years."

My husband Zach got home from work every night at six pm; that was the deal. His last patient was at five. Most days I handed over the boys and went upstairs to take a bath. Sometimes, through pure inertia, I hung around and drank a glass of wine while he gave them dinner, but I got surly if the boys asked me to fetch milk or if Zach asked an easy question like, "Where's the applesauce?" "I'm off duty," I said. In between the hoots and clamor, I filled Zach in on what I'd done that day, giving special emphasis to any adult conversation I might have had, since not every day included it. What I said to Zach rarely seemed to get through; I flung words at him the way the boys threw handfuls of pebbles at pigeons, carelessly, never expecting stone to meet flesh. About his own day Zach always said, "Fine. Long." But for some reason he liked hearing about Selena. He had met her at Margate Park when he took the boys at the weekend, and together he and I formed a picture of Mark Mills.

"I'm guessing he's older," Zach said. "He's high up at Leo Burnett. Right? Selena might be—well, look at her. She's, you know—"

"She's what?" I said and didn't like the sharpness in my voice.

"An attractive woman, wouldn't you say? Haven't you said? I just have a feeling about them. I'm guessing he's a lot older. Maybe she's his second wife—"

"Or third."

Zach reached across the table and wiped the boys' mouths. "Right. What was she before, his secretary?"

I shrugged. Selena didn't seem like anybody's secretary. I divided the stay-at-home mothers into two groups: those who had sacrificed something when they decided to stay at home, and those who gave up their jobs in a flash, no regrets, since they had never liked their work anyway. That was me. I had gotten a degree in library science and was crisp with boredom when I got pregnant. Every time the boys dragged the toilet paper rolls all over the house or dressed the cats in my bras, I reminded myself, At least you're not in that chilly tomb of a library!

"Anyway he sounds miserable," my husband said.

"He probably overworks to avoid himself. Can't slow down or he'll crash. Depressive," I said, then wondered if I'd gone a little too far. Zach takes medication for depression, but for years he threw away the pharmacy bottles and kept the pills in a little brass case. I only learned the extent of the problem after we got married. Partly it's a professional concern; his credibility as a therapist might be compromised if people knew he had a problem. Though I say he doesn't have a problem, just a prescription. Anyway, even though his moods are level as a ruler now, I take care not to throw around the word "depressive."

If it bothered him, he didn't show it.

"How was *your* day?" I asked.

"Fine," Zach said. "Long."

That was all I'd get out of him. I'm not supposed to know who Zach's patients are, and he doesn't tell me, although sometimes I figure it out. We go into a restaurant, for example, and the sixty-year-old man at the next table falls all over himself with gladness: "Nice to see you, Dr. Wagoner!" and later when I say to Zach, "How did you know *him?*" all he does is raise his eyebrows. So I figure. Another person helped by Viagra.

The next time I saw Selena at the park, I asked her what she'd done before she had Lucas.

"Oh, lots of things," she said vaguely. "I'm not from the South, you know. I lived in Montana for a while, and California, before I met Mark."

That didn't answer the question. But it was the first hot day of summer and the boys were tearing off their t-shirts and trying to pitch them into the water fountain. Derek had already got his off and was snapping at his brother with the wet sleeve. "Calm down and get dressed right now," I told them. Lucas stood three feet away, hugging his aardvark, looking at their naked chests.

"Lucas doesn't like being naked," Selena said with a queer sort of pride. "Last week he had a nightmare and I went into his room in just a tee shirt. One minute he's wailing, the next minute he's calm. 'Mama,' he says to me, his face all wrinkled in disgust, 'go put on some pants!'"

Everybody laughed.

"He's just like his father," Selena said.

The laughter died. I swear, it was like a piñata lowered from the sky, only a question of who would take the first-round swing.

"Like his father," Lisa said with deliberate casualness. "Selena, what do you mean?"

"I don't know." Selena flushed. "Just that Mark is a modest person. He doesn't go in for …. gratuitous nakedness. He's a modest person," she repeated. Then the candy rained down. "He prefers to get dressed in the closet."

"Selena!" Jane leaned forward, her hands cupping her face. "That's terrible." Jane, who had sex with her husband three times a week, still found time to masturbate with her electric toothbrush. Probably Jane thought a husband who undressed in the closet constituted emotional abuse.

"Oh no," Selena laughed. "He's all right in that department. I don't mean we have to put a hole in the bed sheet. He's just modest about dressing and undressing."

After that, I felt sorry for Selena in a new way. Jane and Lisa began to call Mark the Puritan. Selena, though she had blushed at that disclosure, seemed unaware of having compromised Mark's image. If anything, she seemed heartened by the confidence and, in the weeks that followed, disclosed detail after detail about Mark's intimate habits. As a teenager, he had been afraid his ears were too big. On their first date, he had eaten a bad flan and gotten diarrhea. Last week, while lifting the lawnmower out of the garage, he had pulled a muscle in his back. Did she have any flattering story to tell about him? She glowed as she spoke of him and intimated that our friendship with Mark was delightfully imminent.

One day, the height of summer, she angled me away from the other women.

"I really want you to meet Mark," she said. "He doesn't warm to everybody, but I have a feeling he'd like you guys."

"Tell him to bring Lucas to the park sometime," I said.

She nodded, but I don't think she heard me. Something about Mark, I supposed, prevented him from taking his own kid to the park. Maybe he was too old to play.

"The trouble is he has no friends here," she said. "I mean he meets people at work he could call friends, but you know how men are. They don't call their friends—do they? It drives me crazy! They just don't do the upkeep."

I'd had the same thought before, but the notion struck me as funny coming from Selena, who never called me or dropped by. We saw each other only in the park. I didn't put her in the class of friends who discreetly labored on behalf of friendship, the women who called as they headed out to the zoo, dropped off bags of clothing that their kids had outgrown, took my boys to the park so I could run errands. A whole world of small selfless social interactions wove me and my friends together, a world in which Selena played no part. The way she spoke of men and women seemed canned.

"So let's make a date, okay?" Selena pressed my hand. "Tell Zach. I think Zach and Mark will get along really well." She suggested we meet for dinner on Friday night.

"Can't you demote it a little?" Zach said when I told him. "Make it a Tuesday. It'll be easy then to leave early."

"She thinks you and Mark will get along. She talks about it like she's arranging a play date."

"What did you tell her about me?"

"Nothing. Nothing! She's going by whatever she liked about you when you two talked in the park."

"Okay. Just wondering." He rolled his eyes.

"She's unbearable really, your Selena."

At five o'clock on Friday night, right after I opened the door for the babysitter, a high school girl with a habit of saying "Okay" to whatever the boys suggested, Zach called and said he had to work late.

"You're kidding," I said. "Come on!"

"Sorry. It was the only time I could fit this patient in. She needs me; she's very distraught. Anyway, you'll have a good time. It's a night out, right? With or without me."

I snickered. He had probably intended to weasel out of the dinner all along.

At the Japanese restaurant, Selena was already seated at a table set for four. She had put on a little make-up and her hair glinted with bobby pins as if she wore some kind of medieval head-plate.

"Where's Zach?" she said.

"Where's Mark?"

"He's parking the car."

I burst out laughing. Selena looked stricken.

"I'm sorry," I said. "I'm just—it's nervous energy. The suspense of another five minutes seemed funny. I mean, that he's *still* not here. But I can wait." I settled my napkin onto my lap.

Selena accepted this explanation with grace. But she blanched when I told her that Zach had to work late. "That's terrible," she said, as if I had told her I might have ovarian cancer. "This evening meant so much to Mark." While she spoke, a waiter appeared and hovered at the table's edge, looking at the wall.

"I'll have a Singha," I said abruptly.

He nodded and turned an opaque face to Selena.

"I'll wait for Mark," she told the waiter, who nodded and glided off.

"Does he know who Mark is?"

"Oh," she waved it aside. "He'll figure it out."

Then she began to talk—oh, how Selena talked!—but I barely pretended to listen, too distracted by the imminent arrival of Mark, whom I pictured first as an ogre—old, grey, stooped—and then as a man in his thirties, with facial hair, a weak body, and a yellowish cast to his skin. The waiter brought my beer and after several large reckless swallows I relaxed and became even more excited. Mark was my mark. He could be anything, but let him be rude, sallow, incompetent, crotchety, prudish, and utterly deficient in charm. Let the evening be awful!

"Ah!" Selena's face lit up like a bride. "There he is!" She began to wave her hands as if he were not six feet away, but on a dock and she on a transatlantic ship, steaming away. Mark came over slowly and sat down in the chair beside her. He was our age. He kissed her cheek before he turned to me. On first glance he seemed neither good-looking nor ugly; neither well dressed nor slovenly. In fact, he seemed decidedly average except for the fact that he wore his sideburns long.

Selena introduced us as if we were two kings, her desire for us to be pleased with each other plain. My impatience suddenly evaporated, and I felt warm and expansive towards them both. They had chosen a simple, unpretentious restaurant. The table was set with ceramic teacups and chopsticks sealed in red and gold wrappers. Like a battered moon, a large paper lampshade glowed above our heads.

"So we meet at last!" said Mark.

He had a nice way of looking at Selena, absent-mindedly patting her arm. He didn't complain about Chicago or give view to any of the qualities Selena had attributed to him. I undressed him with my eyes, and his body seemed all right, not so unworthy it needed to be hidden in the closet.

No more making fun, I thought; I had stepped inside their chalk circle.

Not long after that evening, Selena called up and asked us to a concert—the symphony was doing Rachmaninoff's Second Piano Concerto; it would be torrid, she said, they would sit on the lawn and drink wine; we must come.

"We must, must we?" said Zach. He had taken on new patients at work and hardly seemed to feel the pulse-quickening calls of summer. "You go; they're your friends now."

"All right. I will."

The week before the concert, Selena told me every day how much they were looking forward to it. Her talk had a dampening effect; I don't know if it was her eagerness that was off-putting, or simply that she lived too much in expectation of an event. I only know that as the concert loomed closer, I felt no liveliness about it and wished that, like Zach, I'd said I couldn't come.

The three of us took the train out to Ravinia. Selena and I took two seats together, behind Mark, and I succumbed to the torrent of her talk. Mark made no effort to turn around. I looked at his shoulders and neck as Selena and I spoke of the best places to buy shoes, how to hide vegetables in casseroles, how often our children flossed their teeth. The crowd around us was loud, and Mark either swam in his own thoughts or listened to a woman tell her friend in a berating voice that her boyfriend was a bastard. I half-listened to that conversation, too. It was just getting dark when we got there. We found a place on the grass to spread out our blanket and opened a bottle of wine.

Selena's cell phone vibrated halfway through the Rachmaninoff. Lucas had thrown up and was very upset.

"I'll go back," Mark said.

"No, I'll go," she said. "He'll want me really."

"Is there even a train now?" I said.

We checked the schedule; if she hurried, she could make it back.

"You know, if a kid's thrown up, the worst is probably over," I said. "He'll be asleep by the time you get home."

"No, he throws up in threes. He's a mad vomiter! He'll be up all night."

"You can spare her the details," Mark said.

"I'm sorry." She clutched my arm. "But Lucas! You know how children are. It's better if I go."

I turned away as they said goodbye, lay back on the prickly wool blanket and looked at the stars. After she had gone, Mark stayed seated, as if his posture were a courtesy to someone—but who? Was he counting the minutes until Selena left the park? Then he sighed and lay on the blanket too. I closed my eyes and let my mind unfurl to the music. During the second half, some minor piece by Rimsky-Korsakov, Mark said in a low voice, "Let's go for a walk." He took my hand to thread me through the blankets and bodies on the grass, and even after we had stepped off the lawn and onto the path, neither of us let go. We found a stand of trees, and he pulled me up against one of them and kissed me. There was a smell of bark and beer. On the train we held hands beneath the seat. I was sleepy;

185

I didn't talk much and it didn't matter. We parted at the station without touching and I walked myself home.

For three days after the concert, I didn't see Selena in the park. Possibly Lucas's illness kept them away, but I couldn't help make more of her absence. On the fourth day as I entered the park with the boys, I saw her pretty dark head by the sandbox and approached slowly, as if I were stepping across a driveway that had recently been tarred and might not be dry. She wore a dark blue dress and was, as usual, casually ravishing. The boys, scrambling about at my hips, felt like a shield; when they ran off, I touched my chest as if I were naked. Selena looked up and smiled.

"Don't worry, I'm not contagious," she said. "Oh my god, the first few days, Mark wouldn't come near me. He would only eat Zinc and Airborne!"

"Did he get sick?"

"No, just Lucas and me. But we get everything. Every flu, every cold, don't we, Crazy?" she said with a nod to her son in the sandbox. Lucas was a placid, routine-loving child, and sometimes I wondered if Selena called him "Crazy" to conjure up some wild masculine energy she saw lacking in him. He looked up at his mother, his face calm as a puddle.

"I'm not sick now, Mama."

"How was the concert?" Selena said, turning back to me. "Of course, Mark didn't tell me anything."

"Rachmaninoff, you must know it," I said, suddenly embarrassed. The music came back to me and the pressure of Mark's hands on my body. "Didn't you choose it—"

She talked and talked, her usual flowing self, and told, in the course of things, a few more Mark stories. Your Mark, I thought derisively. Then Jane showed up to push Ellie on the swing, and whatever skeins of melodrama I'd been tangled in—some web I wanted to weave of passion and danger— loosened. None of it felt real to me. There were the boys, running as usual around the playground. Okay, I told myself. So you kissed her husband. Big deal.

I am not a beautiful woman. I have never been deceived, or deceived myself, on the point. The women in my family have long torsos, short legs, no breasts to speak of. We have nice skin and close-set eyes, a sharpness around the chin. When I was a girl, I heard a man say about one of my sisters, "She just missed being pretty," and realized at once that he also had described me. Humiliation turned quickly to relief. Is that all it is? Just missed? Like a B+, I could live with that. Really, there are worse tragedies. As a young woman I developed a habit of being scrupulously generous in bed. I've got heart, I thought, I'm a warm, sensuous, giving woman, and this is how, for years, I consoled myself for my lack of beauty, unaware that I was consoling myself at all.

Mark and I began to meet in the evenings. It was easy to fit him into my life; I told Zach I was going to the movies or grocery shopping. I don't know what Mark told Selena; probably she was used to him working late. We were careful not to go where people could see us. I loved the idea that I might be falling in love, but it was plain from the way Mark and I carried on—even plain from the long and perfectly satisfying intervals between our meetings—that what I loved was the idea of wresting him from Selena. She wrapped him up in a winding sheet every day with her talk, wrapped him up like some kind of mummy, and I unwrapped him and found a live man. A Crackerjack prize! One morning, only hours after he and I had been to a hotel, I sat at the park with Selena, listening to Selena talk, and thought, But we both have to endure her! This talk! This endless river of talk! God! And I longed to sit with Mark in some quiet room in the city.

I took great pains to be kind to my family. I let the boys finger-paint and do mud pies on the porch, and I didn't snap when they let food fall out of their mouths onto the table. I was more than usually solicitous of Zach's feelings, too—asking him about what he read in the newspaper and paying attention as he answered—and I tried to be available for sex. But Zach was not, for his own reasons, much interested in sex those days. He had begun to suspect another doctor in his practice of embezzling money. He told no one besides me his suspicions, but the problem dominated his thoughts. At last he admitted to me that he kept imagining confronting the other doctor in the privacy of her office and forcing her resignation. The suspected doctor was someone he'd long disliked.

"Why don't you just talk to the senior clinicians about her?" I said.

"It wouldn't do to have it all come out. If I'm wrong about it, I'm tainted for having suspected her. If I'm right, there would be reverberations. We'd all be watched more closely as a result."

"Don't you think if Sherry knew, or even Jim Hickling—"

But it was a mistake to try to strategize with him. Even my taking up proper names irritated him. They were his names, they didn't belong in my mouth. Zach's like that. When I take a sip of his wine, he doesn't complain, but he gets up and pours me my own glass.

"It's fine," Zach said. "Let's not talk about it."

I closed my eyes and slid into my own privacies: Mark's hands kneading my ass, the back of my thighs, his mouth on the pulse in my neck.

In my friendships too, I began to find dissatisfaction. I suppose it was my fault; now that I had a secret I noticed with irritation how easily conversation glided over serious topics, how easy, in fact, it was to deceive people. Jane and Lisa would sit down next to me in the park and I would think, But they tell me nothing, I know nothing about them! Their jokes oppressed me, their knowing allusions to my life with Zach.

Of course, all this time Selena was at the park too, soliciting our opinions about healthy snack foods and telling her stories about Mark.

How did she do it? I thought as I listened to her speak without seeming to draw breath. I suppose I envied her confidence, the way she felt free to describe her husband in public to people who had no reason to cherish him. Never mind if she described him accurately or not; she took the liberty to describe. Why all this time had I been so careful to protect my husband's dignity, his profession? How old-fashioned of me, how wifely! Discretion! What was it for and what had it cost me? The pleasure of feeling known?

Selena's Mark stories went on, the usual kinds of stories— Mark had a cold sore on his cheek; Mark had bought himself cargo pants, at his age, could we believe it?— and I became confident that she would not find us out. She seemed to suspect nothing—in fact, she was as fond of me as ever and kept insisting the four of us should get together—which may be why one morning I turned to her and said, with a little too much zeal, "And what's Mark up to these days? Is he still ragging on the Midwest? Has he made any friends yet?" A shadow crossed Selena's face. She knew something—not that I was the one. But maybe that I knew something about where he went those nights. She was hurt. I could see it. "Mark's fine," she said and the river of talk dried up; she changed the subject.

Soon after that, I broke off the affair, for it seemed I had gotten out of it all that I wanted.

THE FROG

Tim Miller

He had already chased one reporter from the porch, but they kept coming, ridiculously dressed young women and their slobby cameramen who looked no better than plumbers. Hughes just didn't answer the door now, and anyhow his neighbors were more obliging and were glad at the chance of being on TV. He of course didn't refuse to speak with the police, but they had only come around once. His statement had been brief: he had only known Allen in passing, a wave if they saw each other driving down the street, that was it. He added that their wives had known each other better, and when the police asked to speak with Carol, he mentioned her passing.

"Only the other month," Hughes said. He wanted to go on and say that, dying in May, she'd had a last sense of spring in her garden, but he knew the police wouldn't care about that. It wouldn't mean anything to them, or help them. Compared to a man whose death required days of police attention at his house, an old woman who had died slowly and predictably—but who had nurtured her marigolds and her herbs, or who had watched from the window as he had done up the trellis for her tomatoes—was nothing to these men. The only time he'd ever had the police's attention was with his daughter Frieda, and he didn't want to mention that either, or that the entire street seemed unlucky.

Three days later, with the police and the news vans still arriving down the street at all hours, Hughes snuck out the side door to get some air. It had been raining all morning, and it still drizzled now, and this made him happy. While he despised the TV people but had nothing against the police, he silently loathed them both for conspiring to ignore Carol. When the ambulance showed up at their house that afternoon, no one had come out onto their lawns to gawk or stand in the street and stare. As he made his way to the backyard, Hughes was annoyed at his own contradictions: he would have hated the attention, yet was jealous that the mere violence of a murder down the street got all of it instead. Apparently his neighbor had been tied to his bed for a week,

190

starved, and a gasoline-soaked rag shoved in his mouth and lit.

"Awful, yes," he said aloud, "but I'm still glad they're getting rained on."

He lifted the latch and entered the fenced-in garden, and immediately remembered putting the crossing path of stepping stones down on the soil, some fifty years ago. The path had never been level or straight, no matter what they did, and Carol had always spoken of the garden's strange moods. Certain vegetables would never grow there, or only would once every few years, and while some flowers never took to the ground, others sprang up and seemed to never die. Carol had loved tending to these idiosyncrasies, but it had also clearly bothered her. Looking towards the corner flowerbed which sat in the lowest ground, Hughes strayed from the stepping stones when he saw something moving there. As always, rainwater had gathered around that bed in a sloggy mush, and peering out from one of the puddles was a frog. Its eyes blinked away the drizzle. Balancing himself with one hand on the fence, Hughes stepped forward and leaned down, and as if he were tugging at a good-sized potato, he grabbed the frog up a little more harshly that he had intended. It seemed shocked to be in his squeezed palm, and seeing its reaction gave him an idea. Taking the frog away from the flooded part of the garden, he knelt down in front of a flowerbed that, while soggy, was still tough with clay-thick earth. With his free hand he dug a good-sized hole, placed the frog inside, covered it over, and stood up as quickly as he could and stamped the ground flat. After another moment, he used both hands to drag some more dirt from another bed, smacked it on top, and packed it tight again with his feet. He found a heavy stone nearby and dropped it, mashing it in again. The thing was buried good.

He had no idea why he was doing this. It had been groundhogs that had always gotten into the garden and been an annoyance, either them or the smallest rabbits that could slip through the bent lip in the gate. Frogs had never been a problem. But he did it anyway, and went back inside.

They had met when he came home from serving overseas. He had done horrible things there—necessary, but still horrible—and he hadn't found a way to understand what he'd done until he met Carol. Many of his friends had taken to drink, or they ran around on their wives, or seemed to take great joy in beating their children, but Hughes had never done this. Even when Frieda was born he had never been anything but gentle, to the both of them. But he had also never been much for speaking, and to his surprise it had all come out once with Carol, when he said he didn't know if he could marry her. "Because when they die," he said, all of twenty years old, "married people want to be buried near one another. And all I want is for my body to be taken back where my friends died."

He'd never cried in front of a woman before, or admitted something so personal. But her love for him had persuaded him against that wish, and they'd been married soon after. From the moment she had accepted his tears, there had never been another woman in his life, and rarely the need for other friends at all.

The next afternoon Hughes went out the side door again, since he was never sure when somebody, like spreading weeds, would show up down the street. Finding the flowerbed, he knelt again to the earth and, removing the stone, began digging with his hands. Recoiling when he felt something soft, he pulled the dirt away more carefully until he could see its entire body, still there. Just then it started to rain again, and the frog blinked away the falling drops.

Hughes didn't know much about frogs, but it didn't make any sense that it was still alive: it had been underground for more than an entire day. He had packed the ground tight, too; it couldn't have moved or eaten, and maybe it was possible but he didn't understand how it could have breathed. Carol had existed for months in the most medicated and precise atmosphere, and yet she had died for want of breath. She had died in the light, she had died loved, she had died with everyone possible trying to prolong her life, and yet she had died anyway.

He snatched the frog up and decided to bring it into the house. At the side door, just as he jiggled the handle he felt the thing struggle in his palm, and he squeezed harder.

"Damn it," he said to himself. He'd forgotten to unlock the handle on his way out, and the wind had blown the door shut, locking him outside. The frog seemed to take some joy in this, and wriggled in his hand some more. It nearly jumped free, and Hughes strained forward to keep it and almost catch it, and his old back—not used to such abrupt movements—suddenly seemed alive with spreading roots of pain.

"Damn it," he said again, and hobbled around to the front door. Hidden just off the stoop and beneath the spreading hastas that no one would tend to anymore was one of Carol's chintzy gardening decorations. It was some piece of plastic made to look like a large rock, with an old-fashioned wheelbarrow and a pitchfork painted on either side of the words, *Gardeners Know All the Best Dirt!* He had always hated it, since even this cheap thing reminded him of wheelbarrows stacked with dead friends, or of dead enemies found after the winter's thaw and gathered with pitchforks. Reaching for the fake stone and shaking it, he heard the extra side-door key fall out of its hollow inside. Grunting and struggling, key in one hand and frog still in the other, he straightened up just as a plumber and his camera, and some woman made up for a night out on the town, were coming up his walk.

"Mr. Hughes?" the woman asked. "Mr. Hughes? Are you Mr. Hughes?" He despised hearing his own name pronounced the way people did it on the news, as if every syllable were crisp and electronic and weighed down with gossip and drama. Nothing about her was natural, she seemed like painted plastic herself, the oaf beside her like some walking landfill. And right on cue he lifted his camera to his shoulder, taking Hughes's silence as assent.

"Get that thing away from me."

"I'm sorry to bother you, Mr. Hughes."

"No you're not, you live to bother people like me."

"We just wondered if you had a moment—"

"Not for you I don't—"

"Just if you had anything to say about your neighbor, what do you remember—"

"I didn't know him from Adam. He lived down the street."

The woman was used to dealing with annoyed people, and even though Hughes hadn't been so angry in a long time, it was clearly nothing compared to other people she had encountered. And so with her plastic voice she continued. "Are you worried about your safety, living here where such a thing happened—"

He wanted to mention Frieda—her death and that of her daughter had been in the papers when it happened—to show the woman who didn't look older than twenty that things like this happened all the time so no, he wasn't worried about it. But the frog nearly jumped out of his hand, and he lurched again to keep hold of it. Only noticing the frog now, this finally surprised the woman and her cameraman both, and Hughes wondered what she would do if he threw it at her. "Please, just leave me alone." He looked around the neighborhood "There're enough idiots around here who will give you whatever you want."

Carol would have been angry with him for saying that; even if it was true he had no way of knowing, since he didn't talk to anybody. Heading back towards the door and clumsy with the key and swearing at himself now, he could still see them standing in the front yard, hoping perhaps he couldn't get in so they'd have another chance at him. Finally the lock gave, but a pair or two of his shoes were still stuck on the other side of the door, and when he rammed it with his shoulder he heard the shoes go flying across the kitchen as he fell to the floor. He cried out, but then realized both his fists were clenched. More disgusted than horrified, he held his hand away from his body and stood up, but saw nothing there. No squashed frog, no imploded frog, just the frog same as it had been. He held it up close to his face. It was clearly breathing. And there it was, blinking again.

Hughes slammed the door, and could see through the front window of the living room that the reporter and cameraman were leaving for somebody else's house, probably to have a laugh at his expense. He drew the shades and turned the kitchen light on, and placed the frog on the counter. He detached the bottom of two of Carol's cake pans and stacked them around the frog, fencing it in. He grabbed a plastic glass that had belonged to his granddaughter and headed for the basement. The giddy cartoon faces and bodies of toy bears were fading on the sides of the cup—it had been one of the few things of hers they'd kept—and in the basement he drilled a series of holes all around it, puncturing the eyes and legs and stomachs of these childrens' bears. With the cup and a handful of nails, he returned to the kitchen.

Hughes stayed up all night watching the frog, but nothing happened. Surrounded by a wall of cloudy but transparent plastic, and pierced on all sides by nails that clearly cut into its flesh, it did nothing except continue to breathe, continue to blink. Hughes wasn't sure how it would indicate any other needs, but it appeared to have no need to eat or move. It wasn't in any pain that he could see, and where the nails had gone in nothing came out, blood or whatever it was a frog had, he wasn't sure. When he removed the nails—sometime in the middle of the night it must have been—there were no traces in its skin that nails had been there at all, or that some of them had been driven in so deep they had met other nails in the middle of its body.

The old man pounded his fist on the kitchen counter, and for once it moved, hopping and sliding back from the force of his hand as he kept hitting the counter. He screamed at the creature and screamed at it, and it blinked. It was so unbearably cruel that he should have a mind filled with monstrous memories, friends holding their guts in with their hands; and Frieda—and their own grandchild, a girl—both dead when she had sealed off this very kitchen and turned the gas on, giving herself and the child sleeping pills; and Carol herself dead finally after years of illness. And she would have certainly taken her own life to ease her pain had her daughter not done so before her. Yet here was this frog, this miniscule, worthless thing; this tiny collection of habits and impulses, without an original thought or need in its body, with no awareness of gardens or side doors or countertops covered in old-fashioned designs of running vines and tendrils, or the time spent building the house and spending decades in the yard, decades redoing the floors and walls, some simplicity and some safety from the outside world, some safety that had never worked.

The doorbell rang. It was no longer the middle of the night, and glancing at the clock on the stove as he went into the other room, he saw that it was nearly eleven. He looked behind the drapes and saw that the daily crowds had already settled in down the street. Hughes was waiting for the moment when they would just bring lawn-chairs and a picnic table, have a barbecue, and play some games while everyone remembered the dead man they hadn't liked in life, and gossiped about how awfully he had died.

The ringing of the doorbell became a pounding, and official voices. "Mr. Hughes? Mr. Hughes?"

Hughes looked through the peep hole and saw two men in uniform, police. He cleared his throat and said through the door, "Yes, gentlemen? Yes?"

"Sir we received a call about a disturbance at your residence?" Despite himself, Hughes laughed out loud, laughed gloriously for a good ten seconds. "Mr. Hughes?"

He opened the door to them and watched from the other side of the screen, their faces broken up into tiny squares. He could see that those who had gathered for the day's festivities, briefly corralled by their curiosity, were drifting over his way. "I'm sorry officers, I was just thinking that you didn't have to travel very far for your call." He glanced down the street.

"Are you okay, Mr. Hughes?"

He wanted to mention that he didn't know what that word meant, or when it could have ever described his emotional state. He wanted to mention what was all old blood, but they wouldn't care. If he had a gun and made a show of it, killed a policeman and acted like a stupid punk, then they'd listen. But he had never been such a person. "I'm good as gold," Hughes replied through the screen-door. "Right as rain." After a moment he added: "Black as coal, drunk as a lord. I'm doing just great, gentlemen."

They were already leaving, and wished him a good day. Hughes shut the door and went to the kitchen, and saw the frog still sitting there, surrounded by his dead granddaughter's plastic cup. But then, as if framing the creature, a handful of photos hanging above the counter caught his attention as well. "I could give a shit," he said, and grabbed the frog up. It was all very strange, but he didn't care. It was a mystery, and made no sense, and he could well spend a few more days prodding the thing, amazed at the how and the why, but so what? What was this mystery to the cold brutality that needed no explanation, that was its own explanation? He went to the front door with the frog and walked with it down his yard and down his driveway and towards the gathered crowd. Still thirty feet away, no one had noticed him, and he put the frog on the pavement, and he shooed it with his hands, and then even kicked it a little with his feet when he stood up. "Go on over there," he said, "go on over to your people."

EYE CANDY

Martin Penman

These days I might come home and my wife will size me up with a furrowed brow and say, "Turn sideways. You look a little chubbier than when you left." Sometimes, if we've been arguing about it, she'll make me lift up my shirt to examine my paunch. She says she isn't trying to humiliate me; she insists I bring all the humiliation upon myself.

I've taken to wearing more layers and baggier clothes. My closet is stuffed with large and extra large sizes, even though I've been a medium most of my life. I don't shower in front of her anymore, and in bed, the lights are out, always out. But she says she sees it in my face.

The truth is I see it in my own face, the way the jowls have bloated and the jaw line has lost its definition. I have less energy to carry me through the day. I fall heavier on each footstep. I feel my wedding ring contracting.

Like every other man, I blame a slowing metabolism or emotional eating due to work stress or less time to exercise, but the skyrocketing male obesity rate cannot be interpreted any other way. I can't tell if I find more or less comfort in being a mere statistic in what is regarded by many as the greatest health crisis of the modern era.

Weight gain through sight sounds like the premise of a bad science fiction movie, but the discovery that vision now transmutes all hormonal activity related to sexual arousal into calories seems fitting of our consumption-crazed times. From a female perspective, it's karmic retribution for the decades (or is it centuries? Millenia?) of catcalls and wolf whistles and body-shaming. Except it's not gender-specific; women are changing too, albeit at a slower rate. The general consensus of the scientific community is that somewhere along the line monogamy has been linked to extended lifespan and wider adaptability, and this is a physical reaction to that association.

In attempting to grasp the implications of this new step in our evolution, which seems to have manifested itself over the last eighteen to twenty-four months, scientists have constructed weight gain

197

models based on the lifestyles of average men and women who "interact socially on a daily basis." The variables are countless, of course, but the studies estimate that the amount of hormonal activity experienced by a man between the ages of twenty-five and sixty-five living with a "domestic partner" and existing in a "mixed gender environment" will generate approximately twenty to thirty pounds of weight per year. They also assure us that this is a viable amount to keep at bay in accordance with a regular exercise routine and a sensible diet. This includes some "wiggle room" for weight gained by "perceiving outside stimuli."

This projection hardly reflects the reality of human nature. Expecting the average Joe to up his exercise game to the level of a fitness instructor is laughable, and I suspect that this "wiggle room" drastically underestimates the resourcefulness of the average Joe to seek out and observe "outside stimuli." But what choice do we have?

The diehard optimists claim this is the dawn of a more responsible mankind. This is the wakeup call our bodies have been waiting for! After we get past this initial negative spike, a new age of awareness will begin, wherein a paradigm shift in consumption patterns and food production and regulation will take root in an effort to offset our bodies' accelerated tendency to gain weight. Our over-sexualized society will begin building a new foundation of mutual respect and moving toward true gender equality. Financial markets and governmental policy alike will be driven by a focus on wellbeing. Conflicts over territory and resources and religious dogma will diminish in significance, and the gears of our mighty war machines will grind to a halt. We will turn back to the nutritious embrace of Mother Earth, and champion sustainable farming, and environmental protection, and finally face up to the perils of climate change and implement practical solutions, and so on and so forth.

They are in the minority. Most people believe we will stay the course and develop into a race of swollen anthropoids with warped psyches and abridged life expectancies. In a way, it's a sweet thing to imagine: a world of dough balls, our similar weights and body shapes overshadowing all other distinctions of skin color and genetic predisposition, sitting around without the energy to fight each other. Not quite what John Lennon had in mind, but certainly closer to his vision than the current situation.

We men are proud. We like to count ourselves as lone success stories and outliers among the crowd. But this "mutation" (as it has affectionately been termed by the media) has leveled the playing field, cutting across racial and class divides and revealing us all to be the perverted trolls we are. I've heard there are pockets of men who have resisted the trend, aside from the very young and very old; these are the monks and other ascetics, as well as a large percentage of the mentally impaired. America's vast prison population has reported only marginal weight gain, as has the Muslim world, whose women are prisoners of restrictive traditional garb. The Dalai Lama is said to be unchanged.

Of course, much of the exponential change, especially among men, can be attributed to pornography. Such pure and instantaneous visual stimulus is like a mono diet of fast food. Anti-obscenity groups finally have the teeth they need to wage their war against porn, citing its tangible correlation to declining health standards and its potential impact upon future generations, and many lawmakers, their flab stretching the seams of their suits, are inclined to listen.

Strip clubs and burlesque acts are on the brink of being outlawed, and their powers of advertisement have been more or less eliminated. Movies have gotten a lot more boring, as nudity has been prohibited, along with most "adult situations." The art world is in chaos, as the very definition of art as personal expression is being reexamined and the parameters of what is considered profane are being revised. It's not that artists ever shied away from the profane and taboo, but now they are being forced to explore it at their own hazard. The fashion industry also has had to reset itself, although it resisted at first, since it has always been the leader and not the follower, but the sea change in human physicality has forced larger sizes into the spotlight and an overall rebranding of what is considered "stylish."

Guerrilla exhibitionism is on the rise, with random men and women exposing themselves for the sake of mayhem, despite penalties for indecency doubling and tripling in severity. The laws on public nudity have become a battleground, and the more liberally-minded the country, the more intense the fight. It's a shame that this is how public breastfeeding, after its own prolonged battle for recognition, has come to its demise.

The walls of my favorite bar, once adorned with tasteful nudes of the 16th century, have been covered with local sports teams' pennants and other uninspired flair.

"Leonard," I say to the bartender, "what gives? I felt no lust when I looked at those paintings. Only pride in the uniqueness of this establishment and in being part of an advanced culture."

"They fell under the category of high-risk imagery," Leonard tells me.

The world is becoming flat again. The curves are disappearing.

Books have retained the right to stir the imagination in this way, and so reading in general is on the rise, although the quality of literature is not rising with it, as paperback romances dominate all aspects of the market. Novels, in an effort to keep up, have gotten much sexier. It's a tradeoff. And you can still write a song about anything you want, as long as you don't make a video that corresponds with it, but it turns out that much of the music made today suffers without some sort of racy or suggestive visual accompaniment.

The mutation has triggered this complex worldwide debate on civil liberties and the power a government yields over its citizens, and yet the real battles are waged at home, within relationships, in those private moments with each other in the hermetic bubble of trust, where nothing is withheld or distorted.

My wife is (or was) not a jealous individual. She harbors the same commonplace insecurities of any confident, ambitious woman. We used to laugh contemptuously at the beauty culture around us and cringe at the Botox-laden faces of celebrities. We would watch shows about cosmetic transformations, Befores and Afters, and we'd think, *Sure, you got a new face but you lost your soul.* We'd agree to embrace the steamroller of age together and watch each other wrinkle and gray.

Now her insecurities bubble to the surface. She sees the effect other women have on me, and she is determined to rage against the passing of time. She tries out new treatments for skin and hair and weight loss. I wonder: if I kept on top of my own weight, would it be enough to convince her that she shouldn't change a thing? Or is it a personal struggle that eats at even the most hardhearted of us? Was it inevitable, despite this new, devastating step in our evolution?

She dares me, tacitly, by setting the scale out on the bathroom floor in the mornings, and I nudge it into the corner with the side of my foot. It's the kind of digital scale with a built-in memory that records your progress, up and down, and I don't want mine recorded. Not if it's only going up, anyway.

We men are now held to this impossible physical standard that our fathers never had to deal with. The stigma of being overweight is all around us, and we hate our own bodies for betraying us this way. I've become so self-conscious about my appearance I can barely concentrate on anything. I shrink from my reflection in store windows and wince at the saggy silhouette of my face on the dark screen of my phone. In public, if my shirt is clinging too tightly to the bulge of my stomach, I know someone somewhere is eyeing it and making assumptions about me. I only hope whoever it is likes what they see and gains a couple ounces.

When I notice a little extra weight on my wife, I'm thrown into a tailspin. Is it from me, or someone else? Has she been literally seeing someone else? Is it someone close to us, a friend we see regularly, or is it a random person she passes on the street? It must not be me, I tell myself, because of the shape I'm in. How could she look at this and be stirred? They say the brain is the largest erogenous zone; now, along with the eyes, it is complicit in sabotaging its physical shell, as if it is trying to transcend it.

My wife, on the other hand, still drives me crazy with an unexpected denuding or random contortion of her body. So the question that I—as well as many other "domestic partners"—now must reckon with is why, after a quiet weekend at home with my soulmate, am I not five pounds heavier?

On this point, we ignore the scientists and turn to the magazines and talk shows, which scramble to reassure us that the strongest relationships have learned to compartmentalize sexual desire in such a way that its freewheeling disruptive power does not hinder the platonic obligations of the partnership. We have built a system of order and respect with our other which does not exist anywhere else.

But we all know the eyes and the imagination are insatiable for the new.

I've learned to discipline my eyes to not immediately sweep over a woman's body the way they used to, the way they would before

I even knew what I was doing, seeking out the curves that thrilled me since I was a boy, feeding that eternal flame of lust and admiration that makes every glimpse feel like the first.

I never wish for blindness, but sometimes I wish that flame would go out.

Other times, when I'm at my lowest, I'll go and sit at a café and ogle women for five full minutes. It's a release of sorts, an indulging of my base instincts. Any longer than that and I begin to feel sluggish and the guilt starts creeping in. I'll return shamefaced to my wife, half-hoping she notices the extra heft, ready to be the tender, committed partner she deserves.

We talk about getting away, just the two of us, to where we can focus on each other, but I think we're scared of what *won't* happen when we get there. We also talk about going back to where we met, which was in a bar full of beautiful people in Oxford, Mississippi, but I think we're scared because it is a college town and the beautiful people are still there, yet we have changed.

I dread our annual beach trip. Each year, usually in early June, we pack up the car and head for one of the glorious ivory stretches near Pensacola. I used to salivate thinking about that time away from the chaotic jumble of the city, those hours spent basking in the swirling palette of blue and white to the sound of my mellow Bob Marley playlist and bottle caps popping open amid the roar of the surf. Now it is a minefield of temptation in neon bikinis and swift and obvious retribution. Until a new swimsuit law is passed which limits the skin on display, I won't do any people-watching. I stare at the oilrigs standing on the horizon or at the insides of my eyelids, red when I'm on my back and black when I'm on my stomach. I don't take my own shirt off anymore, for fear of expanding like an overheated marshmallow in front of everyone. If I get back home within five pounds of my previous weight, I heave a sigh of relief and tell my wife I enjoyed seeing her in a clingy one-piece all weekend.

It's like a great slice of life has been denied us forevermore. Something I thought would provide a constant drip of joie de vivre has been, in essence, forbidden. How many unforgettable songs have been written about seeing a pretty girl walk down the street? How many masterworks of art have been conceived around the glory of the human form? Sonnets, novels, limericks, dirty jokes? Buildings built and rockets launched? How can we begin to quantify the progress attributable to inspiration from wondrous physical presence in our lives, known and unknown?

Now we are made to feel shame at the twinge, like a Catholic schoolboy locked into a vicious cycle of urge and self-loathing. Even the first indelible memories of my youth: a topless woman shaking the sand from her towel in Barbados; the stash of magazines Danny Ford and I stumbled upon in the woods near the ravine, like a pot of flesh-colored gold; these have taken on a sinister undertone that dulls their sweetness.

Now the woman in the elegant dress steps out one evening to be noticed, and the men she encounters avert their eyes or stare with such concentration at her face that the natural electricity between them is extinguished. And on the increasingly rare occasion that I feel like a million bucks, don't I too want to step out and be noticed? Feast your eyes, maidens of my city, upon my upright square-shouldered carriage and the way my rolled-up shirtsleeves barely contain the bulk of my forearms. Observe the way my ass, still relevant, hoists and molds the seat of my pants. What kind of primal impulses am I setting aflame inside you? Look, but don't touch. This is spoken for.

My buddies and I recall the times we could gawk at anything and not gain an ounce. College. Bachelor days. Reckless nights of making eyes at every girl you see. Times when staring was free and clear, and the consequence was little more than an unreturned glance or a middle finger. My buddy Edmund was a player all his life, a man of smoldering looks and athletic build and charisma. A former personal trainer, he is now two hundred and seventy pounds, most of it flowing outward from below the chest, and the teller of many a war story. He'll tell the same ones over and over, and we'll listen because we can, unafraid.

Edmund says, "There was this one who came into my gym just to be stared at. This was before the mutation. She'd do fifteen minutes on the elliptical and then just hang around, doing weird stretches in her yoga pants and purple tank top. She'd position herself in the middle of spaces, in front of windows and wall-sized mirrors, but away from everybody else. She loved it and we loved it. And it never, ever got boring."

We'll all shake our heads and our eyes will glaze over,

something akin to an "Amen" on our lips.

"Is she still there?" someone will ask.

"Naw, man. After the mutation she disappeared. Just quit coming. Out of mercy, I guess."

No one asks what her body was like; it doesn't really matter.

We talk about how we occasionally make time to escape off by ourselves and think, and return home relaxed and unchanged. We talk about the times our wives catch us doing it at home and ask, "What are you thinking about?" and our faces redden. We make guarded jokes about the doomsday scenario, when libidinous thoughts begin to manifest themselves the same way. The healthy spaces that exist between us, how narrow will they become? More importantly, how long will we live?

I look around at my flawed, beloved brothers with worry in my heart. Depression and suicide among men are up. Divorce rates have jumped. Surely this is not what nature intended. Every couple I know, us included, attends weekly therapy. Some claim they are better for it and that their urges have been quelled, but they're all getting fatter too. What is a hundred years of psychoanalysis in the face of eons of evolution?

Scientists predict that the long-term effects will be positive, that it will lead toward stronger, longer-lasting relationships between people. I trust their judgment, but so far it's only proved to drive us farther apart. Will a gender war occur before we reach equilibrium? We men are no match for the resourcefulness of a unified female front.

I know my wife keeps a close watch on our son's weight. He's seven years old, mercifully a few years removed from that time when the world blooms into a sexual cornucopia. She looks to me to help mold him into the kind of man I struggle to be. An improved model. It is of him that I think when I find myself leering at "outside stimuli." I tell myself that I have moved past this point in my development and that my mind must contemplate the tasks pertinent to my elevated status.

It might be argued that this status would be even further evolved if we hadn't had each others' bodies on the brain all this time. Some people are evidence of this. They continue achieving, maintaining a stable weight, as if they have blinders on to the world around them. They excel in their fields and raise well-adjusted sons and daughters. I can tell who they are because they have a peace in their eyes that is all too rare, and it doesn't come from religion or money or uninterrupted sleep cycles. Searching out this peace of mind has become a driving force in my life. I remind myself that this new existence is not a curse or some divine decree, but a destination we have been moving toward all along. I remember we are built to change.

I do have strong days when I ignore all temptation, and other days when I'm so busy I don't have time to think about it. And sometimes I don't mind it at all, like when I'm lying in bed after a week fraught with self-doubt, feeling unsexy and degenerate and worthless, and notice my wife undressing, her image doubly reflected by our bedroom and closet mirrors. She is not trying to be provocative or catch my eye, she is simply unveiling herself because she feels safe here, safe with me, in a way she doesn't feel with anyone else. I will watch and spread my hand across my stomach and try to feel it changing, which I never can, and think, *You are enough for me.*

MEANWHILE THE FORESTS CONTINUE TO DIE

Sandra Hunter

She's seen too many of them, the bonny boys, loud in the way that boys are because they are afraid of not being heard. When they throw their legs over furniture or kick a hole in the screen door what they mean is, *I am here but I don't know if I am here.* They're hit/scolded/thrown out/called a shame to the family, and they land on the other side of the foot/belt/door.
There's a whole tribe that come tromping through the forest in search of drugs or love or sympathy or who knows what kids want these days. She sees them, beating and blatting and tearing through the trees, the city ones who don't know a bush from a bus.

She had one of her own, a time back. Tomo. She would never have let him come up here. If he'd lived. Sometimes, she's out when she hears one coming, and she steps off the path, crouches by a burned out ponderosa pine until he's safely past. Sometimes the boy turns, and she sees Tomo's mouth, his spindly arms, his habit of throwing himself forward as he walked. She knows it's not him beneath the baseball hat, the bandanna. It's just another boy.

The Angeles National Forest camps: Singing Pines and Sulphur Springs and Cooper Canyon that have showers and strings of lights and fire pits and flush toilets. Other camps have no sewers or plumbing or electricity. They are floating islands of plastic and small flags and tentacles, rubber and oozing piles of waste. Home for the homeless, squatters, transients.
Her place is hidden in a dense snarl of old trees and stinging nettles, off the path and well away from the the nearest camp. In the evenings, when the wind blows east, she can hear the muddling voices, sudden sharp scream, braying laughter, whooping, and twining below and

around, apple-cider piano accordion melodies and a crackling banjo. When their drugs kick in it's mostly quiet until it's not.

They're her first line of defense, the ones the police pick up first, and she's usually overlooked. But that may change with the next raid. And there's always another one coming.

From another country, where the forest and its sodden paths and creeping bushes don't exist, this boy comes up, lagging his barely-teen body along. Not even he knows how he got from the flat-roofed beige apartment grey tarmac mini malls to this wet-dirt bushed-out dripping path. He used to skip when he walked but the miles have lacerated the skipping out of him.

The boy lags right past the camp, even though someone is heating soup and someone is playing a three-string ukulele, and the smell of sweet smoke is drifting in the cold, damp December air. He has been rained on for the last however long. One day. One night.

No one sees him because he moves quietly, even though he's been walking for nearly thirty hours. He knows how to approach downwind. He knows how to melt away backwards.

It is hard not to stop and ask if someone will give him a taste of soup. But he knows that even the destitute are discriminating and there are reasons to discriminate against him.

The smell of the soup—tomato—taunts him as he moves on. He tells his stomach to ignore it. A half-mile past, the unmistakable savory smell of chicken drifts in. He gives up. Follows the smell and stops to sit on a tree stump. Should he go back or forward? Back is not appealing. Forward means more pushing the legs to complete the next mile and the next.

--What you want here?

He looks around, almost too tired to be afraid, to slip the knife into his ready hand. The person is short, not much taller than him. Pink and green scarf tied over the head above a shirts-on-top-of-shirts outfit, standard for anyone without a coat. The topmost shirt is red plaid. Drooping mud pants drag over one green Croc and one silver-and-blue Adidas. The hands look old but the eyes are clear, brown. Dark red lipstick.

He can't remember the question.

A woman's voice. Deep pitched but nice-sounding, like you might hear on TV,
--So, what you want?
--I'm hungry.
--We're all hungry.
He looks away,
--I don't know.
--I didn't ask what you know.
She comes closer and holds out a hand,
--Knife. Give.
He clutches it.
-- I'll give it back it when you're on your way. But if you're coming with me you can't have a knife. House rules.
He wasn't aware he was going with her anywhere but she's made her mind up. He hands her the knife.
She leads him through the forest, away from the path, away from the animal trails. They climb over charred, fallen trees, around the remains of burned bush. He wonders if this is where he will die. He has been lured to his death by the smell of chicken. If he does manage to escape he doesn't know where he is. The sun filters weakly through the wet trees. Where is north? What good would it do to know?
And in a thick stand of pines, a family-sized tent. It's the old-fashioned kind that you can stand up in, sheltered by tree branches and a half an old McDonald's billboard. The red and yellow claim of billions served has faded and taken on forest colors. You'd miss it if you weren't looking closely.
She unties the tent-flap, pulls it back, and the smell of chicken nearly makes him drop to his knees.
-- Come in if you're coming.
He steps inside.
A green wicker chair. A cream and brown rug. The rug sits up. An old dog.
--This is Matty.
Matty's front end, hairy as the back end, sticks its nose in for a traditional crotch greeting. The boy jumps back.
The woman unwinds a long scarf,
--Your name? So Matty knows I'm talking to you and not him when it's

time to take a piss.

Her lips pull back as she says the word *piss.* The red lipstick is dark against the unripe-banana teeth.

--Davone.

--That's a name?

Mouth pushes out, he turns from her and stands near the flap,

--Give me my knife. I am going now.

--Already mad, huh? The longer you learn to hold your temper, the longer you'll live. Fact.

She holds out the knife and he takes it.

She turns her back and stumps over to a small stove. She takes off the lid and the smell fills every breathing pore of him.

She picks up a small radio and clicks a switch. *I'm gonna need a friend till I get used to losing you.* Maple-syrupy sound of country guitar.

The longing to sit down makes his legs shiver.

The woman stirs the pot,

--I do love Miss Tammy Wynette.

She glances around,

--You still here?

He puts the knife on the ground next to her.

--Please.

--Aha. So you do have manners. Okay, Davone.

She fills a small yellow plastic bowl and holds it out. He cradles the warm bowl in cold hands. She lifts an elbow towards a card-table,

--Spoon over there.

He picks up the plastic spoon and digs into the food.

She empties a plastic bag of bloody ends onto a metal plate,

--Here, Matty.

Matty follows her out of the tent.

He is eating too fast. He tries to slow down. To remember the taste of the chicken. It isn't Popeye's but it's as good. Better.

She comes back in, serves herself in another yellow bowl and sits on the green chair.

He finishes and puts the bowl on the table,

--Thank you. Uh, very much.

Points her spoon,

--How long you been walking?
--Uh. Yesterday?
She wipes a hand on her pants, holds it out,
--Titania.
Answering the puzzled look,
--*Ill met by moonlight, proud Titania.* No Shakespeare, huh? What school you go to?
He shakes her hand,
--Don't go to no school.
She chews and ejects a small bone,
--You got anyone looking for you? Don't want my place busted up.
Not yes. Not no.
--What's that?
He chins towards a white plastic bucket.
The faintly green teeth gleam in the nest of red lips,
--That's ma Japanese maple.
--It's a tree.
Raised eyebrows,
--You're right. It's a tree.
--I saw them on TV. They need, uh, organic matter and shade. And they gotta be in drained soil. So that bucket's no good. Because, root rot. And they don't like a lot of fertilizer. Too much nitrogen.
Titania tucks her chin,
--Look at you. Give you a piece of chicken and you're all David Attenborough.
--He does *animals*. And he dumped his kids so he could go around the world.
--He's rich, right? So his kids are okay.
--People like him shouldn't have kids. I hate him.
She examines a piece of carrot she's picked from her teeth,
--But he speaks so highly of you.
He scrapes his bowl, one-shoulder shrug,
--Listen, thanks for the food. I better go.
--Okay. But there's no free lunch. You know that?
He watches her, gauges the distance to the tent flap.
--Hey—I want you to re-plant my tree. I only do deviant sexual stuff at weekends. *Jeez.* You're jumpy.
He looks at the plastic bucket,

--Where you want it?

--Outside would be nice.

She puts her bowl down and gets up, points at the bucket. He lifts it. Heavier than it looks. She grabs a shovel and paper sack,

--C'mon.

Titania holds the tent flap for him and leads him behind the tent structure. She stumps ahead of him, body rocking side to side like she doesn't have joints.

Why are they taking the tree so far? Waterfalls down his back. Sweat running into his eyes and ears. Legs burning. Arms on fire. Eyeballs, teeth, ears sweating.

Finally, she stops and turns,

--You okay? I thought that chicken woulda give you some energy. But you done good. Though he be but little he is fierce. Thank you, Mr. Shakespeare. Now let's plant it.

Gasping,

--I'm—not—

--What?

--I'm—not little.

Titania puts the shovel down and rubs her nose,

--Way too sensitive for a--what—twelve year-old?

--Fourteen.

Twelve or fourteen he shouldn't be here at all. This one should have *flee* tattooed across his knuckles. He's the fleeing type.

And he doesn't even look like Tomo. Wrong color for a start. And yet. There's a *something*, standing with his wet arms around a bucket. Boy in his too-large tshirt and too-large pants and too-large shoes, like he mugged a twenty year-old. Boy with running nose running eyes running mouth. You can see where he landed, on the far side of the foot or the belt or the door. There's probably a footmark on the back of that too-large shirt. *Get the fuck out and don't come back.* Yea. Tomo's dad might have said something like that if he'd had the energy after throwing her around.

She digs the shovel into the rain-wet soil. He takes the shovel from

her and makes the hole for the tree. Boy from the other side of the
forest. Maybe he's a sign that police will leave her alone, them and their
sniffy writhing black-and-tan dogs with the let-me-get-at-her teeth.
They lift the Japanese maple out of the bucket, its root ball dragging
pale, naked curls. She adds the fertilizer. They carefully firm the earth
around the tree's stem.
--Well, god's already done his watering.
He sits back on his heels and looks at the tree.
--How often you gotta water it?
--Not that much. The rain'll do it.
--It don't rain here for months.
--We'll cross that bridge. Bring the shovel.

He holds the empty bucket by the rim, stares around at the trees,
the boulders they step around, splintered fallen logs, sprays of
white-flower mushrooms.
--Uh, Titania?
She stops.
--Why we come out here to plant the tree?
Fists on hips,
--Police. Like earthquakes. You never know when but they're coming.
--So they won't get the tree?
--Smart kid.
--But how they find you anyway?
--They always do. Dogs. I don't know.
--Yea. They got my sister.
--What she do?
--Nothing. Hanging with her friends at Popeye's. Got everyone.
Titania clucks,
--Scoop up everyone like a roomba. Like they got nothing better to do.

They arrive at the tent. He hands her the shovel,
--Thanks for the food.
--There's more.
--Nah. I'm good.
--Well. Drop in anytime.
He nods and walks away.
--Davone.

Like his name is a blessing. He raises a hand.

She pulls her lips back against her teeth. Didn't ask how he got here, or why. Sometimes those things matter too much to talk about. Settles the pot of stew in a corner. That'll do for the next couple of days.
He likes trees.
Through the gap in the tent flap, she watches his blue jacket disappearing. Is he on the right path? There's a path that leads to a camp where they fly a rebel flag and grow weed, where he definitely shouldn't show his face.
It's none of her business.
But he's only a boy.
--Okay, Matty. We'll just make sure.

The boy finds a path. It is narrow, maybe an animal track. He ducks under, steps over, pushes through the old growth and the burned branches that break off and splinter, gouge his back. Narrowly misses being stabbed in the eye. It's getting too thick. He might have to go back. The pain up and down his tired legs and spine and knees and face and the path widens and—
He is out on the main road. All the way through the forest. On the far side of the road he can see the world drop away to the wide sweep of the valley floor. Distant, fuzzy shapes of tall buildings. Los Angeles. Guttural throating, two motorbikes, thrusting, accelerating around the bend. He steps back into the grass. His cousin, Jayden, has a bike. Used to come visit in Palmdale and take him for rides up here in the forest. *That's Palmdale, this is the Angeles Forest, and I live over there on the other side.* It made him laugh—the sheer body-feeling of wind and speed. And the laughter papered over the rest of the week, like every week, that began and ended with the brute anger of his mother's boyfriend.

The bikes scud past, spinning their moto-song behind them. He watches them go. Looks back across the road. Over there, that's where Jayden lives. 11829 Chandler Boulevard, North Hollywood. Number 4. It's a studio, Jayden says, but it's got a lot of space. *Come see me, little cuz.*
Despite the curdled leg muscles, he runs across—*I'm coming*

Jayden—
And doesn't hear the third motorbike, song spinning into the chorus of
the other two. Yell-skid-and-squeal, scraping of brake-and-bike, and
the back end clips the boy and he sails, sails, sails

Opens his eyes. Pink scarf and dark red lipstick above him.
--You're alright, Damone. I gotcha.
He makes his mouth move,
--Davone.
--Yea. Course.

She sits with his bloody head in her lap. Doesn't look at the rest of the
body, Da Vinci angles and points.
--Walk through a forest all right, but you're shit at crossing roads. No
roads wherever-the-hell-you-come-from? And Matty's exhausted. He
can't get around like he used to.
--Sorry...
She coughs, clears her throat,
--They're coming right now, Davone. You keep talking to me.
--Okay ...
--You want some water? I can get you some water.
He is so young. The eyes open and close. She keeps talking. The
eyes are black. The dark skin is brushed by the winter sun. Like
Tomo's in the picture where he is always eight. She smoothes the
boy's forehead. His warm skin is supple, clear, soft. Doesn't reflect the
long journey or being thrown through the air like a sock puppet.
He wears the rose of youth upon him.

Other voices around the bike, *Oh god. Is he breathing? Just keep him
still. The ambulance is almost here. I got you buddy. Where'd the kid
come from? Is that his mom?*

The beautiful feral boys, their wild hair and their wide eyes.
My boy was like you, Davone. And that boy over there, broken under
his bike. And the ones standing or kneeling around him.
It will take too long, the wailing siren spiraling up from the valley,
winding up the mountain road to bring the men with the strong hands
to lift him and make him safe. Not the hands that knock small animals

and children, that throw the bottles, chairs, fists, that slam the
doors, that tear hole after hole until all that's left are the spiders
spinning stories.
Where are the strong safe hands?

NONFICTION

AFTER LENNON

Julia Mary Gibson

The Beatles came to us after the day all the adults cried. All
the adults cried the day we were called back to homeroom from
art class and Mrs. Teaford told us the president had been shot and
everybody should go home to be with their families. She was crying,
our sainted funny teacher Mr. Johnson was crying, people we passed
when we were walking home were crying. One man was just standing
in the middle of the block with his face in his hands. We didn't want to
be with our families. We wanted to be with each other, playing
paperdolls that we were too old for and divvying up a pack of M&Ms
by color and throwing away the extras if they didn't come out even.

We got to the corner of Maryland and Newberry. "Maybe he
won't die," Tammy said, but as far as I knew, getting shot equaled
being dead. Medgar Evers had died an hour after being shot. My
parents knew people who knew him. Gunshot meant you were over
and done.

I was too scared to cry. Maybe the Russians had done it and
we were about to be invaded, which would probably be worse than
the president being dead. My friends went down Newberry together
like they always did. I kept on down Maryland another block. My
parents were in the living room standing in front of the television.
Both of them were crying. Even Walter Cronkite was crying. I felt
dizzy and sat down hard on the long couch made of fake leather that
was always cold. My little sister lay on the floor with her head on my
mother's shoe. My mother hadn't taken off her coat. LBJ got sworn in.

The next day was a Saturday. Tammy and I convened at
Debbie's house. Her house was best for sleeping over because they
had potato chips and nobody cared if we ate the whole bag. We
didn't necessarily believe we'd live to be grownups, but if we did, we
intended to have remarkable and thrilling lives.

Thanksgiving was six days later. There were turkeys. There
was pie. There were books and sweaters and mint meltaways for
Christmas. The grownups did their best to assure us. It was terrible

what happened, but the Russians weren't invading. Trains brought grandparents for the holidays. We had electricity and a government. But we knew about precariousness. You could be a carefree schoolgirl one minute and get shipped to a death camp the next. You couldn't outrun a radioactive cloud.

Debbie heard them first. Christmas vacation was over. The three of us were walking to school on a steely Milwaukee morning. "You guys," Debbie said. "There's this new group I heard on the radio last night. They're like a phenomenon in England." We heard them too, crouched over her transistor radio late at night, barely getting the signal from the Chicago station. Our hearts went boom.

The Beatles became our religion. We were under an enchantment, immersed and besotted. We bought every 45, every album, heaps of Beatles bubblegum cards, any magazine with a picture of them. We held hands, closed our eyes, and let ourselves weep and wail and scream as Paul declared his love and John shared his pain. I felt more than I had ever imagined there was to feel. The love was bigger than just for those four brilliant, witty, cute Englishmen. It was for sky, ocean, galaxies, the juice of life. The sadness wasn't just for the unattainableness of a love object. It was for the tragedies and losses of the world. The joy was their music and also the universal dance.

We vowed not to have a favorite Beatle. We had to love each of them for their own particular qualities. Loving one more than the others would break them as a unit somehow and they had to be united to keep on with their crucial mandate. They were saving us and expanding us and giving us a purpose.

But I loved John best because he was wry and wounded. I tried to balance it out with loving Paul best sometimes, but I couldn't work my way into it. He was beautiful and had the big eyes, but John was deep.

That summer, thousands of Black and white students from the North went to Mississippi to help register voters, the worst place in America to end up as a slave and the worst place in America to try to be a Black voter. I thought it was a good thing we weren't old enough to go because I feared my friends would be into it and I'd be too chicken. My mother kept saying she'd go if it weren't for me and my sister. My mother cried when the three civil rights workers disappeared in Mississippi and she cried when their bodies were found six weeks later and she cried because it was only because two of them were white that they made the news, which we watched on the tiny black-and-white television that was brought into the kitchen for the Democratic National Convention, where Bobby Kennedy almost cried when he got a twenty-minute standing ovation before his speech about his brother.

Tammy and Debbie and I cried listening to John growl and wail *baby it's you* and we cried listening to Paul croon *you you you I love you.* I felt guilty for crying wrong. I tried to make myself cry and couldn't when four girls my age were bombed to death in church in Birmingham, one of them with the same curled bangs and arched eyebrows as my best friend in the city we no longer lived in. I was too scared and mad to be sad enough to cry. I hated that my mother cried. It was better when she railed at the honky cracker racists.

My parents were in the paper sometimes for things they did with CORE, trying to make laws about integration and enforce the ones that already existed. We got phone calls calling them lovers of the one taboo word in our household. Racists threw eggs and rocks at our living room windows. I carried the fear that my parents would be accused of treason like the Rosenbergs, or we'd all be rounded up in a midnight raid and sent to an internment camp, or that our house would be bombed like so many houses and churches down south were bombed to scare people out of the movement.

I saw *A Hard Day's Night* eleven times and cried at every slow number, cried at their accents, cried at the way they cradled their guitars, even cried at Ringo's sad eyes. My friends and I would huddle over someone's record player and one of us would cry at the catch in John's voice and the rest of us would work up to crying along. The Beatles were coming to America and they were coming to our city. Someone's father knew how to get tickets when they first went on sale and we got good seats and cried at our incredible fortune and decided to wear our empire waist dresses that weren't all the same but went together. We bought new pale lipsticks like Patti Boyd's in the movie. Every day was an eternity.

It was Debbie who found out where they'd be staying after the show. The show was so loud we couldn't hear ourselves scream. It was really them, bouncing and sweating and showing their teeth. We were close enough to see George's cheekbones. Hundreds of us were sobbing, wailing, pulling at our own hair, clutching one another, reaching for them. After the show, we went to the house of the girl whose father had known about the tickets. She wasn't a close friend, and not an ardent Beatlemaniac like the three of us were. We drank tea to be British and for our raw throats and to stay awake until dawn, when we snuck away and walked the few miles to the hotel. Girls crowded the street. Many had been there all night. Cops encircled us. One girl said she'd gotten into the hotel, but got kicked out without seeing any of them.

"It's them!" someone screamed. A limousine inched down the driveway. We ducked the cops and hurled ourselves onto it. I saw George through a smeared window right before a cop pulled me away and threw me. I stumbled, fell, was almost trampled, but made my way up. I hoped I was injured so I'd have a permanent mark of this day that I was sure would never be surpassed in its glory and intensity. Somehow we got back to someone's house. We were starving. Somebody made us bacon and we ate the whole package. We were cried out.

We started eighth grade two days later. I wrote in my diary that I wanted to marry John. Armed troops on horseback ran down marchers in Selma. Malcolm X was murdered. Viola Liuzzo was murdered. Rev. Reeb was murdered. Dr. King gave the *how long, not long* speech. Family friends Peggy and Dave went to Mississippi and sent back long letters about movement heavies, church ladies, and the local racist power structure. Peggy and Dave were heroes to me and I worried about them being down there where the bigots had guns and ran the show. Every peace and civil rights demonstration was bigger than the one before.

Lennon got melancholy. He had to hide his love away. He didn't want to spoil the party. He needed help. My love for him was no longer desperate. I didn't dream of being his muse. I knew he was trouble as well as unattainable.

My family went to Europe that summer, a longtime dream of my mother's. Her grandmother, still very alive, had emigrated from Cornwall at the turn of the century. I loved her soft accent and the teatimes she orchestrated with bread-and-butter sandwiches and scones. My mother took me to Carnaby Street in London and bought me a fab mod outfit. When I read in the paper that the Beatles would be arriving at Heathrow on a certain day, my mother helped me figure out how to get there by Tube. I went alone and stood in a small crowd for hours before seeing them disembark and be hustled into a car from a distance. I didn't scream or cry. I was there to pay homage, not to be overtaken.

My British miniskirt and black eyeliner helped tamp some of the dread over starting high school. At least I didn't look like the dweeb I felt myself to be. Dweebs were good students, shy and scared. I knew high school would be in every way the opposite of the small progressive school I'd gone to since fifth grade, but before that I'd gone to huge integrated urban schools where teachers hit kids for nothing. I knew the kind of toe the line authoritarian regime I was in for. I constructed a balustrade of chill and cool in order to brave the stern teachers and scary jock seniors who would bump into you on purpose while passing in the hall.

There were a few kindred folk – creative, serious, funny. A sweet, poetic boy liked me and I liked him back, but I didn't want to love him or any boy. I was after sophisticated adventure. I was reading Colette and Edna O'Brien and the lives of Isadora Duncan and Emma Goldman, women who loved freely and fiercely. You could have lovers here and there and never marry any of them. They could be old and jaded or young and careless. They could be lifelong tender comrades or flings.

Rubber Soul came out that winter, and *Revolver* a few months later. Lennon was threatening to kill a girl if he caught her with another man, and showing everybody the light by telling us to *say the word love.* Our family drove in our red VW bus from Milwaukee to San Francisco and made a pilgrimage to the place in Berkeley where the Free Speech Movement started. We wandered in the Haight and and saw guerrilla theater in Golden Gate Park and met Lawrence Ferlinghetti and rode the cable cars.

I embarked on sophomore year wearing the necklace of tiny bells that I'd bought from a hippie street vendor in the Haight. All I wanted to be was artistic, but I couldn't get past a few chords on the guitar, didn't have the grace or rhythm to dance, couldn't draw beyond cartoons, had nothing to write about. I hated the war and warmongers and racism and poverty and materialism and there was nothing I could do about any of it except show up for demonstrations. My friends and I saw *Juliet of the Spirits* at the university film society and hung out at the bohemian coffeehouse to hear John Lee Hooker and Howlin' Wolf. I was long past yearning for Lennon, but I missed the passion he'd once provided. I needed a replacement. Man, not boy. Fire.

A stranger came to the house one evening. He had longish hair and wore all black, as I often did myself. He had weary, deep eyes. His name was John, which bolstered my belief that he'd been provided to me by a thoughtful universe. He had come to Milwaukee from New York for a few days to shoot a film for the upcoming Expo 67. The director was a friend of my parents. Our family played a family in the film.

New York John didn't say much, but what he did say was pithy and witty. He held his light meter at my chin. I pretended to ignore his sculpted cheekbones and long fingers. My plan was to have a night or two of passion with him that would forever be a bittersweet memory. At fifteen I considered myself sophisticated enough to negotiate such a thing.

One evening when we were done filming, he and the other filmmaker guys were staying for dinner. Everybody else was in the kitchen drinking wine and talking to my mother while she made lamb curry. John was kneeling by the hi-fi, paging through the stack of albums that leaned against the wall.

"What do you like?" he said to me.

You, I thought. You you and you.

"Musically," he added, as if I'd spoken. I knew that our minds and souls had mingled. We were meant to be. The half-stack that he'd leafed through leaned against his black Beatle boot, adorably scuffed at the toe. I was in love with his lean thighs in the black trousers and his manly blond stubble and his weary eyes.

I dared to reach for the albums. Our shoulders were an inch apart.

"This," I said. It wasn't my ultimate fave, but I liked it and because we were one consciousness together, I knew he did too.

He lifted the album with two long nicotine-stained fingers. "Yeah. Modern Jazz Quartet. Excellent. Will anyone mind if I put it on?"

I told him to go ahead. He was graceful rising from his crouch.

He slid the record on top of the turntable and lined up the hole.

New York John left town before I got up the nerve to let him know who we could be to one another, but that was okay because my parents had both taught summer school so we could afford to visit New York in the spring. My mother had let me go alone to Heathrow Airport to greet the Beatles when I was fourteen. There would be no problem with me going off by myself on some manufactured adventure.

I had snagged his address. Writing was better than talking anyway. There would be no blushing or saying the wrong thing. I drafted many versions and picked out stationery that wasn't pink or flowery. I wrote it out in my best handwriting that wasn't too schoolgirly neat. It looked good. I was aware that a lot could go wrong. Our rendezvous could turn out to be sordid, or he might give me the freeze, or I could fall for him like a dumb chick and have a nervous breakdown. I didn't worry about my parents finding out. I doubted they'd mind. I was taking birth control pills even though I'd barely done anything with anybody. My mother thought I might pair up with one of the boys who were my friends and had made me go to the Commie gynecologist. The worst would be if New York John felt sorry for me. I held the envelope in the post box slit for a long time before finally letting it drop.

Every day I checked the mail when I got home from school, even though I'd told him to write me at a friend's address on the off chance that my father, who always leapt on the mail as soon as it arrived, would wonder at the New York postmark. John wrote me back in short order, a gorgeous poetic heartful letter about Sisyphus and jazz and the collective unconscious. It was poetic but not obtuse, kind but clear. He didn't say I was too young or too far away or that he was with someone else or that he liked me but not like that. Our phases were not congruent. He didn't say that any of it could change with time. It was a gentle dismissal and a kind farewell.

I was disappointed, but not insulted. I'd made a stab because I was compelled to and I knew he wouldn't make the first move because if he had, he'd have been a perv and I would have been repulsed. I had to be the one to point out what I was sure was obvious to him. There was spark. If we got to know each other, we'd discover all the commonality, more than just liking the same album. But, sadly, he was right. Our realms were foreign to each other.

Of course I loved him all the more for his finesse and depth of understanding. He could have had me, harmed me, haunted me, kept me on the hook, left me hanging, hung me out, hung me up, flung me, stung me, slung me to the curb. Maybe he was icked out by the age difference. Maybe it was too much trouble. Maybe he just wasn't into it. Whichever way, he let me down easy, didn't lead me on, didn't lie, didn't take advantage.

I lost track of both Johns. Lennon became an ex-Beatle, a househusband, an exile from his homeland, an enemy of the state. I became a cultural revolutionary and a mother. My parents lost their university teaching jobs due to their antiwar activism. Our family and our lives splintered. I'd once been close to my mother and told her of my inner life, but I was mad at her for being wild and outrageous and not caring what anybody thought of her life decisions. I lost my radical community and there wasn't another one to join up with. I struggled artistically, financially, emotionally. Nixon resigned and the war finally was over. I moved to Los Angeles with my five-year-old daughter and no car and got my first full-time job. Eventually I lucked myself onto the visual effects crew of a feature film. Former movie star Reagan was governor and everybody I knew considered him to be a fascist monster. He had just been elected president of the country. I was in the production office requisitioning fog filters when someone said that Lennon was dead. I made myself keep it together. I was the only female on the crew and I definitely couldn't cry on the job.

I didn't cry later, either. I was more in shock than grief. The Lennon who was murdered was such a different Lennon from the one I had given myself over to. I wasn't sure how much I liked the John who was now dead. His confessional, primal songs reminded me of my mother's poetry that told the world too much. My mother visited soon after his murder and couldn't believe I wasn't devastated. She adored the latter-day John. She loved that he made bread, loved his bare screaming anguish, loved him curled naked around Yoko. I thought the baking bread thing was bogus, and his declarations that he and Yoko were one person freaked me out.

Until the end of her life, tears would come to my mother's eyes if she saw a picture of him or heard his music in a restaurant. I finally extricated myself from her relationship with Lennon so that I could reclaim my own. Lennon the Beatle had been a gateway to ritual madness. Then he was a template for the romance I hoped to have one day, until I saw what a terrible boyfriend he would make. Listening to *Sgt. Pepper* with the boys from algebra class, I knew Lennon was a DaVinci. His artistry, work ethic, and creative courage have inspired me ever since. A beautiful photograph of him hangs in my kitchen, where I see it every day. He's in a sharp striped jacket and shades, cigarette between his fingers, slouched with his head resting on the wall of a dressing room cubicle after a show on the first tour of the States. My heartthrob partner in life gave it to me. Like Lennon, he's an imaginative, clever, wisecracking, hardworking champion of love.

John's on a stamp now, his face in rainbow colors. "People always ask why he's the only Beatle with a stamp," the post office guy said as he rang me up. "Because he's American! Nixon tried to get rid of him, but he couldn't." In promoting peace, John Winston Ono Lennon worked to heal his own violence. The murderous land of guns for all killed him.

Yoko built him the Peace Tower. He always wanted fame and then he had enough of it and didn't care if peace art made him a dime, but it became his eternal brand.

Imagine.

VISIBILITY

Sarah Priestman

My son wears the word "visible," tattooed in Times Roman, on his right arm. The tattoo was a present from me for his 18th birthday. A handwritten sign reading, "Visible for those who can't be," hangs on his dorm room door. He is transgender, and to him, visibility is an antidote to stigma; it's refusing what most of the world still wants trans people to do: disappear. By wearing this word on his sleeve (his skin, really), he claims the power of being seen. And isn't this what we all want? To be perceived – even cared about – for who we are?

Let me say at the outset that Evie is more than visible. He is also convivial and smart, wrapped-up with friends, looking into a future that is sometimes blinding with possibilities, occasionally stupefying with the amount of work it might take to reach his dreams, which, as is the norm for his age, change regularly. In other words, a typical college kid, but also, and intentionally, visible. His visibility is less about an indignant, "this is me, what are you going to do about it," and more about a simple statement: "This is me, others are like me." It is also his visibility, and not mine, but being his mother has allowed me to also feel seen.

He and I attended monthly support groups for gender non-conforming kids and their parents during the first two years of his transition. The pediatric psychiatric department, which hosted the groups, was located in a hospital basement, so the evenings began with polite greetings in an elevator, parents nodding to familiar faces, kids fist-bumping their found tribe. We'd all assemble in a cramped lobby, and then the counselors would appear, filing kids into in one room, parents into another.

Evie and I compared notes on our drive home. In his stories, the group reported bullying and family resistance, but they were excited to be with other trans kids. In my group, there was no excitement. Parents were stymied by legal requirements and medical options, weary from the skepticism of friends, and, primarily, terrified for their kids. Mothers sometimes wept. Men spoke in anger, staring into their hands, helpless to shield a child from the struggle that living one's truth can entail.

My son told me he was trans a few weeks into his freshman year of high school, after identifying as gender-queer in middle school. I am a mother; my first reaction is to protect. I believed then that being transgender meant having a bull's eye on your back, which for some – especially trans women of color – it often does. I suggested he give the idea some time.

The next weekend, he casually told me, in an aisle of Home Depot, that he'd given it time and, yes, this was his identity. He would transition.

Was that ok with me, he asked, and I told him yes, but let's learn more, all the while thinking, as we wandered past paint cans and floor tile, let's learn more because I want to find a reason to prevent this. In elementary school, he'd rarely presented as a girl. He'd shopped in the boys' departments and was a regular at the barber, always requesting a crew cut. I was nonplussed. You can be whomever you want to be, I'd told him. Listen to what's true for you. I had joined friends in a number of PRIDE parades over the years, and danced at countless gay bars. The possibility of my having a gay child, which was my assumption then, when he dressed as a boy, felt "normal." His being transgender, however, was new. It was a risk, and I was afraid.

The next Monday, he politely asked the teacher in each of his classes if he could make an announcement, and then informed everyone to use male pronouns with him. His classmates agreed, easily. We launched ourselves into the galaxy of legal and medical issues that comprise transitioning, and started attending the groups. I was tentative in the beginning, unfamiliarity underscoring my fear. I could not have known, then, that within a few years I would be in awe of the way my son managed his transition; that eventually I would bask, not in his difference, but in his having the gall to live candidly. Though I'd been wary of him being burdened by social challenges when he first told me, I eventually witnessed him rise as an advocate, untethered from these challenges by his openness. He appeared in print, on stage and, yes, screen. He wowed with truth. His visibility, I saw, could illuminate the path for other transitioning kids, still in shadow. I freely admit to luxuriating in his spotlight. He'd not been outspoken as a child, but now brought a depth of empathy unique to adolescence, and an intent to mitigate the struggle I had anticipated for him -- but he did it for others.

I first moved from my fear about his transition long before Evie became a public spokesperson, as I was motivated by another mother in the support group. We'd been surprised to recognize one another from years before, when both of our boys – who then each identified as their gender assigned at birth, presenting as little girls—trained with the same Suzuki teacher. Then, we sat in a cavernous church every Saturday morning, comparing notes on raising our four-year old daughters. What did we read to them, what playgrounds did we visit, which teachers would we consider for violin lessons next year? Now, reunited, we sat across a conference table in a windowless room, taking our turns with other parents to report-out about paperwork and testosterone shots. I had regarded her as more traditional than I all those years ago, but had enjoyed our conversations, whispered to avoid interrupting the Twinkle, Twinkle, Little Star practiced diligently in the front of the sanctuary.

I would have expected this mother to give an eye-roll to the notion of transitioning, so she intrigued me, her isolated voice urging the rest of us to leave our doubts behind and move forward, honoring what was true for our kids.

Her son had started transitioning a year before mine, and I hung on her every knowledgeable word as she spoke of his positive changes. I remembered him as a stony-faced girl, glowering, never bouncing down the church aisle as the other young musicians did. Now, when we waited in the lobby, I saw a jocular, confident young man. This behavior emerged, his mother told me, as he transitioned.

"I now see that this is who he was all along," she told me. "It's like transitioning was not a matter of him changing. It just allowed him to be who he really is."

I thought this could be possible for my own son – not that he would mirror this boy, but that he would also reveal his own strengths.

These were the early days of my son's transition, before visibility became routine. Neither he nor I could have known how positive the next few years would be as he was able to live as the gender, like this other boy, he had always been.

As a three-year-old, he'd asked, sitting in the car's back-seat booster, if he could get a penis sewn on to his body. I'd told him, yes, but that he'd have to pay for it, which was my answer, back then, for most things he'd wanted. In elementary school, his life had revolved around sports, music, and friends. We now laugh at videos of he and other kids dancing to "Soldier Boy" at sleepovers, jumping into the neighborhood pool, frosting cupcakes. For his 11th birthday party, he invited 17 guests, not wanting anyone to feel left out. What was one more, two more, three more? I admired his sensitivity to inclusion. His classmates and teachers all knew him as a "tomboy," as this was before the reality of transgender kids exploded into the mainstream, so there was no other way to explain his male affinity with appearing male. I had been fine with his choosing neck ties for school pictures, but I cringe to remember my response when he begged to be called "John" on a beach trip, trying to be recognized, I now understand, as the boy he knew he was. As a pre-adolescent, he wore baggy surfer shorts and a swim shirt, or no top at all. I accepted him, then, as a girl, just pretending to be a boy. Calling him a boy's name within earshot of others felt like this was no longer an imaginary game. I had refused.

A neighbor tells the story of meeting us at the playground when Evie was in kindergarten. After introductions, she says, he pulled her aside and whispered, "I'm a boy." I listened, a decade later, as he described the disconnect of being seen as one gender while knowing he was another. This was when the steps of transitioning were behind him, and he was preparing his script for a TEDx Talk entitled "It Takes a Village to Transition," in which he presented stories of support from his school district, hoping to encourage other districts to do the same. His recited his lines aloud, pacing back and forth in the living room. "Transgender individuals are often asked when they realized they were not a boy or not a girl. It's a good question," he read, "but it doesn't make sense to all of us." He acknowledged that other tomboys move out of their "phases," and become more girlish, but that, as he watched that happening, "I knew inside that I was truly a boy all along, and now I just wanted to live like one."

As my friend spoke in the support group, I began to acknowledge that my son – like hers – was not pretending to be male, but that it was, in fact, his gender. I needed to honor this truth. I decided to move beyond my fear – dread, really -- and be the accepting mom that my son needed.

There is a second thing that helped me to get past my fear, and it's a phenomenon that's often overlooked when any of us negotiate change: the fluke of winning a bet on the unknown at other points in my life made me confident enough to risk this unknown, as well. Fate deals us a hand, and it's easy to think, if it's good once, of course we'll win twice. If it's bad, we may avoid ever sticking our necks out again. I once bought a ticket to Nepal, with plans of following the Annapurna Circuit. This was in 1983, when flights were booked through travel agents, and itineraries handed to customers, folded crisply into an envelope. After arranging the flight, I walked to the ticket office on my lunch break at least ten times, my travel receipt tucked into my shoulder bag, planning to cancel the trip. I was afraid. Not of the hiking—I'd been an avid backpacker – and not of the solo travel, as that came easily to me. I didn't know why I wanted a refund on the ticket I'd worked so hard to afford, I just knew I was afraid, and not going on the trip was one way to handle my fear. I eventually decided to take the risk and go. I flew into Kathmandu, completed the trek, and, yes, my gamble on an unknown exceeded my dreams.

Evie and I had started attending the support groups in early-October, and by the time the receptionist's desk was festooned with paper turkeys, I'd resolved to gamble on this unknown, as well. I would be the mother who supported her son's transition 100%. It was an intentional, conscious choice, like the resolution to stop staring at the travel agent's door and just do what I knew, deep inside, was right. It may be hubris, or faith, or the biggest leap of all – love – but I chose to believe that everything would turn out well. I made the decision, silently, sitting in that airless conference room. I paused, waiting for trepidation to rise. Instead, I felt peaceful. I was doing the right thing. For him, yes, and also for me.

In middle school, when my son had first abandoned the tomboy moniker and called himself gender-queer, I'd brought him to Provincetown, MA, a famously LGBTQ-inclusive village on the tip of Cape Cod. He'd stopped in his tracks our first afternoon walking down Commercial Street and thanked me for bringing him.

"This is where I belong," he'd told me. I'd been to P'town many times before I became a mother, and was familiar with its affirming spirit, so knew he'd feel welcomed in this town full of rainbows.

We visited P'town again, this time with his girlfriend, when he was in high school. He'd identified as transgender for almost two years. Driving north, he'd asked if I could accompany him into a sex toy shop to buy a cock ring for his packer. I agreed to go with him, but why, I thought to myself, does he need one?

We met-up one evening at EROS, a sex shop in the middle of town. He was waiting with an open face, not unlike the one he wore when he was very little and awaiting a first visit with Santa. It's the look of a little anxiety – this is new – and thrill – this is what I've heard so much about, and now it's my turn! When Santa had asked him what he'd wanted, he had just stared, blank-face. "Well, sweetie," Santa had asked again, using the prompt he probably tried on any pre-school kid, "What's your favorite thing?"

And my child had answered, sincerely, "The number ten."

This time, his face was, again, anxious. What if his mother vetoed this purchase?

It was a balmy summer night. Vacationers strolled around us as. "What is this ring for?" I asked, knowing it would be irrelevant as a sex toy, and with the same unabashed response he brought to Santa, Evie answered, "To fix my packer. It's for a construction issue."

We entered the store -- his girlfriend waited outside, people-watching -- and approached a slip of a woman with blond dreadlocks and a medley of piercings. She seemed genuine; I liked her immediately. Evie glanced at me with a look that I knew meant he wanted me to do the talking, so I explained: he has a packer and needs a cock ring to fix it, but I don't really understand what's broken.

This gave him an opening, as now he could correct me. "It's not to fix the packer," he said. "It's to keep it in my underwear."

The clerk understood dutifully; seemed impressed. She grabbed a pair of underwear, smoothed them over the glass counter, handed my son a packer, and he said, "Like this," slipping the ring onto the rub-ber phallus, pressing it against the fabric, and demonstrating how he could stich the ring onto the underwear to secure his packer in place. I am so glad I taught my kid to sew.

"So it won't slip out, right?" I asked, and the sales clerk, nodding, added, "This seems like a really good idea. I've never seen this done before."

"Thanks," my son said, and then, "See, Mom?"

"Okay, but this is what I have concerns about," I continued. "He'll be sitting in the bathroom at school and his packer will fall onto the floor and then someone will see it lying there, and it will be so weird that he'll have to change schools. I just don't want to go through that."

"That makes sense," she agreed. "It's like when you don't want it to slip down the pant leg."

"Please, no," I said. "No slipping down the pant leg."

"It never slips down the pant leg," my son answered.

"It can if you don't have the right underwear," the clerk replied. My son looked shocked. How could he be wrong about something?

"But this set-up will prevent that," she said, yanking at the cock ring as if it was already sewn to the fabric. "This is a really good idea."

"Yeah, he's a smart kid," I replied. "Industrious." I picked up the ring. It was pliable, purple, about the size you'd imagine would fit over a shaft. I ask about the price.

"Twelve dollars."

I was shocked. Almost more shocked by the price than to find myself in this store in the first place. I didn't mind spending twelve dollars, but it seemed so over-priced that I had to say something.

"This thing probably costs four cents to make," I said. "Why is it so expensive?"

The store manager, ringing up at the next register, overheard us.

"This is the going price for pleasure toys," she called over. "This is what people will pay."

"Mom, come on, it's a good idea," my son pleaded.

The manager wandered off.

"Six dollars," the salesclerk whispered to us. "This is not for pleasure." I paid her, we both thanked her, and she said, "I'm giving you this discount because you're both amazing. I never met a mom and son like you guys. This conversation practically made my summer."

"Wow, thanks," I said. My son headed out the door, into the August night, but I paused, taking-in the clerk's words. By that time in his transition, I'd heard this a lot. It was about my support, of course, especially in a world where so many parents linger in their discomfort, delaying the approval their child craves. But this sales clerk was, I believe, touched most by my son's visibility.

There's a quote by the author Marianne Williamson that reads, in part, "...We are all meant to shine... as we let our own light shine, we unconsciously give other people permission to do the same. As we are liberated from our own fear, our presence automatically liberates others."

I saw this liberation happen again and again. I watched Evie's transparency help others feel comfortable, from his personal conversations to his public speeches. People tell me that I gave him a gift with my support, and maybe I did, but I see more clearly the gift his visibility gave to me.

As parents, we're told to push our kids, and then to feign modesty when they succeed. Neither makes sense to me. I didn't push, nor do I pretend to be modest. I revel in my brave, accomplished kid. "Your playing small does not serve the world," Williamson writes. "There is nothing enlightened about shrinking so that other people won't feel insecure around you." Evie saw that "playing small" would not serve him, or other transitioning kids, so he cast a wide net. He published a piece in The New York Times. When NBC wanted commentary on a study about transgender youth, they interviewed him. When a regional magazine celebrated its tenth-year anniversary, it profiled him to mark the progress of the local LGBTQ community. He addressed a roomful of lawyers whose firms provided pro bono services. Another group gave him a scholarship and an "Equality Award" at a black-tie dinner. His face is prominent in an ad campaign, encouraging trans youth to seek the healthcare they need. Together, we spoke to advocacy organizations, and to classes of graduate students training to be counselors, helping them appreciate transitioning from the parent/child perspectives. And, together, we got locked in a parking garage moments before his TedX Talk. He had asked, as we downed the Cosi sandwiches provided to presenters, if he could rehearse just one more time, so we'd slipped through a stage door into the garage. As he practiced his lines, now for the hundredth time, gesturing at the grimy cinder block walls as if to his Power Point, we heard the click of a lock. Astonished, we sprinted past the rows of cars and onto the street, dashed through the theatre lobby, and slipped into the green room, our laughter shushed by the techies back stage.

This was his gift to me – the chance to participate in his joy of visibility. The invitation to share, as Williamson says, his light. And this was, I now see, a chance for my visibility, as well.

I loved, without apology, being seen as his mom. I learned that as parents, we must do what Williamson tells us: do not shrink. Shine. We must allow ourselves, as parents, to be visible and to play big. In doing so, others — especially our kids – can do the same.

One year my son tied a transgender flag around his shoulders, letting it float behind him like a cape as he joined in the PRIDE parade. It was a steamy day in June. We'd started marching in this parade together when he was in middle school, the route guiding us through the gauntlet of love that is that day. The year he wore his cape it was so hot that I watched from an air-conditioned bar, waving as he walked by, his pink, blue and white striped flag buoyant, visible in a sea of superheroes.

SHARING RUS

Michele Feeney

The first birthday our son Rus celebrated in our home was his twelfth: October 24, 2009. This was Rus's "real" birthday, not the January-1-of-the-year-following-birth-birthday the U.S. government assigns to all refugees without papers. I remember feeling proud that I understood that distinction. I'd ordered a big, professionally-decorated chocolate cake. My husband Matt, our other four children, and I watched as Rus blew out the candles, then ate the large slice I cut for him.

When I asked what kind of cake Rus wanted the next year, he said, "Not chocolate." He'd been given chocolate on the plane when he came to the United States at age seven, and it made him sick to his stomach. The taste of partly-digested chocolate was forever entwined with the memory of leaving Africa.

This is what it's like to mother a child one does not meet until he's ten. You don't know that he hates chocolate. Add that he was raised in a different culture, religion, and economic circumstance. One tries to get it right, but it's often wrong.

Milan Kundera, in *The Book of Laughter and Forgetting,* wrote, "...love is a continual interrogation. I don't know a better definition of love." With Rus, my interrogation goes like this: Do I show my love for him the same as to my other children? Have I blended culture and race? Have I celebrated his differences? Has Rus had a good childhood?

Have I at least done no harm?

The first time I met refugees was the summer of 1980. I was between college and law school and got a job preparing twelve refugee children to enter the public-school system in the fall.

The children were "boat people" from Cambodia, Laos, and Vietnam. The youngest was seven. The oldest, in her early twenties, was older than me. We had no common language. They'd been in the

United States for a few weeks. I had grown up in a small farm town, mostly Irish Catholic.

We labelled everything in their house with English words, read all my favorite children's books, and went on a field trip every day. They soaked up English like sponges; by August, they were ready for school.

But, their trauma was evident. One family had lost their mother because dialysis wasn't available in their refugee camp in Thailand. I couldn't imagine such a thing; for me, the child of Michigan teachers, health care had always been a given.

A young girl introduced herself as "Snow." I questioned that—I didn't think it snowed in Vietnam and snow is an English word. She explained that the church that sponsored them had given each child a new name because their Vietnamese names were "too difficult to pronounce."

I sobbed the day I left that job, traumatized by the separation from the students. I don't know that I've ever felt that pain leaving a job since. Snow sat across the kitchen table from me; she'd left everything she'd known only a few short months earlier, including her mother. Including her real, hard-to-pronounce name.

Rus' full name is Rusamarirwa. For longer than I care to admit, I had no idea how to say it. Like Snow, Rus had early on been given something short and easy, so we Americans wouldn't be challenged by the pronunciation.

Rus entered our lives in 2008, when he and my son Mike were ten. Matt came home from Mike's club basketball practice and told me about "a new African kid" who'd been there. The coach had seen Rus shooting hoops in a YMCA parking lot, and invited him to practice. Rus had come from Africa two years earlier, as a refugee, with his grandparents. His parents were presumed dead.

I met Rus shortly after. He was a head taller than Mike and very thin, unpredictable on the court, oftentimes erratic and temperamental. When I looked at him, he looked away.

The parent who'd been driving Rus to practice lived the opposite direction, and the apartment where Rus lived with his grandparents was on our way home. We became Rus's regular ride.

Those first several months, I had the impression Rus ran his own life, at least as far as club sports went. Often, we'd be halfway to a practice or game when he called us, asking for a ride. Sometimes, we'd get to the apartment to pick him up, and someone else already had. Though there was a landline in his grandparents' apartment, the phone often went unanswered, or the person who answered was unable to speak any English besides "Hello," and "Call back later?" Leaving messages at that number was futile.

I don't remember which transportation snafu resulted in me asking Matt, "Should we get Rus a cell phone?" but I do remember that Matt agreed right away. I asked Rus to get his grandparents' permission. They immediately agreed. The cell phone was the first important thing we bought Rus. It was life-changing for him, and for our connection and communication, it was an artery.

Long before Rus became our son, he became Mike's closest friend. Mike, like me, needs few friends, but is all-in with the ones he has. Mike and Rus didn't look like brothers in the beginning. Along with the height difference, Mike has my Irish-white complexion. But now, they are exactly the same size—shirt, shoes, waist and inseam. When at home, they still sleep in their identical twin beds just a few feet from one another. They even weigh the same.

One evening in mid-May of 2010, I drove Rus home from a game by myself. Car rides with Rus, without Mike, were a long slog of me asking questions to try to make conversation, and Rus giving short answers, staring straight ahead.

I asked, "Are you excited for the summer?" My boys were already signed up for multiple camps. Our family vacation was planned. We'd spend July in Michigan on the farm where I grew up.

I can still remember Rus's sidelong look at me. "Not really," he said. "Not much to do."

Why would I assume that summer is preferable to winter, for all children? That all families do fun things over the summer? Then, I thought about food—did Rus's family even have enough food over the summer?

"Would you want to go to basketball camp with Mike in June?" I was trying to cover up my embarrassment at my stupid question. Brophy, where the camp was, is a Catholic boys' college preparatory school near our home. "I mean," I added, "if your grandparents agree. I could help with transportation. Maybe you could spend the night sometimes."

"Yes," he said. "I want to go."

The papers were due shortly, maybe even overdue, when we had that conversation. That is when I met Rus's grandparents, Jason and Thereza. I brought the forms to the apartment, and with Rus translating, they signed their consent.

The last day of basketball camp, Rus and I sat in the pick-up lane at the north end of Brophy's campus. I asked Rus if he'd liked the camp.

"Yes," Rus said. "It's so green here. So clean."

"Would you ever want to go to a school like this?" I blurted out, without regard for whether he could qualify, what his grandparents might think, or finances.

"Yes," Rus said. "I want to go here."

"Okay," I answered, as my left brain overtook my right. The application process was exhaustive, boys who went to Brophy were prepared, and Rus had already had enough disappointment and trauma. "Talk to your grandparents," I said.

After that first basketball camp, Rus's grandparents also agreed to allow Rus to travel to Michigan with us later that summer. My mother was still alive then. Rus, like all the grandchildren, called her "Grandma Helen."

Over morning coffee, while the three boys slept, I asked my mother what she thought about the way Rus seemed to be joining our family by degrees. I discussed my self-interrogation. What if I got Rus excited, and Brophy rejected him? As Rus spent more time with our family, and less with his grandparents, was I doing more harm than good?

My mother reminded me of what she'd said when we'd adopted Joe, our youngest. "In all my years of teaching," she said, "I only met one or two children I couldn't have taken home with me and loved. You just have to go all-in."

The fall of Rus's eighth grade year, he collected recommendations, pulled up his grades, and took a course to prepare for the admission exam. I asked for help from anyone who had influence, and drove him back and forth to the preparation course. Together, we met with the admissions director at Brophy. I remember the director asking Rus what his grandfather did for a job. Rus somehow avoided saying he washed dishes at a hotel.

The decision about applying to Brophy required a meeting with Rus's uncle, Daniel. Daniel is the person in Rus's family who has been in the United States the longest. I know, from reading news stories about Daniel available on the internet, that he was brutalized in his early teens in Africa and was somehow able to get to the United States. He was in terrible physical condition when he arrived and was placed with a foster family. He became a college track star, eventually earning a master's degree. Somehow Daniel got his parents, Jason and Thereza, their minor children, and Rus, their grandchild, to the United States.

Daniel told me the family agreed—Brophy was a good idea for Rus.

By early January, as the application deadline approached, I'd been bugging Rus for days to give me a draft of his essay. Finally, he explained, "I've never written an essay."

I remembered the work I'd done with my refugee students in 1980, long before computers and printers. I had the students tell me a story in the best English they could. I'd write the story with proper penmanship, spelling, punctuation, and grammar, and they would illustrate. Then, they'd read the story back to me over and over again. We did that every day for weeks.

I asked Rus to face the wall of my home office and tell me the story of how he got to the United States. I typed word-for-word as he talked.

I learned that his family had been well established in his village of Rumagaza in the Democratic Republic of the Congo. Jason and Thereza married at fourteen and had eleven children. Jason was the headmaster of a Catholic School. Rus's parents were sixteen when he was born. They were at school when the village was invaded. Rus's grandparents, who were babysitting, fled with him. He was one. They moved from camp to camp until Rus was seven. No one knew where his parents were, or what had happened to them.

Rus had some positive memories of playing with other children in the more stable refugee camps, and "liked the cats there." When I asked for the name of his favorite cat, he gave me the same incredulous look he'd given me when I asked about plans for the summer, six months earlier. He told me that in one camp, his grandfather was able to have cows, the thing he loved best. He told me only one specific bad memory of that time—while running, he saw a mother shot, and then drowned in a river while her daughter cried on the banks—but general bad memories of moving from camp to camp as one after another was attacked.

At the end of that story, which I had never heard before, I handed Rus a printed-out copy, and said, "Here's your first draft."

Rus earned his acceptance to Brophy. His teachers wrote glowing recommendations. In the test preparation course, he improved more from the pre-test to the final test than any other student. His essay, the one I typed the first draft of, still brings tears to my eyes.

In early 2011, just after Rus's application package was complete, the landline next to our bed rang at two o'clock a.m. The caller asked for Rus. Matt roused Rus, who spoke in his native language, then told us he "had to go home right now." He didn't know why. It wasn't until the next morning that I reached Rus to find out what had happened.

"They found my parents," he said. "In Uganda. I have four younger siblings."

I asked a hundred questions, I'm sure, but can only remember that Rus told me he'd been able to speak to his mother and father for the first time he could remember, and his oldest brother, Thierry.

For a long time, it seemed like nothing changed. No one had any hope Rus's parents and siblings could emigrate. The man, Sasha, who had helped Daniel get the rest of the family to the United States years before couldn't help, because he'd already shown "preference" that could get him in trouble. Rus's parents called every couple of months, when they had access to a phone.

Rus stayed with us, aware his parents lived, probably suffering, on the other side of the world. As we prepared for the beginning of Rus's freshman year, I addressed the transportation issue. "I see three options," I said. "You can try to ride a city bus, we can join a carpool and I'll drive from your neighborhood once a week, or you can stay with us."

"I want to stay with you," Rus said.

In retrospect, it seems especially cruel that Rus moved in with us within a few months of learning his family was alive. I am in awe of this resilience—a boy, age fourteen, leaving his grandparents and the home he knows, finding out he has parents he has no memory of, and siblings too, and yet integrating into our family and home, as well as a new school, all at the same time. It was only much later I learned how scared Rus was to stay with us. Other than some trips for sports, he'd never spent a night away from his grandparents.

In 2011, when Rus had been living with us for the few months since school started, his grandparents, uncles, aunts, and cousins came to our house for Thanksgiving. His grandfather, Jason, offered the prayer before dinner. Jason is tall, maybe 6'4", and elegant. Jason prays with gusto and flailing arms, in an African dialect. Rus translates—but only a short sentence at the end of what sounds like whole paragraphs. That Thanksgiving, Jason was thankful Rus's parents and siblings were alive.

After dinner, Rus said, "My grandparents want to talk to you guys. I'll translate."

We sat on the sofas in our living room. Rus sat on a chair near the fireplace.

Jason spoke for a few minutes.

Rus said, "My grandfather says you are my parents now."

Thereza nodded.

Matt and I both teared up, thinking this was a polite way of thanking us for helping to take care of Rus. Later, as months passed, we realized that this was the moment where his grandparents stopped behaving as parents and started behaving as grandparents. Maybe it was the African way of accomplishing an adoption.

Rus's parents and siblings became even more real for me in early 2012 when a family member planned a trip to Uganda to visit their camp. She took a long letter from me and a camera. She returned with dozens of pictures, including several of Rus' parents with his siblings. No one in the pictures smiled. Everyone was very thin. Rus's mother wore a traditional colorful African dress. His father wore a suit. His siblings wore American-style play clothes. I had a group shot framed and hung it over Rus's bed. The photo was a daily reminder there were people on the other side of the world who belonged to Rus, and who he belonged to. In addition to belonging to us.

We began to explore whether there was any way Rus's parents and siblings could come to the United States. When we dug into paperwork, we learned Rus had been considered one of Jason and Thereza's children when they emigrated back in 2006. The fact Rus' parents had a minor child in the United States from whom they'd been forcibly separated might give us an argument to support permission.

But, I worried. What if Rus had to go back to his parents, to a county he barely remembered, rather than them coming to the United States? What if they came here, and wanted Rus to live with them? By then, he'd been with us for almost two years. He was part of our family.

I took one of Rus's uncles, Bizi, out for coffee. He answered my question—"In our culture, we don't break things that are working. Rus is thriving. People move from family to family. Nothing will change."

Through a young lawyer's creative pro bono work at Matt's law firm, we were able to complete an immigration application for Rus' family. This required blood samples from Rus's parents and siblings, in Kampala, and Rus, in Phoenix, to prove the relationship through DNA testing. It required health exams for everyone. It took over a year. It was held up by Rus's mother's medical issues.

But, in December 2013, Rus's parents and siblings arrived, first in New York, then at Sky Harbor airport in Phoenix. Rus had just received his learner's permit—I let him drive to the airport. We agreed, laughing, that I should drive home. It was "too much" to subject his family to an inexperienced driver on their first day in America. When we met them outside security, they were all wearing heavy winter clothing, which whoever greeted them in New York had provided. I remember only one small suitcase among the six of them.

Only days after they arrived, Rus's parents came to our house for Christmas. The letter I'd sent years earlier had a picture of Rus's bed and our dogs, as well as our children. But, their reactions to a very large home in North Central Phoenix and more food than our crowd of thirty could possibly consume were concealed. If they were shocked, they kept it to themselves.

They had given me a dress from Africa, made of the kind of oilcloth the French use for tablecloths. I assumed it came in that very small suitcase. It was red with a bright pattern and gold braid and fell to the floor.

I wore it Christmas day. Of course, I felt totally off. It was not my dress. The fabric didn't breathe. I felt foolish, awkward. The dress was the only African thing in my home, aside from Rus. I knew almost as little about life in Africa as I'd known about life in Vietnam, Cambodia and Laos so many years ago.

I recall Rus's father, Bizimana, hugging the young lawyer, Irina, who'd done all the work on their immigration. Rus translated: his father couldn't believe how "young" she was, or that anyone would have the "power" to make their immigration happen. Sadly, there was no power involved. Just access to legal help and a legitimate path to entry.

Late in the day, I decided to make an effort to talk with Rus's sisters. "Can you translate?" I asked Rus.

"Oh, they speak English," Rus said.

Rus's sister Migone, who I've since learned is the feisty one, cracked open a book of children's poetry on our living room coffee table. She read aloud, start to finish, Robert Louis Stevenson's, "My Little Shadow."

"We learned to read in the camps," she explained. "It was a safe thing for us to do."

Rus was a junior in high school at this point. He was part of his high school community, and playing high school basketball and club soccer. He was living like most American high school students, thinking about the SATs and colleges.

By then, soccer had become Rus's sport of choice: though I tried to enjoy it, I never really learned the rules. Not like basketball—I was there for the elementary stage of three-year-old basketball with my other two boys. There is something about being there from the beginning, skin-to-skin, with a child.

Rus told me he'd forgotten African words, and he was busy and self-centered the way adolescents can be. Between his family's arrival and his departure for University of New Mexico, where he was recruited to play Division One soccer, he never spent a night at their apartment, as far as I know.

I remember once after some shenanigan Rus asked me if he'd embarrassed me. "No," I said. "You've only embarrassed me once."

"When was that?"

"Way back in eighth grade, at the interview to get into Brophy, when you wouldn't say what your grandfather did to support your family."

Rus nodded.

"There is no shame in washing dishes," I said.

For his junior year of college, Rus elected to return to Phoenix to attend Grand Canyon University. With all the political changes and ugly rhetoric around immigration, we became insistent that he complete the steps for U.S. citizenship. He became a citizen in mid-October of 2017, on his twentieth birthday.

It didn't strike me as strange at the time that only Matt, our children, and I were present at his citizenship ceremony. Though there was never any question Rus's African family loved him, it didn't seem part of their culture to attend games or ceremonies. I remember laughing with Rus at the rabid cheering of some parents at AAU basketball games, and him saying, "Makes me glad they don't come." Still, citizenship is a big deal. I asked him if he'd invited them.

"They're working," was all he said.

In November 2017, Alyce and Bizimana had their sixth child, a boy. They named him Matthew, after my husband. They told us this while seated in the very same seats Jason and Thereza sat, six years before, when they told us we were now Rus's parents.

Rus stopped playing college soccer in the late spring of 2018. The places he first excelled in the United States were the soccer field and the basketball court. Sports was his entry point. The immediacy of athletics was his escape, like when I lose myself in a good book. I took him out to dinner the day he made that sad decision, realizing his playing time didn't justify the many hours of practice required, while putting academics a distant second. "Imagining you not playing a sport," I said, "is like imagining me without a book."

Yet, the end of soccer opened in Rus a desire to talk to me. He wanted to talk about his personal history, for the first time ever. We started reading a book by a Somali refugee titled, Call Me American. Many of the experiences of the author, Abdi Nor Iftin, who fled war when in Somalia beginning at age six, mirror Rus's family's experiences.

In the course of discussing the book, I realized I didn't know how to pronounce Rus' full name, Rusamarirwa. I'd seen it in print many times, but never said it aloud.   .

"How do you say your name?" I asked.

Rus answers: "Roos—ee—mar—ee—wa."

The first attempt, I butchered it terribly.

Rus repeated: "Roos—ee—mar—ee-wa."

I got it the second time, but accented the wrong syllable.

"Help me learn," I said. "I want to say it right."

He repeated and I repeated until it finally came out right. Like water. Like music.

"That's it," he said.

Mothers' Day, 2018, Rus asked me for money to go to Walgreen's to get "cards."

"How many do you need?" I asked.

"Three," he said. "You, my mom and my grandma."

This is where I wonder if we three together create a whole that is more or less than the sum of its parts.

The long-ago July when my mother met Rus on our Michigan farm, we had all read Paddle to the Sea each night before bed. My mother's mother had read the book to her when she was a girl. It is the story of a young boy who carves the wooden figure of an Indian paddling a canoe, then releases the little boat into the Great Lakes system in the far north. The boat makes its journey through the Great Lakes, miraculously returning to the boy when he's a man. We sat in the dark breakfast room of my mother's farmhouse, homesteaded by our family since the 1850s, and traced the canoe's path in heavy black marker on a map, advancing the line a little bit each day. It is only as I write this essay that I connect all the many miracles, the frank magic, that made Rus' and my life entwine. It is more miraculous than the little boat making its way back to the boy, now a man.

Just a few weeks ago, my family attended the wedding of Ruganza Mugisha, Rus's uncle. When we met Rus, Ruganza was in high school. The bride, Esperance, had recently emigrated from Rwanda to marry Ruganza. Many members of her family had travelled from Rwanda for the event.

At the wedding, Rus sat with our family. When it came time for each family to get a picture with Ruganza and Esperance, Rus was in the picture with Matt, me, our daughters, my son Joe, my daughters' husbands, and my granddaughter Maggie. Mike was away at college. I can't recall if Rus also joined the photo of Bizimana, Alyce, and his other siblings.

The reception was managed by an emcee, in a language I don't understand. Most of the adult women were dressed in traditional African outfits—brightly-colored cotton dresses to the floor and headscarves. I was seated next to a lovely young woman from Massachusetts named Grace, who spoke English with a thick accent.

"What is he talking about?" I asked, as the emcee continued.

"He is saying that they will help her learn to cook, to prepare the foods he likes. He's talking about the dowry and such. About cows."

I nodded.

"It's mostly for the old people," Grace added, then laughed. "Who do you know here?" she asked.

We were the only white people in the room. Probably the only adults born in the United States. Grace rightly figured there was a story to our presence. It's the kind of story that can go on for a minute or hours.

"We share Rus," I finally said.

Her eyebrows raised.

"With Jason and Thereza," I continued. "And Alyce and Bizimana."

Across the table, Rus caught my eye and smiled.

Grace continued to translate. There was a lot of prayer, and talk about how the two families are now joined together. That seems to be the main point of an African wedding. It is a celebration of families joining their fates.

Everyone in the room, other than us, was an immigrant or the young child of an immigrant. Most, maybe all, fled war-torn countries. They built lives here and thrived. These people, most notably Rus, had so enriched my life. It was obvious to me that the richness of immigration really is a two-way street. In its best form, immigration involves movement from not only the culture of the people who've embraced a new home, but the people who welcome them. It requires a fluidity that benefits us all.

Once, when I had made some rule for Rus in high school, and he resisted, I suggested he "call his grandmother and see what she thought."

"Why bother?" Rus said. "You and my grandmother agree about everything."

On October 24, 2018, Rus turned twenty-one. He is an adult. All I ever wanted for him was to have a real childhood. At the celebration, with vanilla cake, of course, were Rus's mother, Alyce; siblings, Theirry (17), Angelique (16), Migone (15), Mediatrice (9) and baby Matthew (2). Bizimana was at church. Our family was there. All of us were his family.

Before dinner, in a quiet conversation with Alyce, I asked, "How did you pick the name Rusamarirwa?" Just like that, his whole, real, African name. "What does it mean?"

Rus' sister Angelique translated. "It means beautiful man."

"Can you tell me the story of the day Rus was born?" I asked.

He was born at home, and it took two days. No medicine, no doctor. Just "old ladies," who didn't expect Rus to be healthy as the hours wore on. But he was a "strong" baby. Rus was born when Alyce was sixteen; they were separated when she was seventeen.

It is a perfectly ordinary birthday. Yet, when the house is quiet, Rus thanks me. We know how extraordinary it all is.

Of course, there are things I wish—I wish I'd learned the rules of soccer, organically, like with basketball. I wish I'd worn the dress more than once. I wish I'd learned to say Rus's name earlier. But, at

Rus's twenty-first birthday, I'm mostly in awe of the wonderful turn my life took with Rus, a turn I never could have expected.

Milan Kundera, who wrote about love's interrogation, also wrote that, "The novelist teaches the reader to comprehend the world as a question." I believe parenting teaches us to accept children as a mystery, whether biological, adopted, or in Rus's case, shared. One never knows exactly how they will turn out, or even what they're thinking. Even on my deathbed, I suspect worries for my children— wondering how life will turn out for them—will still be top of mind. But, Rus's twenty-first birthday seems a fair time to take stock. My takeaway from this magical but unusual parenting experience is that people of good will who undertake to act in the best interests of a child, will find a way.

In that simple human endeavor, we all speak the same language.

THROUGH THE DOG DOOR, A MEMOIR

Elizabeth Hellstern

My son has finished his macaroni and cheese, won't touch the avocado or coleslaw or anything really that's not yellow, soft and mushy. He stretches his arms to lifted out of the highchair. I gesture a washcloth over his face and pull him to the hip-dock while I move dirty plates to the sink.

My husband lies on the couch, two steps away from the hallway kitchen, just off the front door in our dark rural house with no insulation.

I have on a cotton Indian dress with geometric patterns that I must hand-wash and mend every time it's worn. I roll on mauve lipstick and wave on mascara. I finger lift my pregnancy-thick hair and ask for the car keys.

"I'm not going to be the babysitter tonight," he says.
"But I want to go out. I'm the Arts Editor." I flip my purse strap over my shoulder.
"No, you don't." He walks to the hook near the door, snatches the car keys and blocks me. He won't look away.
"Fine." I say.

I talk my neighbor into driving me downtown to the art walk. We stay for two hours. It's okay, same-o, same-o. When I come home, everything's bolted like we're in Southside Chicago, not off a dirt road. I crawl in the dog door. I spoon my son in his twin bed, find comfort in his tangly hair and suckling reflex.

We're asleep, two warm bodies who still remember how to be as one, snuggled in Buzz Lightyear sheets and a comforter with planets on it.

The planets get yanked away.

"Where were you?" my husband snaps, and I snap-bean towards
Isaac, see if he's awake.
"Downtown. With Brandy."
"You just don't listen, do you?"

I want to leave Isaac here on his own special earth, so I try to dance
past Jason in the narrow door-frame, but like a drowning man he
snags my upper arm, squeezing mamma-fat through his fingers.

"I can go where I want to, you don't own me."

I'm suddenly smacked on the sofa, the shadow of the streetlamp
haloing his head, my shoulders stuck like pinned bugs under his meat
hands.

"You can't tell me what to do." He shakes me like a crack-baby.
"You think you're a big man."
His hand collides with my face. I feel blood sprint in.
"Bitch, you think you're so smart!"

I can't hear what he says anymore; smell the sour aluminum of his
sweaty mouth.
Isaac stays asleep.

CLOSE KNIT

Jane Hipkins Sobie

A Navajo weaver leaves a flaw in the pattern of a blanket or rug so
that the soul has a way out.

For Steven Sobie and Robin Williams

When I heard on the evening news that you died of suicide, Robin, I
felt I had lost a member of the fold. They reported you had bipolar.
No one had to tell me. I knew the threads of the insidious bipolar gene
were generously woven through our veins like intricate French lace.
We understood the depths of depression and mania.

Whenever I didn't see you performing comedy on television for long
stretches, I wondered if you were tangled in the weft of melancholy.

Did you find comfort playing Chopin like me? He was a melancholy
baby, too.

Listening to the news about your death, I was taking a fresh peach
pie out of the oven, made from juice-swollen South Carolina peaches
I bought a few days before in a roadside stand coming home from
Litchfield Beach. After placing the pie on a potholder to cool, I sat on
the counter stool.

And wept. My tears tasting the ocean waves I had just left.

Shivers shot through me like Fourth of July sparklers. Our spirits were
more closely knit together than I thought.   A few days earlier, after
crossing the border from South Carolina to North Carolina, thoughts of
you, gentle as a secret, drifted up out of my subconscious.

I wondered, "What's Robin Williams doing? His absence from movies
and television meant to me he fell into a snake pit abyss. Fans love

you when you are up, funny, entertaining. They forget you and write you off when you are down.

But I didn't realize the fabric of your being was unraveling. Edges fraying fast.

Driving my Mazda Protégé up the interstate to Winston-Salem, I murmured, "Thinking of you, Robin. Sending love."

After you died, my only consolation was knowing that one of my twin sons Steven, who also had bipolar, took his life and had a slap stick sense humor, would take the opportunity to perform sketches with you in the comedy club of heaven.

Robin, two days before Steven died, he found a box of my magazine articles and poetry that had been published when he was in elementary school.

"I didn't know you wrote all of this," he said. "And all these press awards? You must keep writing, Mom. You have a lot to say."

After he died I never thought I could write through the pain. I haven't.

Three nights after you died, Robin, I had a dream. One that has everything to do with why I am sitting at my computer.

I'm walking down a path in a lush green forest on a spring morning when sun, like a theatre footlight speared between trees, illuminated the path. Bluebirds serenade me, Thumper thumps. The whole Disney crew.

> *Two figures walk towards me, laughing like grade school buddies.*
> *It's you and Steven. My heart breaks and swells. In front of me are two pairs of eyes like icons fluid with love. A book opens in the palms of both your hands. A pine scented breeze flips through the blank pages. Alphabet letters, like raindrops sprinkle the pages.*

"It's time, Mom," says Steven. Robin and Steven smile at each other.

"Write."

A TRAGEDY ON THE MEXICAN BORDER

Donley Watt

Tornillo, Texas, is a small town, a place of a couple of thousand people just 20 or so miles Southeast of El Paso, whose claim now to fame (or notoriety) is being home to a new detention camp. This tent encampment, established by the Unaccompanied Alien Children program, is a prison for children, by any other name. Those children being detained there in Tornillo, now, as I write this in January of 2019, are being held forcibly in tents with cots enough to sleep 2400 detainees. Its location on the north edge of the Rio Grande is only a short swim and wade away from Mexico. Or, in more proper terms, it is located adjacent to the Marcelina Serna port of entry between the US and Mexico.

The children are detained there by our federal government, separated from their parents for a variety of reasons, all of which fall under the general term of being illegal immigrants. But the reasons more accurately result from other more complex causes and reasons: primarily fear of staying in their Central American countries of origin with their out-of-control drug cultures, hope for a safer home with more opportunities in America, and having suffered (along with their ancestors, for centuries) under the harsh, prejudicial and discriminatory fact of being indigenous peoples. So sometimes alone, sometimes with their families, they have endured a hazardous and difficult journey hoping for a better life and now are incarcerated in limbo as criminals whose only crimes are fear, naive hope, and trust that has been betrayed.

This encampment and others like it are administered not by the federal government, but by Christian charities, such as BCFS Health and Human Services (historically affiliated with the ultra-conservative Baptist General Convention of Texas) funded by hundreds of millions of government dollars and with minimum oversight.

Tornillo is a five hour drive south of my home in Santa Fe, a drive not to be taken frivolously by a man of my years (78) and the years and miles (15 & 185,000) on my Ford Ranger pickup. And the drive will take me through the daunting (for me) haphazard traffic and inevitable congestion of both Albuquerque and El Paso. Because of my history of heart problems and eyesight I cleared this trip with Dr. Tom (I call him), my local GP. He is a wise and caring young doctor, one who understands me, knows my precarious health and also my deep-seated need not to give up—not only writing, but also my still flickering need for small adventures and just causes. He did advise me to take two or three days at least for the round trip, and no more than five hours driving at a stretch. He doesn't lecture me about the risks for a man with my years and medical history. I guess he figures being depressed at home on my sofa carries more danger for me than a road trip.

The continuing need to write manifests itself for numerous reasons, most of them—anger, pride, ego, and stubbornness—do not have places on most folks' list of virtues. Not honorable at all. But that anger for me now, concerning what is happening on the border with Mexico, and especially with the detention of children, is intense and rises above the others to join passion on the side of the more admirable traits. I feel justified to move that intense feeling over into the category of "almost virtuous".

For the encampment at Tornillo is not the first refugee encampment I will have seen. In 1990 on a trip even farther south, towards Guatemala where that country's internal war would rage on for five or so more years, my wife and I made our way in southern Mexico, past San Cristobal de las Casas and farther on. Then, finally, thanks to directions from a priest in San Cristobal, up a rugged side road to Glorieta, an encampment just twenty kilometers north of the Guatemala/Mexico border. There, refugees from the mountainous villages of Guatemala whose homes were burned and men were slaughtered by the dictator's military fled north into Mexico over the Guatemalan border. Several hundred of them found temporary, relative safety, with conditions, in Glorieta.

As we eased our car up that side road, the land finally flattened out as a barren plateau, a rocky outcropping above a fertile valley. A few twisted, stunted trees clung to crevices in the rock like the last survivors from another age. The houses there, squat squares with walls of dried cane and crooked tree limbs, stood starkly on the land, which appeared too poor to support even a single flower, much less a small garden or orchard. The refugee camp held one well with only enough water to be pumped less than an hour a day.

When we drove up a dozen or so women had gathered by that water well, waiting. A score of colorful striped jugs and empty plastic buckets sat tilted on a rocky ledge. Young children hid in their mothers' skirts and stared at us as we passed.

We met with the village elders in a metal storage barn where burlap sacks of beans and rice rose head-high against one wall. I listened to their stories, and later incorporated their bare existence that they angrily described into my first novel, *The Journey of Hector Rabinal*. A harsh existence, but some of the families seemed to be intact and most had fled across the Mexican border to Glorieta from villages in the same mountainous area of Guatemala. I could sense the presence of a frustrated, helpless, but determined and cohesive society.

Men could leave Glorieta only for seasonal day labor in the fields below, when their work was needed. But no one had the freedom to walk away from Glorieta other than for that, and Mexican agents patrolled the highway that ran from the Guatemalan border north to Comitán. There were no guards, no fences or razor wire. They were held captive by their helplessness, their fear and lack of resources, and until the war in their country ended, the absence of better options.

It wasn't until after the war was over, in the mid-nineties, that some of those refugees forced out of their villages and off their land began to be repatriated with a chance to return to their home country and reclaim what was rightfully theirs. To this day that dispossession is still not fully resolved.

And others, even in the late 1990s, began to look northward, to America, as a place to escape the methodical persecution and repression of Guatemala's (American-backed) right-wing leaders. That combination of fear, hope, and helplessness in the face of brutal power has been a driving force in creating what some in America now call the "border crisis."

Flash forward twenty-eight years to Tornillo. For being 20 miles from the thriving city of El Paso, the encampment there is remote and mostly inaccessible except for those directly involved in the government dictated operation. From the road that leads to the border crossing only the tops of a few tents can be seen and access is severely limited—even members of Congress cannot just stop by and gain entrance. And the major press outlets only have an occasional press release or a staged limited visit—or a furtive conversation with a worker after hours for an inside version of the true conditions.

Some similarities exist between these children in "detention" in Tornillo and the Guatemalans who were held for years in the Glorieta refugee camp in southern Mexico in the 1990s. They include the Tornillo childrens' absence of power, their dependence on others for basic sustenance, their confinement to that one facility, the uncertainty of what awaits them in the future, and their lack of meaningful resources and advocates for their defense.

But unlike the Glorieta refugees, the children at Tornillo are confined by walls and fences and guards; they are separated and isolated from their families. They have lost everything of importance in their lives—family, friends, familiar towns and villages, and even their native food. In fact, they are lost in a bureaucratic confinement deprived of their entire culture and systems of support, even as lacking as they may have been.

The detention camp at Tornillo is a petri dish where anger and hopelessness, fear and impotence will, I fear, inevitably ferment and lead to the formation of substitute support networks that are in effect, what our political leaders fear most: organized gangs.

A cruel, misguided, flawed and politically motivated reaction to an ongoing social problem, with children as victims.

BOOK REVIEWS

Quiet Courage: A review of Violet by **Leslie Tate**
Reviewed by Emma Claire Sweeney
Magic Oxygen, imprint of Lyme Regis, Dorset, Great Britain, March 2018
223 pages

The final novel in the *Lavender Blues* trilogy by British author Leslie
Tate moves us beyond the earlier books' explorations of free love,
traditional courtship and open marriage into a lyrical and poignant
meditation on late-life love.

Functioning perfectly as a stand-alone novel as well as drawing
the trilogy to a close, *Violet* is narrated by deep-thinking Beth and
high-spirited James. It opens with the blind date that changes the remaining course of both their lives, capturing the childlike exuberance
of early-stage romance as well as the inevitable trepidation of those
on whom love has already left a deep scar. And it turns out that both
Beth and James have good reason to fear.

Structured to resemble the workings of memory, *Violet* reaches backwards as well as forwards in time, finally excavating the dark pit of
Beth's past. The warmth offered by her parents and the wider family
of their liberal church, it turns out, has done little to help her resist
the magnetism of Conrad, an aspiring preacher. After they wed, her
husband's enigma soon shades into coldness, his conviction into
the exertion of an unbending will. The romantic Beth, whose parents
provided her with such a fine example of enduring love, has always
believed in the sanctity of marriage. But her own experiences as both
a wife and mother force her to face up to life's complexity.

Easy-going James has made his peace with his previous marriage
before he embarks on the romance with Beth. But, for him, the future
will prove more perilous than the past, and Beth will be the source of
both his sorrow and solace.

Although *Violet's* setting and characters are unmistakably and endear-
ingly British, in its insistence on nuance, its insight into the extraordi-
nariness of the ordinary, and its investigation of faith, it shares its DNA
with great North American novelists. Bringing to mind writers such as

Carol Shields and Marilynne Robinson, *Violet* dares to offer neither the false consolation of easy answers nor the luxury of adolescent despair – a quietly courageous novel about the bravery of the everyday.

Author's website: www.leslietate.com

What Does Not Return by Tami Haaland
Reviewed by Austin Bennett

Lost Horse Press, Sand Point, Idaho, March 2018 (paper)
ISBN 978-0-9981963-6-7
80 pages

What is left when memory fails? Tami Haaland suggests companionship. In her third collection, *What Does Not Return,* the former Montana Poet Laureate naturally unfolds four interrelated parts that teeter
on the spectrum of time. Early, we encounter the role reversal of
mother and daughter due to dementia. As memory fails, the daughter
faces the burden of becoming "a third person across the table/a listener who hears about my other self/my name, the secrets she would
not say." The dizzying effect implores the daughter to investigate their
shared life—recall what can be known—only to discover the limits of
memory for both the healthy and the diseased. In an even, unpretentious tone these limits expand outward from the personal to the
collective. Cold War missile silos, Chappaquiddick Bridge, and school
shootings surface and "never go away;" even when the mind of the
one she most desires does.

After the mother's death, the tension of absence continues to
grow in light of companionship's binding ties. She keeps her mother's
wrist watch and confesses, "Now, I see time/in a glance and I think
you must have/something to do with it, still marching me/through the
hours and days." This onward marching leads the daughter through
a series of companion poems featuring deer, mosquito, and squirrel
that culminate in the title poem with "a hinged wonder." She collects
an oyster from the shoreline "noting that without water/it lost part of its
shine." Feeling responsible for its death, she keeps forgetting to return
it to the water captivated by the shoreline full of "open shells. . .their
fragments catching the sun/I had to walk away from so much light."
This interplay of death and light reflects the daughter's overall acceptance of living with death, of absence and companionship—of "what
cannot be undone."

Haaland's magic is in her consistency. She steers clear of
flash-in-the-pan poems to offer something greater. For the caretak-
ers of 5.5 million sufferers of Alzheimer's/dementia, Haaland's poetry
serves as an empathetic companion. She offers strength through
calmness. Hope through accepting life's tensions.

Morsel of Bread, a Knife by Roberta Feins
Reviewed by Lindsey Royce
CoCa: Center on Contemporary Art, Seattle, WA, April 2018
82 pages

A Morsel of Bread, a Knife, Roberta Feins' poetry collection, explores a woman's coming of age in the 50s, 60s and 70s. Feins examines what it is to be a woman in light of familial and sociocultural expectations. She scrutinizes the nature of womanhood in a sexist world and how—during times of civil rights, the sexual revolution, and first- and second- wave feminism—she chooses what kind of woman, and person, she'll become.

In "My Mother Muses at the Louvre: Gabrielle d'Estrees and One of her Sisters," Feins employs ekphrasis using comparison/contrast to illustrate the mother's childhood abuses, particularly sexual abuse, as contrasted with historical ideas about fecundity. In unindented stanzas, Feins tells the innocent story of Gabrielle bathing with a sister, while in indented stanzas, she juxtaposes her mother's bathing with sister, Sylvia, and witnessing an incident of sexual abuse:

The sisters [in the painting] bathe together
in a marble tub, a sheet draped
over one edge.

Sylvia and I [the mother and *her* sister] bathing
in Grossvater's house on West 113th.
Thin towels across a tile floor.

These juxtapositions continue until we come to the crime:

Uncle Sol came in. I [the mother] couldn't
protect you [Sylvia] from his groping hands.
I watched the soot on the sill.

Throughout this collection, Feins questions familial and sociocultural choices. In "The Medicine Cabinet," Feins' narrator's struggles to choose "a side" (male or female) to emulate:

The searing gray bonnet over my hair
would test me for the side I'd chosen. I had to bear

the heat, the bite of plastic curlers,
unlike the princess who could not bear the hidden pea.

In other poems, Feins takes on issues such as slut shaming, female empowerment, sexism in religion, and celebrations of female sexuality. Overall, Feins' collection is not facile in its examination of sexism but offers a somewhat complex, dual trajectory that combines fairly straightforward narrative poems about self and family with those employing ekphrasis and a variety of forms to reveal inherited sexist oppression in family, culture, and history. In poetry that offers musical lines and startling word choices, Feins digs deep to find original, fresh images. This collection is not only for feminists, women and men, but for anyone interested in his or her identity in the world.

Mississippi, Ann Fisher-Wirth and Maude Schuyler Clay
Reviewed by Danielle Sellers
Wings Press, 2018, hardback
$34.95.

As collaborations go, this one is a hit. Comprised of photographs by Maude Schuyler Clay and poems by California-born Mississippi eco-poet Ann Fisher-Wirth, Mississippi seeks to discover the many different faces of this complicated state. With this collection, one is not merely a reader, but a participant as the photos are woven with voice and figurative images to create an immersive experience.

Schuyler Clay's photographs are often nature-driven: a still pollen-covered pond at midday that Fisher-Wirth says you can walk on, an impossibly orange sunset looming over a mass of black trees, which Fisher-Wirth calls "a lifting up/ an exaltation." Fisher-Wirth's poems speak from the center of these photographs. Many of the poems take on a persona, the result of which is a myriad of voices that express a deep understanding of the complicated historical and racial intersections of Mississippi, as many know is fraught with violence. What is surprising here, though, is the organic marriage of the two arts.

In the poem "Thirty-five years," the speaker remembers how as a resident of Berkley in the 60s, she vowed "never never never/to live in the South." As fate would have it, that vow was soon broken, as the speaker muses on living in Mississippi for many decades. In the poem, the speaker recalls Lightnin' Hopkins desire to walk "down by the riverside," proving that the love for Mississippi is strong, even though it is often a symbol of danger and fear for African Americans.

The voices Fisher-Wirth adopt tell stories of danger and fear, like in the poem "I do not like snake…," the speaker says, "after that boy got shot/ I heard him/ in among the skeeters/ and the peepers…moanin' for mercy." Superstition, ghost stories, Old World traditions and beliefs are always under the surface. The dead are long with us. These are intimate stories you won't get just by visiting. These are stories told only by the long-time listener, told from the open heart of the poet, with love and understanding for the difficult experience of being.

But there are stories of love and light here, too, as in the poem "We was walking home from prom." In this poem, a female speaker describes the moment her husband proposed. He had bought the ring for another girl, but changed his mind when he saw her. "I don't care," she says, "never had much/ folks say I'm pretty/ but shy as the back of the moon." She decides to love him for a dimple. In Mississippi, vows are easily taken up, easily broken, proving that nothing is ever set in stone. Change is possible, which is the hope for not only Mississippi but the south in general.

Ann Fisher-Wirth's poems and Maude Schuyler-Clay's photographs make sense of an often misunderstood place. If you're from Mississippi, this book can take you home and if you're not, this book will make you wish you were.

WEST OF PHOEBE, Stories by Lawrence Judson Reynolds

Reviewed by Donley Watt
Rainbow Ridge Books, Faber, Virginia. 2017 (paper).
ISBN 978-1-937907-50-1
185 pgs.

The stories of Lawrence Judson Reynolds in his collection, West of Phoebe, feel as if they sprouted from the red earth of rural Virginia, the ground that nourished tobacco and corn and both blessed and cursed those men and women—and their children—of the 1940s and 1950s who struggled there.

Some of the stories are powerful, especially those such as "The Man with the Gun" and "My Father's Necktie," both told from a boy's point of view. These capture the dreaminess, isolation and confusion, the innocence and loss and uncertainty that are further developed, mostly successfully in other stories as the narrators age. But as they age, those early traits often evolve over time into other, more adult disappointments as in ("That Grand Canyon" and "The Half-Life of Holidays").

Reynolds writes these stories with sensitivity and grace, and most of the tales seem to be not so much about the surface action, but as ways to touch the undercurrents of emotion, of painful and mostly unsuccessful attempts by the characters to find a place of comfort in those small worlds where they never quite fit. These outsiders always appear puzzled how others seem to find relationships and ways of belonging, but where they can only attempt—often—to reconcile themselves with their isolation and their fates, an uncomfortable alienation and even bitterness can result.

But the writing, the words and sentences that stream by like the highway that cuts through the heart of Phoebe, captures times and characters in ways that beautifully, and importantly, evoke those mostly forgotten decades in a particular and important part of America.

CONTRIBUTORS NOTES

Tony Barnstone teaches at Whittier College and is the author of 20 books and a music CD, *Tokyo's Burning: WWII Songs.* His poetry books include *Pulp Sonnets; Tongue of War: From Pearl Harbor to Nagasaki; The Golem of Los Angeles; Sad Jazz;* and *Impure.* Forthcoming are a translation of the selected poems of the Urdu poet Ghalib, the collected poems of Mary Ellen Solt, and an anthology of Chinese and American Ecopoetry, University of Hawaii Press. Barnstone is a distinguished translator of Chinese literature, anthologist, and world literature textbook editor. Among his awards: The Grand Prize of the Strokestown International Poetry Contest, Pushcart Prize, John Ciardi Prize, Benjamin Saltman Award, and fellowships from the NEA, NEH, and California Arts Council.

Daniel Barnum lives and writes in Columbus, Ohio. His work has appeared in or is forthcoming from *RHINO, Barrow Street, Ninth Letter, The Adirondack Review, The Matador Review,* and elsewhere. He serves as associate poetry editor for *The Journal*, and as poetry editor for *The White Elephant.* This is his first published translation from the Swedish.

Austin Grant Bennett (MFA Wilkes University) is a son, brother, friend, husband, and father. He teaches writing at Montana State University Billings and is crafting his first novel.

Kimberly Blaeser, writer, photographer, and scholar, is Professor at the University of Wisconsin—Milwaukee and serves on faculty for the Institute of American Indian Arts low res MFA program in Santa Fe. She is the author of four books including the poetry collection *Apprenticed to Justice.* Her short fiction has appeared recently in Wasafiri and has been anthologized in collections such as *Reckoning: Contemporary Short Fiction by Native American Women.* An enrolled member of the Minnesota Chippewa Tribe, she is also the editor of *Traces in Blood, Bone, and Stone: Contemporary Ojibwe Poetry.* Blaeser served as Wisconsin Poet Laureate for 2015-16. A fourth collection of poetry, *Copper Yearning,* will be released in fall 2019.

Chris Bullard lives in Philadelphia, PA. He received his B.A. in English from the University of Pennsylvania and his M.F.A. from Wilkes University. Finishing Line Press published his poetry chapbook, *Leviathan*, in 2016 and Kattywompus Press published *High Pulp,* a collection of his flash fiction, in 2017. His work has appeared in publications such as *32 Poems, Green Mountains Review, Rattle, Pleiades, River Styx* and *Nimrod.*

.chisaraokwu. is an American Igbo poet, artist & healthcare futurist. She has been published in literary and academic journals, including *Obsidian* and the *New England Journal of Medicine*. She is currently developing two poetry collections about (im)migration and the Nigerian Civil War.

Stewe Claeson is a Swedish writer, translator and educator. His first book, a poetry collection, came out in 1969 and he has since written four short story collections, eleven novels and a long traveldiary on trips to see US writers, mostly in the Southwest *(Snow Falls in Cochise County* (2017). He has translated around 30 American poets - from Ezra Pound, H.D. and William Carlos Williams to poets Louis Simpson, James Wright, Mark Strand, Russell Edson to Stephen Dobyns, William Heyen, Bruce Weigl, Joy Harjo and also this magazine's editors William Pitt Root and Pamela Uschuk. He has just finished a translation of Louise Glück's *Ararat.* He has recieved many prizes, been runner-up for the Strindberg Prize and recently won the Selma Lagerlöf Prize. He was for many years a college director, has three grown-up children, and now lives with his wife Ingela on the West coast of Sweden.

Tyler Dettloff is an Anishinaabe Métis, Irish, and Italian poet, professor, musician, and water protector raised on the edge of the Delirium Wilderness. He lives in Gnoozhekaaning (Bay Mills, Michigan). Tyler teaches College Composition at LSSU and is the NF Editor for Border Crossing Literature Magazine. His work has been featured in *Voice on the Water: Great Lakes Native America Now, Crab Fat Magazine,* and *Heartwood Literature Magazine*. Mostly, he enjoys walking along rivers with his wife Daraka and through swamps with his dogs Banjo and Fiddle.

D.E. St. John is a poet residing in Atlanta, GA. His poetry has been nominated for Best of the Net and has previously appeared in *Atlanta Review, B O D Y, Prairie Schooner,* and *Hunger Mountain.* Currently a PhD candidate in English literature at Georgia State University, he is also the Associate Director of the school's writing center.

Chard DeNiord is the poet laureate of Vermont and author of six books of poetry, including *Interstate,* (The University of Pittsburgh Press, 2015) *The Double Truth* (University of Pittsburgh Press, 2011), and *Night Mowing* (University of Pittsburgh Press, 2005). He is also the author of two books of interviews with American poets *I Would Lie To You If I Could* (University of Pittsburgh Press, 2018) and *Sad Friends, Drowned Lovers, Stapled Song* (Marick Press, 2011). deNiord is a professor of English and Creative Writing at Providence College and a trustee of the Ruth Stone Trust. He lives in Westminster West, Vermont with his wife Liz.

Richard Dinges, Jr. has an MA in literary studies from University of Iowa, and manages information security risk at an insurance company. *Blue Unicorn, Red River Review, Abbey, Oddville Press,* and *Ship of Fools* most recently accepted his poems publication.

Anita Endrezze is an award-winning poet, writer, and artist. Her work is influenced by her Yaqui and European heritage. In 2012, University of Arizona Press published her book of short stories, *Butterfly Moon.* Anita's work has been translated into ten lanuages. Her new poetry book, *Enigma,* is due to be published in 2019 by Press 53. Anita lives, writes and paints in the Pacific Northwest.

Michele Feeney practices law, teaches at Arizona State University's College of Law ("Creative Writing for Lawyers"), and helps to manage a clinic at ASU College of law. She is on the editorial board of *Narrative Magazine.* Her short stories have been published in the *Arizona Attorney Magazine, Moses' Basket, Quality Women's Fiction,* and *Bear River Review.* Her work has received awards from *The Arizona Attorney Magazine, Glimmer Train* (Family Matters Contest, Honorable Mention) and *The New Millennium* (Fiction Contest, Honorable Mention). She will attend the 2019 Tucson

Festival of Books in 2018 and the Sirenland Writing Conference is Positano, Italy in March 2019.

Courtney Felle lives in the margins between the Northeast and the Midwest. Her work currently focuses on the landscape of queerness, illness, and gender, and can be found in *Blue Marble Review, Chautauqua Literary Journal*, and *Brain Mill Press*, among other publications. In addition to writing, she edits *Body Without Organs Literary Journal,* reads poetry for *Helen: A Lit Mag*, and interns for Senator Kirsten Gillibrand.

Ann Fisher-Wirth's sixth book of poems, *Bones of Winter Birds*, is winner of Terrapin Books' 2018 open reading contest. Her fifth book, *Mississippi,* (Wings Press 2018) is a poetry/photography collaboration with the Delta photographer Maude Schuyler Clay. Ann is coeditor of *The Ecopoetry Anthology* (Trinity UP 2013). 2017 Poet in Residence at Randolph College, she is a senior fellow and board member of The Black Earth Institute. She teaches at the University of Mississippi, where she also directs the Environmental Studies program; and she teaches yoga in Oxford, MS.

Susan Foster writes poetry and nonfiction and is currently a candidate for the MFA in Creative Writing-Poetry at Vermont College of Fine Arts. Her degrees and career have been in accounting, teaching (grades K-college), higher education administration, and classical music education. Mother and grandmother of many, Susan is a fifth-generation descendant of Southwestern pioneers and lives on the edge of the beautiful Mohave Desert, where her greatest passion is exploring and writing about Nature and family.

An avid fly fisherman and lover of the wild, **Jerry Gates** is a visual artist who has shown his paintings and oil pastels internationally. His work appears in permanent collections around the U.S., in Canada and in Mexico. Jerry has taught art at every level, in a public schools and at the university level. A Native Michigander, Jerry lives and paints in Williamsburg, Michigan, near Northern Lake Michigan and Traverse City.

Julia Mary Gibson grew up on the shores of Lake Michigan, where her novel *Copper Magic* takes place. Her fiction and nonfiction work has been published in *The Michigan Quarterly* and elsewhere. A personal essay about her intense relationship with John Lennon, who she never met in real life, appears in *Cutthroat* and won its 2018 Barry Lopez Nonfiction Prize. www.juliamarygibson.com

Jennifer Givhan is a Mexican-American poet, recently graduated with her Master's Degree in Literature with an emphasis on Latina women's poetry and motherhood from CSU, Fullerton,. Jennifer was the recipient of their Graduate Equity Fellowship. She teaches composition at Fullerton and Cerritos Colleges. She has a beautiful baby son, who recently learned to walk and keeps her on her toes chasing after him. She is married to a wonderful man who helps keep her grounded (and does the dishes) so she can concentrate on writing. She is working on a full-length collection of poetry that focuses on infertility, adoption, and the healing power of family. Her poems have been published or are forthcoming in *Verdad, Dash, Caesura, Mom Writer's Literary Magazine, Third Wednesday,* and *Pinyon,* amongst others.

Joy Harjo is a Mvskoke poet, musician, writer, playwright, memoirist and performer She's the author of nine books of poetry, including her most recent, *An American Sunrise.* Her awards include the Ruth Lilly Prize from the Poetry Foundation, the Wallace Stevens Award from the Academy of American Poets, and a Guggenheim Fellowship. Her memoir Crazy Brave won the PEN USA Literary Award for Creative Non-Fiction. Joy's music has been awarded a NAMMY for Best Female Artist of the Year. She is co-founder with Jennifer Foerster of an arts mentorship program for Mvskoke citizens.

Elizabeth Hellstern is a writer and artist who lives off-grid on 44 acres in Cerrillos, NM. She received her MFA in Creative Writing from Northern Arizona University. Her multi-genre writing work has appeared in places such as *Hotel Amerika, Slag Glass City, New World Writing* and *The Tusculum Review.* Hellstern's experimental poetry book, *"How to Live: A Suggestive Guide"* is forthcoming from Tolsun Books and she is the editor of T*elepoem Booth Anthology*

(Burning Books, 2019.) Hellstern is the creator of the public art installation the *Telepoem Booth*, where members of the public can dial-a-poem on a rotary phone in a 1970s phone booth. When she's not writing or dreaming up interactive experiences, she's melting welding tips to her shipping container house.

Sandra Hunter's fiction has won the 2018 Lorian Hemingway Short Story Competition, 2017 Leapfrog Press Fiction Contest, 2016 Gold Line Press Chapbook Prize, and three Pushcart Prize nominations. Her fiction collection *Trip Wires* was published in 2018. She is currently working on a novel trilogy set in Johannesburg, Los Angeles, and Berlin. www.sandrajhunter.com

Richard Jackson is the author of 15 books of poems and ten of criticism, anthologies and translations. His latest collection is *Broken Horizons* from Press 53. He is winner of Guggenheim, Fulbright, NEA, NEH, Witter-Bynner Fellowships, the AWP George Garrett Award, and the Order of Freedom from the President of Slovenia for Literary and Humanitarian work in the Balkan wars. His poems have been translated into 17 languages, and he has lectured and given readings widely both here and abroad. He teaches at UT-Chattanooga where he lives with his wife, Terri, and their dog, Wilbur.

Patricia Spears Jones is a Black American poet who is the 2017 Poets & Writers Jackson Poetry Prize Winner. Her collection, *A Lucent Fire: New and Seleced Poems* was a finalist for the Paterson Poetry Prize. She is author of ten additional publications. Her work has appeared in *The New Yorker, Ocean State Review, the Brooklyn Rail* and in prestigious anthologies such as *Of Poetry and Protest: From Emmett Till to Trayvon Martin; BAX: Best American Experimental Writing, 2016: 2017 Pushcart Prize XLI, Best of Small Presses; Truth to Power: Writers Respond to The Rhetoric of Hate and Fear;* and *Angles of Ascent: A Norton Anthology of Contemporary African American Poetry.* She edited *Ordinary Women: An Anthology of New York City Women* (1978) and *THINK: Poems for Aretha Franklin's Inauguration Day Hat* (2009). She teaches at Barnard College. She is a senior fellow emeritus of Black Earth Institute and is the founder organizer of The American Poets Congress. www.psjones.com.

Whitney Judd lives and works in Tucson, AZ, works to support writing and regrets that working impinges so much on the love of poetry and its writing, but probably (if it is possible) writes too much and submits too little.

Sarah Kaminski teaches middle school math in downtown Kansas City. She lives in a nearby suburb with her husband and two boys. When she can, she loves to lose herself in a good book, and she'll read almost anything—from the classics to nonfiction to contemporary YA romance. She is devoted to her students, and her work as a teacher has led her to believe that every person has a story worth telling.

Barry Kitterman is the author of a novel, *The Baker's Boy,* and a collection of stories, *From the San Joaquin.* He has received grants from the Tennessee Arts Council and the NEA, has been a writing fellow at the Fine Arts Work Center in Provincetown and the Hambidge Center in Georgia. He currently teaches writing at Austin Peay State University in Clarksville, Tennessee. Recent work has appeared in *The Hawaii Review* and *The Green Hills Literary Lantern.*

Joan Larkin's most recent collections are *Blue Hanuman* and *My Body: New and Selected Poems*, both published by Hanging Loose Press. A teacher for many decades, she has taught at Brooklyn College, Sarah Lawrence, and Smith, among others. Her honors include the Shelley Memorial Award and the Academy of American Poets Fellowship. A longtime resident of Brooklyn, she now lives in southern Arizona.

Following a near-fatal whitewater accident, **Angela La Voie** gained the courage to pursue her creative writing. Since then, she's earned an MFA in poetry and creative nonfiction from Antioch University Los Angeles. She's revising a memoir and a poetry collection, and has two novels pending revision. She holds a B.A. in English and Communication (Phi Beta Kappa) from Rutgers, The State University of New Jersey in New Brunswick. She lives near Denver, Colorado with her husband and their two dogs. www.angelalavoie.com

Sara Levine is the author of the novel *Treasure Island!!!* (Europa Editions) and a collection of short stories, *Short Dark Oracles* (Caketrain Press). Her essays have been anthologized in *The Touchstone Anthology of Contemporary Creative Nonfiction, Understanding the Essay,* and *Essayists on the Essay: Montaigne to Our Time.*

Jennifer Martelli is the author of *My Tarantella* (Bordighera Press), as well as the chapbook, *After Bird* (Grey Book Press, winner of the open reading, 2016). Her work has appeared or will appear in *Verse Daily, The Sonora Review,* and *Iron Horse Review* (winner, Photo Finish contest). Jennifer Martelli is the recipient of the Massachusetts Cultural Council Grant in Poetry. She is co-poetry editor for *The Mom Egg Review.*

Tim Miller's most recent books are *Bone Antler Stone* (poetry, The High Window Press) and The *Lonely Young & the Lonely Old* (stories, Pelekinesis Books). *"The Frog"* is part of a larger cycle of stories and a novel, called *School of Night.* He writes about art, religion and history at wordandsilence.com.

Born and raised in Romania, **Mihaela Moscaliuc** is the author of the poetry collections *Immigrant Model* (University of Pittsburgh Press, 2015) and *Father Dirt* (Alice James Books, 2010), translator of Carmelia Leonte's *The Hiss of the Viper* (Carnegie Mellon University Press, 2015) and Liliana Ursu's *Clay and Star* (Etruscan Press, forthcoming 2020), and editor of *Insane Devotion: On the Writing of Gerald Stern* (Trinity University Press, 2016). She is associate professor of English at Monmouth University.

Patricia Colleen Murphy founded *Superstition Review* at Arizona State University, where she teaches creative writing and magazine production. Her book *Bully Love* won the 2019 Press 53 Poetry Award. Her book *Hemming Flames* (Utah State University Press) won the 2016 May Swenson Poetry Award judged by Stephen Dunn, and the 2017 Milt Kessler Poetry Award. A chapter from her memoir in progress was published as a chapbook by New Orleans Review. Her writing has appeared in many literary journals, including *The Iowa Review, Quarterly West, American Poetry Review,* and has received awards from *Gulf Coast, Bellevue Literary Review,* among others. She lives in Phoenix, AZ.

Refering to herself as the wandering poet, **Naomi Shihab Nye** is the author of thirty books, including *19 Varieties of Gazelle: Poems of the Middle East* and *Red Suitcase.* Naomi's awards include a Lavan Award from the Academy of American Poets, four Pushcart Prizes, The Robert Creeley Award, and many others. Naomi's poem will be included in *The Tiny Journalist,* due out in April 2019 from BOA Editions LTD.

Martin Penman writes, plays drums, raises his kids and loves his wife in New Orleans.

Samuel Piccone is the author of the chapbook *Pupa,* which was awarded Editors' Choice in the 2017 Rick Campbell Chapbook Prize with Anhinga Press. His work has appeared or is forthcoming in publications including, *Southern Indiana Review, Passages North, American Literary Review,* and *Midwestern Gothic.* He received an MFA in poetry from North Carolina State University and serves on the poetry staff at Raleigh Review. Currently, he resides and teaches in Nevada.

Herbert Plummer earned an M.A. in British & American Literature from Hunter College, writing his thesis on aesthetics of war in Yusef Komunyakaa's poetry. He has taken several poetry workshops in the NYC area with various poets, including Jenny Xie. He works for Columbia University Press, where he manages subscriptions to research databases, including the *Granger's World of Poetry.* His work has been published in Unbroken Journal and is forthcoming in Aethlon. Poetry editor of *FishFood Magazine,* Plummer lives in Hoboken and runs with the Central Park Track Club.

Sarah Priestman's essays have been published in *The Hudson Review, Common Boundary magazine,* and *The Washingtonian.* Her work has also been awarded for Literary Excellence by the DC Commission on the Arts, listed in *America's Best Essays,* and nominated for a Pushcart Prize. Priestman lives outside of

Washington, DC, where she teaches English to recently-arrived immigrant students in the public schools.

Lindsey Royce's poems have appeared in many American periodicals and anthologies, including *Cutthroat: A Journal of the Arts, Poet Lore,* and *Washington Square Review.* Her first poetry collection, *Bare Hands,* was published by Turning Point in September of 2016. Her second collection, *Writing Bareback,* has been accepted for publication by Press 53. Royce teaches writing and literature at Colorado Mountain College in Steamboat Springs, Colorado.

Anele Rubin's poetry has appeared in *New Ohio Review, Chariton Review, Rattle, december, Mudfish, Raleigh Review, Paterson Literary Review, San Pedro River Review, Chattahoochee Review* and many other places. Her poetry collection, *Trying to Speak*, was published by Kent State University Press.

Sarah Elizabeth Schantz lives outside of Boulder, Colorado in an old farmhouse with her family where they are surrounded by open sky and century-old cottonwoods. Her first novel *Fig* debuted from Simon & Schuster in 2015 and was selected by NPR as A Best Read of the Year before it won the 2016 Colorado Book Award. She teaches creative writing at Front Range Community College. Her short stories appear in *Third Coast, Midwestern Gothic, The Los Angeles Review,* and *Hunger Mountain*. She is working on her second novel, *Roadside Altars.* She literally grew up in a bookstore where she was taught to worship at the altar of literature and all things art.

Danielle Sellers is from Key West, FL. She has an MA from The Writing Seminars at Johns Hopkins University and an MFA from the University of Mississippi where she held the John Grisham Poetry Fellowship. Her poems have appeared in *Prairie Schooner, Subtropics, Smartish Pace, The Cimarron Review, Poet Lore,* and elsewhere. She is the author of two collections of poetry: *Bone Key Elegies* (Main Street Rag 2009) and *The Minor Territories* (Sundress Publications 2018). She teaches Literature and Creative Writing at Trinity Valley School in Fort Worth, Texas.

Jane Hipkins Sobie is a journalist and essayist whose work has earned a dozen press awards, including a first place national press award for magazine editorial. She taught high school English Lit. and journalism in Virginia Beach, and creative writing in a North Carolina women's prison. She's an occasional newspaper guest columnist. Jane lives in Winston-Salem, North Carolina.

Sharon Solwitz' novel in stories *Abra Cadabra* won the 2018 Christopher Dohenny Award from the Center for Fiction. Her novel, *Once,* in Lourdes (Spiegel and Grau 2017) won first prize in adult fiction from the Society of Midland Authors. She is the author of a novel, *Bloody Mary,* and a collection of stories, *Blood and Milk*, which won the Carl Sandburg Prize from Friends of the Chicago Public Library, and the prize for adult fiction from the Society of Midland Authors, and was a finalist for the National Jewish Book Award. Reprinted, her short stories and essays can be found in creative writing textbooks, and in *Best American Short Stories* and the *Pushcart Prize Anthology.* Solwitz teaches fiction writing at Purdue University and lives in Chicago with her husband, the poet Barry Silesky.

Meredith Stricker is a visual artist and poet working in cross-genre media. She is the author of *Our Animal*, Omnidawn Open Book Prize; *Tenderness Shore* which received the National Poetry Series Award; *Alphabet Theater*, mixed-media performance poetry from Wesleyan University Press; *Mistake,* Caketrain Chapbook Award and Anemochore selected for the Gloria Anzaldua chapbook prize, Newfound Press. Work will appear in the *2019 Best American Experimental Writing* anthology from Wesleyan. She is co-director of visual poetry studio, a collaborative that focuses on architecture in Big Sur, California and projects to bring together artists, writers, musicians and experimental forms.   https://www.meredithstricker.com

Melissa Studdard is the author of the poetry collection *I Ate the Cosmos for Breakfast* and the young adult novel *Six Weeks to Yehidah.* Her writings have appeared or are forthcoming in *The Guardian, The New York Times, Psychology Today, Poetry, Harvard Review, New Ohio Review, Poets & Writers,* and more. In addition to writing, she serves as executive producer and host of VIDA Voices & Views for VIDA: Women in Literary Arts and president of the Women's Caucus for AWP. To learn more, visit www.melissastuddard.com

Emma Claire Sweeney is author of the award-winning novel, *Owl Song at Dawn,* and she co-authored with Emily Midorikawa *A Secret Sisterhood: The Literary Friendships of Jane Austen, Charlotte Brontë, George Eliot and Virginia Woolf.* Together Emily and Emma also run the literary friendship site SomethingRhymed.com.

John Tait's stories have appeared in journals such as *TriQuarterly, Crazyhorse, Fiction, Prairie Schooner,* and *The Sun* and have been anthologized in *The Crazyhorse 50th Anniversary Issue* and *New Stories from the Southwest.* His work has won four national awards including the Tobias Wolff Award and the H.E. Francis Award for Fiction. He is an Associate Professor of fiction writing at the University of North Texas.

Shelly Taylor is the author of two full-length poetry collections, *Lions, Remonstrance* (Coconut Books Braddock Book Prize, 2014) and *Black-Eyed Heifer* (Tarpaulin Sky, 2010), and co-editor, with Abraham Smith, of the anthology of rural American poetry and essays, *Hick Poetics* (Lost Roads Press, 2015). Recent work appears in Guernica's "The Future of Language" special issue, *Pinwheel,* and *Volt.*

Marina Tsvetaeva (1982-1941), admired by Joseph Brodsky: "Well, if you are talking about the twentieth century, I'll give you a list of poets. Akhmatova, Mandelstam, Tsvetaeva and she is the greatest one, in my view. The greatest poet in the twentieth century was a woman."

Heidi Vanderbilt is an award-winning writer who lives on and manages a horse ranch in southern Arizona where she cares for a dozen horses (Seafarer, Friars Moon, Wasabi, Oracle Rose, Ike, Jamie, Lucky Hunter), donkeys (Xote and Pepine), and goats (Malachi and Samson), and three female dogs: HiJinx, Ivy and Homer.. Her work has appeared in national, local and literary publications, including *Lear's , Stone Country* and *Ellery Queen's Mystery Magazine*, which won her a special Edgar Award from Mystery Writers of America. Her poem, "Ode to Moonlight and Sperm" appeared in the first issue of *Cutthroat.*

George Wallace is Writer-in-residence at the Walt Whitman Birthplace, author of 34 chapbooks of poetry, and the first American to be awarded the Alexander Gold Medal, UNESCO-Piraeus Islands.

Editor of *Poetrybay* and co-editor of *Great Weather for Media*, he lives in New York and travels worldwide to perform his work.

Donley Watt lives in Santa Fe, NM. His collection of short stories, "Can You Get There from Here?" won the Texas Institute of Letters' prize for best first book of fiction. Since then he has had four more book-length works of fiction published, along with many other stories, and recent essays in the *Los Angeles Review* and *Texas Monthly*. A former vice-president of the Texas Institute of Letters, his collected papers are a part of the Witliff Collections at Texas State University.

Patricia Jabbeh Wesley is the author of five collections of poetry, including *When the Wanderers Come Home, Where the Road Turns, The River is Rising,* and *Becoming Ebony*. Her sixth collection of poems, "Praise Song for My Children: New and Selected Poems," is forthcoming from Autumn House Press in 2020. Her work has appeared in *Harvard Review, Harvard Divinity Review, Transition Magazine, Prairie Schooner, Crab Orchard Review,* among others, and her work has been translated in Italian, Spanish, and Finnish. She teaches Creative Writing and African Literature at Penn State Altoona. Mary Jane White, MFA Iowa Writers' Workshop, NEA Fellowships (in poetry and translation). Tsvetaeva translations: *Starry Sky to Starry Sky* (Holy Cow! Press, 1988) *New Year's, an elegy for Rilke* (Adastra Press, 2007); *Poem of the Hill* (The New England Review); *Poem of the End* (The Hudson Review), reprinted in *Poets Translate Poets,* (Syracuse 2013).

Ann Leshy Wood is a Middle Eastern American poet, art-photographer, and vocalist. Her work has been published in many peer reviewed journals and magazines. She studied in the creative writing department at the University of Florida. She reads her poetry at many conferences. She has had 2 shows of her photography. She also sings with a master chorale that preforms in several languages. Ann lives on 8 isolated acres in a house she built in the old Florida woods.

MOON DANCE
Black and White Photo
Ann Leshy Wood

ONE ON ONE online/SKYPE Mentor Writing Program

Choose a four week One-on-one online Mentorship with the Master Writer of your choice in poetry, short story, flash fiction, mixed genre, memoir, poetry-in-translation and the novel or a six week critical full-length manuscript evaluation of short story and poetry collections, poetry-in- translation collections, and novels.

DISTINGUISHED FACULTY

Patricia Smith, Donley Watt, Naomi Benaron, TR Hummer, Melissa Pritchard, Doug Anderson, Sean Thomas Dougherty, Beth Alvarado, Pam Uschuk, Richard Jackson, Linda Hogan, Marilyn Kallet, Patricia Spears Jones, Darlin' Neal, Annie Finch, William Pitt Root, William Luvaas

"I am grateful for Don Watt's help with this book of mine. He not only edited what I had but taught me how to improve it and gave me tools to go ahead with it on my own." *Heidi Vanderbilt*

"I cannot express enough the fantastic, constructive time I spent in my mentorship with Marilyn Kallet. Not only practical and helpful, she has a generosity of spirit that was significant in aiding my work. I absolutely recom-mend this mentorship to others," *KB Ballentine*

"Patricia Spears Jones has given me so much armor for the page. Each session was enriching and I learned so much about my work (and myself) with her guidance." *Ali McClain*

There are no travel, no housing, no meal costs, just one flat fee for a high quality mentorship or manuscript evaluation. $1,000 for each four week one-on-one mentor session. These can be repeated or extended. $2,000 for a six week intensive manuscript critique. For more information, or to register go to www.cutthroatmag.com or call 970-903-7914.

2018 JOY HARJO POETRY PRIZE
BARRY LOPEZ CREATIVE NONFICTION PRIZE
RICK DEMARINIS SHORT STORY PRIZE
$1200 1st PRIZE, $250 2nd PRIZE, $100 Honorable Mention

FINAL JUDGES To Be Announced

GUIDELINES:
Go to www.cutthroatmag.com and submit poems and stories through our online submission manager. We no longer accept mailed-in or emailed entries. Submit up to 3 poems (100 line limit/one poem per page) or one short story or nonfiction piece (5000 word limit/double spaced) in 12 point font. NO AUTHOR NAME ALLOWED ON ANY MS. There is a $20 nonrefundable entry fee per submission. Make checks to Ravens Word Writers. READING PERIOD: August1, 2019- November 1, 2019. UNPUBLISHED WORK ONLY! No work that has already won a prize is eligible. No former CUTTHROAT prize-winning author may enter the contest he/or she has previously won. Enter as often as you wish. Multiple submissions okay, but we must be informed immediately of acceptances elsewhere. Finalists considered for publication. Winners published in CUTTHROAT and an-nounced on our website, in POETS & WRITERS and AWP CHRONICLE. No staff relatives or staff members of CUT-THROAT nor close friends, relatives or students of judges are eligible to enter our contests. See www.cutthroatmag.com for more information.WE HIGHLY RECOMMEND READING A COPY OF CUTTHROAT BEFORE ENTERING OUR CONTESTS.

2019 LORIAN HEMINGWAY SHORT STORY COMPETITION

$2,500 Awaits Winners of 2019 Lorian Hemingway Short Story Competition

• Writers of short fiction are encouraged to enter the 2019 Lorian Hemingway Short Story Competition. The competition has a thirty-one year history of literary excellence, and its organizers are dedicated to enthusiastically supporting the efforts and talent of emerg-ing writers of short fiction whose voices have yet to be heard. Lorian Hemingway, granddaughter of Nobel laureate Ernest Hemingway, is the author of three critically acclaimed books: Walking into the River, Walk on Water, and A World Turned Over. Ms. Hemingway is the competition's final judge.

Prizes and Publication:
• The first-place winner will receive $1,500 and publication of his or her winning story in Cutthroat: A Journal of the Arts. The second – and third-place winners will receive $500 each. Honorable mentions will also be awarded to entrants whose work demonstrates promise. Cutthroat: A Journal of the Arts was founded by Editor-In-Chief Pa-mela Uschuk, winner of the 2010 American Book Award for her book of poems Crazy Love, and by poet William Pitt Root, Guggenheim Fellow and NEA recipient. The journal contains some of the finest contemporary fiction and poetry and nonfiction in print, and the Lorian Hemingway Short Story Competition is both proud and grateful to be associated with such a reputable publication.

Eligibility requirements for our 2019 competition are as follows:

What to submit:
• Stories must be original unpublished fiction, typed and dou-ble-spaced, and may not exceed 3,500 words in length. We have extended our word limit for the first time in thirty years to 3,500 words rather than 3,000. There are no theme or genre restrictions. Copyright remains property of the author.
Who may submit:
• The literary competition is open to all U.S. and international writers whose fiction has not appeared in a nationally distributed publication with a circulation of 5,000 or more. Writers who have been published by an online magazine or who have self-published will be considered on an individual basis.

Submission requirements:

• Submissions may be sent via regular mail or submitted online. Please visit our online submissions page for complete instructions regarding online submissions. Writers may submit multi-ple entries, but each must be accompanied by an entry fee and separate cover sheet. We do accept simultaneous submissions; however, the writer must notify us if a story is accepted for publication or wins an award prior to our July announcements. No entry confirmation will be given unless requested. No SASE is required.

• The author's name should not appear on the story. Our entrants are judged anonymously. Each story must be accompanied by a separate cover sheet with the writer's name, complete mailing address, e-mail address, phone number, the title of the piece, and the word count. Manuscripts will not be returned. These requirements apply for online submissions as well.

Deadlines and Entry Fees:

• The entry fee is $15 for each story postmarked by May 1, 2019. The late entry fee is $20 for each story postmarked by May 15, 2019. We encourage you to enter by May 1 if at all possible, but please know that your story will still be accepted if you meet the later deadline. Entries postmarked after May 15, 2019 will not be accepted. Entries submitted online after May 15, 2019 will not be accepted. Writers may submit for the 2018 competition beginning May 16, 2019.

How to pay your entry fee:

• Entry fees submitted by mail with their accompanying stories may be paid -- in U.S. funds -- via a personal check, cashier's check, or money order. Please make checks payable to LHSSC or The Lorian Hemingway Short Story Competition. Entry fees for online submis-sions may be paid with PayPal.

Announcement of Winners and Honorable Mentions:

• Winners of the 2019 competition will be announced at the end of July 2019 in Key West, Florida, and posted on our website soon afterward. Only the first-place entrant will be noti-fied personally. All entrants will receive a letter from Lorian Hemingway and a list of winners, either via regular mail or e-mail, by October 1, 2019. All manuscripts and their accompanying entry fees should be sent to The Lorian Hemingway Short Story Competition, P.O. Box 993, Key West, FL 33041 or submitted on- line.

For more information, please explore our website at:
www. shortstorycompetition.com
or e-mail: shortstorykw@gmail.com

NEW FROM PRESS 53, SILVER CONCHO POETRY SERIES, 2018

Kelly Cherry, Howard Faerstein and Willie James King

"This bare-boned scalpel-edged verse reversed and heals the mad maladies of our time."   Michael Martone

I know of no other contemporary poet who has quite her gifts. Hers is a passionate intellection, and she embodies it in a bright tough music no one else matches or even approaches.   Fred Chappell

"these poems 'never refuse love's lure,' never forget 'the great glory' of creation. *Googootz* is a large-souled book that gives us courage to "go on living."   Jay Udall

CPSIA information can be obtained
at www.ICGtesting.com
Printed in the USA
LVHW041608040820
662390LV00003B/357